FELICIA KETCHESON

Sketching Rebellion

To Grandpa.

Receive a Free Short Story

Receive the exclusive and free short story *Warning* by subscribing to my newsletter at https://feliciaketcheson.com/nlsketching/. You'll also receive news about upcoming releases and exclusive content, and your email will never be shared. If you only want to read the story, simply unsubscribe after downloading your copy.

Can sixteen-year-old Cafrec avoid the consequences of disrespecting the president of his oppressed society?

In a society where obedience is expected and defiance is punished, Cafrec is a dissatisfied teenager searching for a way out. When he takes a small, impulsive action in class, he quickly learns that even the slightest deviation from the norm can have consequences.

Takes place two years before *Sketching Rebellion*.

Author's Note

As a Canadian, I use Canadian spellings throughout.

Chapter One

When Breel Sorep entered the classroom, Mr. Progrio wasn't at the front of the room. She frowned.

That's strange…

"Nice not having Mr. Progrio ordering us to hurry," said Sero, evidently not concerned.

He followed Breel to the first row of computers and sat beside her. Most of their fellow computer programming students were already in their seats.

The classroom had four rows of tables, each with ten computers. There was a small window overlooking the walkway into the school. Students raced to get to the classroom first and claim one of the two seats beside the window.

"True," Breel said. She bit her lip. "But… where is he?"

Sero shrugged as Breel turned on her computer.

Around the room, fellow Leaders of Tomorrow whispered. "Where is he?" "What's going on?" "Oh no… not again." It was more conversation than the group usually had with each other. It seemed the only one not concerned was Sero. Mr. Progrio had chewed him out the other day for finding an error in the assignment.

The computer beeped as the login screen appeared. Breel entered her information.

"Oh!" said Sero.

An unfamiliar man stood at the front. He wore the same cobalt-blue pants, dress shirt, and smoky-gray sweater as everyone else who worked for the Department of Teaching. His career stripings, around each bicep, were two thick cherry-coloured stripes sandwiched between two thin lemon-coloured ones.

Breel and Sero exchanged glances, the latter's brow furrowed. "A computer programming teacher we've never met before?" she asked in a whisper.

"I guess so."

The man cleared his throat and clapped his hands once. "Class will come to order."

All whispering stopped.

He straightened his posture and placed his hands on his hips. "I'm Mr. Stitus. I'll be teaching this class for the remainder of the year."

Breel raised an eyebrow. *For two days, then?* When he said nothing more, Breel raised a hand.

"Yes?" Mr. Stitus said.

"What's wrong with Mr. Progrio?"

Mr. Stitus frowned. "That's none of your concern, because he'll no longer be teaching this class. I expect you to continue with the assignment he already gave you."

No one moved. Breel and her classmates looked around, as if exchanging puzzled glances would solve the mystery.

Mr. Stitus slammed a hand on the teacher's desk. Everyone jumped. "Get to work!"

Yesterday, Mr. Progrio had looked healthy. He'd strutted around the room, referring to President Tatem as "our hero," and towered over Breel as he waited for her to answer a question. He hadn't been sick. There was only one explanation.

Another disappearance.

Breel had never liked Mr. Progrio, but he didn't deserve this.

Something touched her arm—Sero poking her with a pen. "Breel." He pointed to her monitor.

Right. She was supposed to be working on a programming assignment.

But concentrating on it was impossible when there was another hushed-up disappearance. The second in as many months.

Disappearances were easy to forget when she didn't personally know who disappeared. This time was different...

There was a chance Mr. Progrio was a Vucapi, that he hadn't disappeared. But since a new Mortae hadn't been scheduled and it was already Thursday afternoon, that was doubtful.

Like with all the other missing citizens, President Tatem wouldn't mention the disappearance on the evening news. Nor would he or anyone else explain the reasoning for it. But from hearing other Leaders of Today talk, many citizens figured it meant the government had murdered them because they were too dangerous to keep alive.

Just like Uncle Famut.

Tears burned Breel's eyes, but she blinked them away.

Famut had been high in the governmental echelon. That was the reason the government gave Breel's father for classifying the details of his disappearance. But Mr. Progrio was an ordinary teacher.

Everyone was typing their programs. Breel exhaled and forced her breathing to slow. Finishing her final assignment was the most important thing right now.

She forced her brain to forget about Mr. Progrio and concentrate on programming instead.

Chapter Two

Breel cringed at her use of rambling *if* statements and other programming atrocities. Before she could fix them, the bell echoed throughout Lexum Secondary School. She'd done the best she could, given the distraction of Mr. Progrio's disappearance.

She clicked the button to send her file for marking and shut down her computer, collected her advanced computer programming textbook, and began to head to her next class.

Everyone else had finished their work and was silently exiting the room.

Every classmate but Sero.

He was still typing even though he had previously received two warnings for being late to class. Due to the nature of the warnings, Breel and their other Computer Programming Career Group classmates knew about them. Teachers encouraged Leaders of Tomorrow to report any illegal or suspicious behaviour to them, but, lucky for Sero, he was well-liked by his peers. They didn't want him to be caught again and receive Mortae for something preventable.

"Hey, Sero, fix your code later," Breel said.

He looked up from his screen, eyes widening at the empty seats. "Thanks, Breel."

The hallway was a sea of students wearing their black pants and dress shirts and the occasional teacher in cobalt blue and smoky gray.

Beige lockers lined the hallway. Few clanged shut, since most Leaders of Tomorrow carried their books to every class. A lighter load wasn't worth the risk of receiving a warning for lateness.

Ahead, at the end of the hall, her best friend Ami's long blonde hair disappeared into a classroom. Breel followed, the last of twenty Leaders of Tomorrow to arrive. She slipped into her usual desk beside Ami.

Breel's body tensed. *What annoying thing is Ami going to say this time?*

"How was programming?" Ami asked.

Breel's shoulders relaxed at the mundane question. Breel shrugged as she pulled her hair back to disentangle the black curls from her glasses. She didn't mention Mr. Progrio. If citizens talked about disappearances in front of the wrong people, Department of Enforcement officers would arrest them.

"Programming was okay. How was stats?" Breel asked.

"Easy."

As Ami was in the Mathematician Career Group, she and Breel only had logic and one or two mathematics classes together per year.

Breel opened her advanced discrete mathematics textbook, grinning. It'd be one of her last times sitting in the classroom. In a couple of weeks, she'd be done with school until starting the mandatory Department of Expansion classes next month.

Mr. Gaimster, their thirtysomething-year-old teacher, leaned against the whiteboard, speaking to a few Leaders of Tomorrow before class started. He was one of the few teachers who talked to their students about things not in the curriculum. Overall, Mr. Gaimster made the horrid subject more bearable.

Breel's ears picked up the word "Demna," pulling her attention away from Ami and her textbook.

Mr. Gaimster laughed. "I say Demna, and every pair of eyes is on me!"

"We're writing it soon, so anything you can tell us..." said Curia from the front. Her elbows were on her desk, head in her hands as she leaned forward.

Breel rolled her eyes. *Could she be any more obvious?*

Leaders of Tomorrow wrote an exam covering the year's material every June. But the Demna Exam was different. It was three days long and covered every class ever taken. For those like Breel, in academic Career Groups, this meant studying twelve years of material.

"What if we fail?" Curia asked.

Mr. Gaimster shook his head, his chestnut-brown curls bouncing. "Impossible. Years ago, failure wasn't uncommon. But the Nito Test and Career Group curricula have improved."

"But what if we do?"

Mr. Gaimster opened his mouth then closed it, his lips pursed. The answer was obvious—Mortae.

The bell rang. He turned to teaching mathematics.

* * *

"Imagine failing the Demna?" Breel said to Ami. Her arms ached from holding her textbooks as she waited for Ami to get her things from her locker. Heavy math textbooks meant Ami used her locker more than most. She often ran to and from her classes.

"No," Ami said.

Breel rolled her eyes. *There's the annoying comment. Ami has no imagination.*

Not that anyone did.

"Why?" asked Ami. "Do you worry about it?"

"Never," said Breel. "I've studied courses from prior grades at least an hour each night and at least eight hours every Saturday and Sunday for nine months. And that's on top of my current classes."

Ami removed her head from her locker to gape at Breel, eyes wide.

"An hour on previous grades? Nine months? Gee, Breel. I've studied at least two hours a day every weekday and twelve hours on Saturday and Sunday for over three years."

Breel shrugged. "I'm not worried."

When Ami returned her head to her locker, Breel rolled her eyes. *It's so unfair that academic Career Groups study so much.*

Then there were the non-academic groups. They learned the basics and had a year, if that, of career-specific material. Unlike the academic groups, they didn't study like robots for nothing in return except having higher demands placed on them. Breel wanted to shake her five-year-old self for her performance on the Nito Test.

During the Nito, an examiner asked situational and practical questions to test IQ and aptitude. The results alone determined one's Career Group.

If I lied, I'd be in a better Career Group.

Ami finished her daily ritual of stuffing her textbooks into her backpack. Somehow, her sanity stayed intact despite her nearly pure mathematics course load. Even though her parents spent Lexum Catalog points to upgrade from the standard-issue backpack, the straps were fraying and the zipper splitting.

They arrived at Breel's locker next. Her arms sang in relief as she dumped her discrete mathematics, *History of Lexum* volume twelve, computer networks, algorithm analysis, and software architecture textbooks on a shelf. Breel and Ami often joked that they didn't need to do push-ups during the daily exercises—their textbooks were weighty enough. Breel stuffed them into her second standard-issue backpack of the year and donned her standard-issue lightweight black jacket.

Breel and Ami walked through the main hallway. As usual, Breel cringed as she ignored a poster of a teacher, arms crossed, standing in front of a whiteboard with the words *Everything you need to know, the Government of Lexum directly provides.* From what she heard, there were a collection of posters in strategic places and they were rotated every few months.

They parted ways at the school entrance. Lexum Secondary School—grades nine through twelve—was smaller than Lexum Elementary School, though comparable in layout. While everyone attended the elementary school, some Career Groups didn't go to the secondary school whereas others attended for a year or more.

The entrance was a set of four doors. A walkway lined with birch trees led to the sidewalk. The school was one floor and made of the same red brick as most structures in Lexum.

Breel was alone for a moment, among the sea of other Leaders of Tomorrow heading for the sidewalk, before Trafis put an arm around her, the weight pulling her backpack.

"Hey, big sis!" he said.

"Hey! It's heavy enough without you doing that."

Trafis laughed and bodychecked her. She moved but an inch because of her textbooks.

"Training for something with that weight?" he asked.

"Oh yeah. I'll have fit shoulders and arms."

"Big, bulging, and beefy."

"Ew."

Next year, her brother would teach English classes at Lexum Elementary School, a two-minute walk away. His backpack only carried small grammar books and teaching manuals.

Wish I were lucky enough to have such a light load, Breel thought.

They started their ten-minute walk home, first passing two-bedroom homes for three-person families. Every house was the same size and identical in appearance: redbrick bungalow, driveway the dimensions of a delivery van, birch tree on the patch of grass at the front, and two rows of purple chrysanthemums lining the walkway to the white door. All that distinguished the neighbourhood from others were the flower colours and sizes of homes. If one didn't read street signs, getting lost was a certainty.

The wind moved Trafis's hair, which he fixed even though it was too short to fly into his face.

"My programming teacher disappeared," Breel said. She kept her voice low.

"Maybe he's a Vucapi?"

"Then why isn't there a Mortae?"

Trafis thought about that. "There's one tomorrow."

"It was announced before he disappeared."

"Oh." He frowned. "That sucks. Ready for the Demna?"

Breel didn't need Trafis to tell her he was changing the subject on purpose.

"Of course," she said.

"Most people in my classes are already studying hours a day."

That wasn't surprising. Like Ami, most studied for years, increasing to daily no later than the four-week summer break before the last school year. Breel had spent those weeks in her bedroom pretending to pour over textbooks. Her father had beamed every time she'd emerged from hibernation, unaware she hadn't opened a single book since her grade eleven exams.

She hadn't wanted to squander her last four weeks of freedom before finishing school and working as a Leader of Today. Of course, she didn't tell her father, since he'd only question Famut's influence.

"Duknum, I don't think Famut is dangerous," her mother had told her father. But he wouldn't listen.

If Duknum did question Famut's influence, he'd be right. Famut had told Breel and Trafis that studying was important, but so was enjoying life.

"The way the government makes us work and study all hours of every day is a travesty," Famut had said. "Take a night off and just talk. Play a game."

"Game?" Breel had asked.

She could define "game" but wasn't sure what it meant. No one had ever suggested playing one. But Famut had taught them a game that involved flicking smooth stones into the centre of a circle to knock out their opponents' stones. In another, they described a Career Group in a ridiculous manner ("someone who pokes people with sharp objects") and others guessed which it was. Breel's favourite was inventing new Career Groups.

Since nights and weekends were for studying, playing games with Famut was rare. Plus, Famut had never suggested games when his brother was within earshot. From an early age, Breel had never considered spilling the secret to her father.

Breel and Trafis stopped at a traffic light along with half a dozen other Leaders of Tomorrow. A delivery van, the only vehicles on the road, rumbled past. Regardless of what it was delivering, every van was a white box with the words "Lexum Delivery" on both sides in black block letters.

"I've been studying once a week for over a year," said Trafis, bringing Breel back to the reality of school. "Should I start studying daily after my exams?"

Breel shrugged as they waited for five more delivery vans.

"What's with the shrug? It was a rhetorical question! Obviously, I will. Duh. You're stupid not to start then! Nothing else to do, anyway."

Breel laughed. That was for sure.

Trafis glanced at Breel, ignoring the now-green light. "You didn't study during break, did you?" Breel strained to hear him above the cacophony of delivery van engines.

"I didn't say that." She stepped onto the street with Trafis.

"Breel, how could you?" He kept his voice low.

"Don't tell anyone."

He groaned. "Do I look like an idiot?" He leaned in and whispered, "You were drawing, weren't you?"

Breel didn't respond—Trafis already knew the answer.

She considered herself a portrait artist—if there were such a thing, which there wasn't. In her preschool days, her portraits were stick figures. They soon turned into rough pictures, and in time, something more realistic and recognizable. If she were to put her drawing of Trafis onto an ID card, it'd be difficult to differentiate it from his actual one.

Years ago, a future illustrator was in Breel's fifth History of Lexum class. He had complained about the difficulty in perfecting his drawing skills on different mediums. Breel had clenched her teeth, unable to respond. He didn't realize how lucky was. Not only did he get to finish school early, but he'd become an illustrator in the Department of Teaching or Expansion.

"You know I'd never tell," Trafis said. "But you shouldn't be doing it! What if you're caught again?"

It was a bright, cloudless, twenty-five-degree centigrade day and the chrysanthemums were in full bloom, but Breel shivered at the thought. "I'm careful."

"But, Breel, it's not worth it! You've already had one warning. Just one more and after that... Mortae."

Unlike Trafis and her parents, Breel chose not to ruminate about it. After her warning, she had started taking greater precautions to avoid a second. But she had to make allowances for Trafis. This wasn't an uncommon conversation with him. He blew every warning out of proportion.

"You'd think that nearly being a Leader of Today, I'd be too valuable for Mortae," she said.

"Everyone's valuable because we've all had our utility maximized. Well, I'd argue yours isn't since you draw instead of study."

There he goes, spewing propaganda at me. "I get straight As."

"But how're you supposed to get the highest marks possible if you're—" He paused as a middle-aged teacher walked past. Once she was a few strides away, he said in a whisper, "If you're doing other things, your marks aren't the highest possible. Don't you want to get a more prestigious department or have more job variety?"

"It's not fair we're supposed to spend every hour studying. Don't you remember Uncle Famut?" Back then, Trafis had played the games.

But Breel and Trafis had done more than just play games with Famut. Throughout his life, their uncle's education had been more rigorous than other Career Groups. He worked as a geneticist and enjoyed sharing what he learned about medicine and genetics with his niece and nephew. However, he never told them what his job entailed, as details of every citizen's job were on a need-to-know basis. Depending upon the necessary level of privacy and security, telling someone could even mean Mortae. Still, his brother had hated Famut teaching his children these things and had often quoted the saying "everything you need to know, the Government of Lexum directly provides." As Lexum wasn't teaching his children these things, they didn't need to know about it.

"Yeah," said Trafis. "I remember what Uncle Famut told us. But he's dead. Well, disappeared. Likely dead. Like him, you forget it's not about you. What about fairness to society? Everyone needs to do their part and 'embrace the collective'."

Breel rolled her eyes at Lexum's motto. "Uncle Famut thought that was ridiculous."

Trafis gasped, stopping midstride. "Don't say that! It's not worth it."

He was right, of course, but she was careful. After all, she'd received her only warning years ago. She didn't need her younger brother to pretend to be the older, protective brother.

"Just do the right thing, Breel," he said.

"More and more you're sounding like Ami. Please don't become annoying like her."

He scoffed. "But who'd report you in a heartbeat?"

Ami—without a doubt. Like with Famut, she trusted Trafis with such information. He would never report her.

Breel's thoughts returned to her uncle. *I still can't believe it's been five years...*

Duknum had sat the family down in the living room to break the news. Void of emotion, he said his brother had disappeared—and therefore was likely dead. Hearing her father use the word "death" rather than "disappearance" was the last thing Breel expected. She assumed her father was one of the citizens who believed everyone who disappeared sat in jail for the rest of their lives or was an actual disappearance.

A couple of minutes later, the emotionless façade crumbled when his voice caught mid-sentence. Breel buried her head into the couch, soaking it with her tears as her mother rubbed her back. For the rest of the day her body shook, heart pounding as she processed her uncle's likely death.

Famut had visited their house only two days before. And when he left, since it was half an hour before the Leader of Tomorrow curfew, Breel and Trafis walked him to the end of Chrysanthemum Lane.

Breel had favoured moments alone with Famut and Trafis. That was when he told them about Intercludae. He invented the world for Breel to fantasize drawing in a society in which the government allowed hobbies. Instead of a dictator, Intercludae had a leadership elected by its residents; Leaders of Tomorrow could take whatever classes they wanted; and everyone chose their Career Group.

"But I don't understand it, Uncle Famut," she said. "That's not how the world works."

"That's what makes it fantasy, Ree," he said, using his pet name for her. "Intercludae's a fantastical place I created based on how the world used to work."

The concept of a fantasy started making sense when Breel turned twelve. But Famut's view was different from everyone else's. He didn't consider archaic concepts like choosing one's Career Group or elections or money as individualistic and detrimental to society. The ways in which Intercludae differed from Lexum made it alluring. Breel still spent many evenings daydreaming about a life in which she could draw whenever and wherever she wanted.

After Famut's death, Trafis and their father hadn't condoned Famut's disobedience, since his beliefs had likely caused his death. As for Famut being in the upper echelon of the government, Duknum had said, "Rebels like him shouldn't get to such a status."

Breel's stomach tightened as they turned onto their street. It was what she experienced whenever she thought too hard about Famut.

They passed the Chrysanthemum Lane street sign and the beginning of the four-person homes neighbourhood. The only visual difference from the three-person houses, other than size, were the red chrysanthemums lining the walkways. Like elsewhere in Lexum, every lawn was weedless and green, thanks to weekly maintenance from gardeners in the Department of Households.

"I don't understand why you give me such a hard time about my marks," she said to Trafis.

"Because it's dangerous! Uncle Famut was a bad influence on you."

"If he was, why'd I have high marks?"

"Because you're smart. Smarter than me."

True.

Trafis worked hard to get his B-plus average—nearly a failing grade by Lexum standards.

"Your grades don't mean you're dumber than me," she said. "Your Nito Test results don't make sense."

He gasped. "Breel! That's practically blasphemy!"

But it was true. Trafis didn't need to tell her he disliked his Career Group. However, Trafis wouldn't tell anyone what he'd prefer to do.

Poor Trafis, living like a mindless drone. I bet he's never even thought about what he'd rather do.

Clearly, Famut's influence didn't take. Trafis was as brainwashed as the rest of the masses.

Chapter Three

The air on Chrysanthemum Lane was thick with the aroma of cut grass. Breel breathed in deeply through her diaphragm, allowing the fresh, potent pollen to fill her lungs. Trafis sneezed and removed a tissue from his pocket.

"I hate Thursdays," he said and blew his nose.

"Imagine if the Nito Test assigned you as a gardener?" Breel said.

Trafis groaned. "That'd be awful!"

They walked up the small driveway and down the flower-lined path to the porch. The bronze "5" above the door distinguished it from the other forty-two houses on Chrysanthemum Lane.

Breel held her ID to the boxy charcoal door scanner, which were ubiquitous around Lexum.

Hideous and obtrusive things.

The scanner beeped and unlocked the door. They walked onto the standard-issue charcoal rug and deposited their standard-issue shoes and jackets in the closet, which was just big enough for four people. The entryway was square and didn't quite comfortably fit all four of them at once.

They headed to their bedrooms to do homework and study. As they walked through the living room, Breel tuned out the continuous newsreel from their forty-inch TV. There was no need to listen to the previous day's news, since watching it daily at 7:00 p.m. was mandatory.

Trafis closed his bedroom door. The *thud* of his backpack hitting the floor reverberated into Breel's bedroom. Breel never dropped her bag like that—it'd surely smash through the floor and into... something unknown. Unlike a small number of governmental buildings, houses didn't have basements—in fact, Breel had never been in one.

Breel tossed her backpack onto her twin bed in the middle of the room and retrieved her books from the wide four-shelf bookcase. All twelve years of books and notes fit with only a couple of inches to spare. She moved her keyboard and mouse to one side of her desk and set her books onto it. She opened one and pushed it against the wall. Next, she removed half the books from her bottom shelf, reached to the back to pull out a notebook, and replaced the books.

Sitting at her desk, she opened the notebook to her last picture. It was of Famut—well, how she remembered him.

Why was memorializing his appearance a bad thing? After all, her drawings were all she had of him. His hair had been wavy and as black as ink on a page. Sometimes, if the light hit his head just right, it'd dance across the waves like sunrays on open water. His chiselled face was the same as Duknum's.

It was her sixth attempt at drawing Famut in as many days. His face—chiselled and weathered—and long black hair were easy to draw. But his eyes didn't look right. It was impossible to remember the colour of his glasses frames, or the colour and shape of his eyes. She couldn't recall the contour of his mouth. After five years, it was unlikely she'd ever be able to draw him to true form.

After turning to a blank page, she picked up a pencil and began a portrait of someone else. She refrained from drawing when her parents were home, so she had a couple of hours until they arrived after five. Trafis would be horrified she wasn't preparing for tomorrow's weekly exams, but drawing gave her a clear enough head to study the rest of the evening.

Not that Breel disliked programming. She liked it well enough and was a good a programmer as anyone in her Career Group. But, like everyone else, it meant an inability to develop other skills.

"But why doesn't the government allow me to draw?" she'd asked Famut one day.

"You've taken a history class every year. You know why it's law. President Tatem isn't changing it."

History class... more like propaganda class.

Gripping the pencil in her hand and moving it purposefully across a page filled Breel with contentment in a way nothing else did. Her muscles relaxed the further she got into her picture. Drawing meant doing something for herself, something of her own volition. She made the rules, not the government. It provided an outlet for creativity. Sometimes programming allowed for creative design and coding, but most of the time, restraints in class zapped creativity like an errant firefly.

Drawing was an escape from the daily pressures of Lexum. It freed her mind, allowing her to reminisce about Famut or fantasize about Intercludae or consider what life would be like if the Nito Test had assigned her to be an illustrator. Then, like magic, a portrait would appear.

Breel held up her finished work. It was as if Mr. Gaimster was smiling at her. She had started with his round face and hooked nose, then added his eyes and thin lips. Drawing his curly hair had been fun, but like all her drawings, his hair was charcoal, as the government allowed only illustrators to have coloured pencils.

Satisfied, Breel slipped into the bathroom and scrubbed her hands to wash away the pencil marks, turning the water black. Her drawing finished, her mind relaxed, she slipped into her desk chair, brushing eraser bits into the small garbage pail underneath the desk. She pulled her opened textbook toward her at the metallic whirring of a lock disengaging. Her parents were home—she had finished just in time.

Breel attempted to concentrate on studying. The weekly exams were simple if you paid attention in class (which everyone did), finished your homework (which everyone did), and understood the material (which everyone usually did). For Breel, needing to cram during the night was rare.

This weekly exam would be her last. Then she had a week off to study for the Demna Exam—written exams on Monday and Tuesday and a practical exam on Wednesday. The government mailed results on Friday, along with her assigned department, a general job description, and moving instructions for relocating to her own home. Instructions for the first day of work would be on her dining room table.

She'd be a Leader of Today and finally have her own house. A place to draw without fear of her family catching her. Waiting to learn what her job would entail was unbearable. But the hardest wait of all was learning of her assigned governmental department.

Every computer programmer had three dream jobs, that, not coincidentally, were in the most prestigious of the twelve departments. The first was working in the Department of Education writing programs to analyze Nito Test scores and assign Career Groups. Second was the Department of Enforcement writing programs that analyzed Mortae trends. The third was the Department of Health writing programs to analyze various hospital data.

Breel didn't prefer a particular department; rather, she preferred to *not* work in two departments. The first was the Department of Enforcement. With luck, her previous warning disqualified her. But what kept her up at night was the fear of being in the Department of Occupation alongside her father, writing programs to assist in determining the supply and demand of Career Groups. After seventeen years of fearing this possibility, she had only fifteen more days before learning her fate. Just thinking about it made her limbs tingle and her heart pound.

A knock on the door brought her back to her open textbook. "Supper's here," her mother, Criba, said in her soft voice.

Breel was glad to leave her textbooks. She walked into a hallway filled with the smell of pasta, freshly prepared by a cook from the Department of Food. Her parents and Trafis sat at their small chocolate-brown dining table, which fit just so into the square dining room off the living room. Breel joined them, facing the small patio and patch of grass that was their backyard.

Trafis had straight brown hair like their mother and the same chiselled face as Duknum and Famut. As for Breel, other than wearing glasses and having black hair like her father, she was physically out of place with her curls and slender form. Criba was often out of place as well—though that was because she was a hair under five feet, whereas the others were at least six inches taller.

Breel dug into the fettuccini Alfredo. It was everyone's favourite, so whenever it was on the menu, they all chose it.

"Your last weekly exam's tomorrow," Duknum said.

Since Leaders of Today could only say so much about work, school was the typical topic of their supper conversation. Duknum beamed as she twirled her noodles, flipping a zucchini off her fork. She stabbed it.

"I can hardly believe it," Breel said.

He nodded, glasses slipping. He pushed them up the bridge of his nose. "I remember the excitement, the anticipation. Almost ready to do my part for Lexum."

"You're forgetting the anxiety," Criba said. She was like a mouse beside Duknum's booming voice.

"Criba, is there a need for anxiety given Breel's marks?" Duknum asked.

He was ever the logician.

"I'd be anxious," said Trafis. "I *will* be anxious."

Their mother nodded. "I was. I was sick the entire week leading up to it."

Criba's parents had been hard on her. She had been studious but received even worse marks than Trafis. Years ago, Breel had asked her father about her maternal grandparents. In confidence, he had confirmed they were alive, but Breel's mother had cut contact the day she moved out to start working as the secretary in the Programming Section of the Department of Occupation.

Breel's parents worked in the same section, but their paths rarely crossed. However, sometimes they reminisced about old times socializing with coworkers. Since having children, they said they would rather spend the precious few spare minutes Lexum afforded them together as a family. That usually meant supper conversations and sometimes reading textbooks in companionable silence.

"No point in being anxious," Duknum said. "Just study, study, study."

Breel didn't bother to say she wasn't anxious. Instead, she enjoyed her meal—especially the creaminess of the sauce, which coated every square inch of noodle and vegetable.

Ten minutes later, she was placing her fork on her empty plate when there was a knock. Everyone exchanged glances. Her father's eyebrows raised. No one paid visits to homes unless it was serious business.

Duknum walked to the door, the others lingering at the table. An unseen man said, "We need a word."

A moment later, a man wearing black pants and a sunshine-yellow sweater uniform came into view. Two thick neon-orange stripes wrapped around his biceps. He was an officer from the Department of Enforcement. Breel's jaw dropped.

What's the DOE doing here?

The DOE officer instructed everyone to sit in the living room. Stomach knotted, Breel got up from the table and sank into the couch beside Trafis.

"I think you have the wrong house," Duknum said as he sat beside Criba.

"Silence," said the officer. He tucked a clipboard under his arm. "Is this not the Sorep house?"

Duknum's eyes widened, and he nodded. "Yes, I'm Duknum Sorep."

"And Breel Sorep lives here?"

Breel's stomach squirmed.

"That's my daughter," Duknum said. He glanced at Breel; his pupils dilated.

The officer stroked his mustache. "Then I'm at the right house."

He walked down the hall. The only sound was that of the TV replaying yesterday's news. The silence was too much. Breel's heart thudded against her rib cage. She glanced at her parents. They stared at her unmoving, Criba with a hand to her mouth. Her face was pale. Breel looked to the ground.

"What'd you do?" Duknum asked. His tone was higher pitched than normal. "Breel?"

She didn't answer. He'd find out soon enough. Waves of nausea coursed through Breel's stomach. It was like she had just run a marathon. She breathed deeply through her nose to control her breathing. If it weren't for the officer undoubtedly being in her bedroom, she would've fled to it.

The officer returned a couple of minutes later and stood in front of them, hands on his hips, feet spread. Breel's heart tried to beat itself free of her ribcage.

"Breel?" the officer asked.

It was as if someone had tied a rope around her stomach and pulled the ends. "Yes," she said, voice squeaking.

"Recognize this?"

It took an eternity for him to open his clipboard and reveal her drawing notebook.

It was as she expected. Her parents hadn't moved, and neither looked surprised. Her father shook his head, lips pursed, as her mother let out a soft cry. Trafis stared at her, eyes wide.

"Oh, Breel," Criba said.

Flipping to a page, the DOE officer showed one of her later portraits of Famut. Duknum gasped. Before the officer could speak, her mother burst into tears.

"Breel Sorep," the officer said, speaking over Criba, "you've been reported for and found guilty of engaging in unlawful activities. You broke the law that reads 'you shall not engage in behaviour that places individual benefit over societal benefit.' This is your second warning for drawing, an activity only permitted for illustrators. If you're caught engaging in any other unlawful activities, drawing or otherwise, it means Mortae."

Breel stared into the abyss of the TV. How'd this happen? She'd been so careful. She gripped the end of the couch, knuckles whitening. As she dared a look at the officer, his lip curled. The worst were her mother's cries, ripping open the silence and Breel's heart. She swallowed bile. Her body shook. Duknum had his arm around Criba as she cried into his chest—a rare moment of public physical contact.

The DOE officer cleared his throat. "You know the laws. You're nearly a Leader of Today with high marks in history classes, but you clearly forget the material. Imagine if everyone drew? What would happen?"

Breel answered as taught from the propaganda. "No one would work." Her voice shook and was as soft as Criba's.

"Exactly. President Tatem changed the laws forty-nine years ago for a reason. By drawing, you're not 'embracing the collective.' Yet, as a citizen, 'embracing the collective' is your duty. For your sake, I hope you start understanding that."

Notebook in hand, the officer bid farewell—as if he'd come for a social call—and left. Breel took deep breaths. Her fingers dug into her leg until she drew blood. She released.

"I don't even know where to begin," Duknum said.

Criba was still crying into his chest.

"Father, I—"

"Silence!" His face reddened, and his nostrils flared. "You're out of warnings, not that it matters, since you're nearly a Leader of Today. One more mistake and Mortae, Breel, Mortae!"

"I know. I'll be careful." Her voice quavered.

"Careful? By careful you better mean no more drawing, *ever*! I can only presume you carelessly left your notebook for the housekeeper to find."

No. Breel was always sure not to do that. But he was right—the only explanation was the housekeeper. Everyone knew that housekeepers were more likely than any other Career Group to be in the Platinum section, since they were in prime positions to learn about illegality and report citizens to the DOE. While her parents, her father especially, were paranoid about their children following the law, they'd never report her. It seemed a housekeeper had snooped and found the notebook. Seeing her textbooks, the housekeeper would've known she wasn't permitted to draw. Or—and Famut had always suspected as much—the government told housekeepers the Career Groups of everyone in each house they entered.

Her family didn't understand that drawing was her life. But if drawing meant potential Mortae... Just the thought of Mortae caused her stomach to twist.

Nonetheless, the gravity of the situation hit her. Before, at least there was the cushion of another warning. Now that was gone. Once she became a Leader of Today, Breel had planned to keep drawing. However, it was a guarantee the government would tell housekeepers to keep a close eye on her. No way could she draw and risk Mortae.

"Yes, I won't draw again." Tears welled in her eyes, but she meant it.

Duknum studied her, then nodded. Criba removed herself from her husband and wiped her red eyes. Her lower lip trembled.

"Good," said Duknum. "Your drawing doesn't benefit society. What benefits society is your programming. How're you supposed to do that if you draw the night before your last weekly exam? Even worse, the week before the Demna Exam? Then soon, you'll be a Leader of Today taking Department of Expansion courses, and those assignments will require your attention as well. You think it's unfair, but these laws exist for a reason. We can't return to the old ways."

Responding was pointless. Heart hammering in her chest, she stood.

"I have studying to do." Her voice was monotone.

Her father pointed at her. "Be sure that's all you do."

"I promise."

It was a promise she intended to keep.

Chapter Four

All Breel wanted to do was cry and punch her pillow. Instead, she sat at her desk, mind swirling as she attempted to study.

Every movement was an effort—even turning the page in her textbook. Drawing was her life, and now she couldn't do it.

Stupid law... how can drawing an hour per day destroy society?

After the evening news, Duknum entered without permission and sat on her bed's standard-issue baby-blue sheets. He adjusted his shirt, the upper arms of which had a thick scarlet stripe flanked by two thin white stripes.

"We need to talk," he said.

Taking a deep breath, Breel spun in her chair to face him.

He shook his head, jaw set. "I'm proud of your accomplishments, Breel. You're a fantastic computer programmer. However, you don't recognize the seriousness of this."

"I do."

He frowned. "I sure hope so. Your mother's been crying all evening, terrified the DOE will catch you drawing again."

Breel's chest tightened as tears stung her eyes. She stared at her father's foot to avoid his gaze. "I said I won't draw. I promise."

"You'll be moving out next week and won't have me to keep you in line. How do I know you won't draw then?"

Breel suppressed a smirk. Her father had never successfully kept her "in line." Not even after taking the first few history classes when she learned why President Tatem reformed Lexum.

Breel had aced those classes like all the others. During some history classes, she challenged the teacher to the point that Ami demanded she stop, referencing Mortae—that was before Breel feared Ami wouldn't stop at reporting her. Every teacher she challenged pulled her aside, saying this was a reportable offense, but they'd let it go this time. Teachers failed to convince her to believe in and want to follow the laws of Lexum. With time, her ability to hide her beliefs improved. Despite having the tenth-highest mark in her year in History of Lexum XII and learning about the purported dangers of hobbies, Breel's nonconformity remained.

Until now.

"I won't break the law," Breel said.

Another frown. "Your record doesn't reassure me."

"After today, I've learned my lesson. I won't do anything. I... I'm terrified of Mortae." Her voice caught.

Duknum's piercing green-eyed stare softened, and he gave her a rare hug. "Good. That's good. Oh, and your mother's right. It's too bad you didn't test for illustrator, because your drawing of Famut was... well, it was nice to see his face."

Brushing a hand over his eyes, he left.

Is he wiping away tears? Wow. Guess there's a first for everything.

Even though it was the last thing she wanted to do, Breel returned to her textbooks.

* * *

A life-sized drawing of Famut chasing her plagued Breel's sleep. She fled through the nearly identical city streets until reaching the Quaddro—the public square in the middle of town.

Dream Quaddro was the same as real-life Quaddro. The ground was cobblestone and there were three roped-off sections holding the population of Lexum. At one end of the square, a fifty-metre-long raised platform with a wall at the back faced the populace. Television screens large enough for those at the back to see were on either side of the platform.

The drawing chased Breel to the edge of the platform. The crowd awaited the scheduled *Mortae* in their roped-off sections. President Tatem stood in the middle of the platform flanked by his four personal security officers. A glass wall separated him from the crowd. He spoke into a microphone, screens broadcasting his image.

Breel covered her ears as the crowd chanted "Mortae! Mortae!", punching the air with each word.

President Tatem grinned and ran his hand through his salt-and-pepper hair. Then he turned to Breel, smile widening. It bore into her very soul. A shiver jolted her spine.

Before she could discover if she was the Vucapi, the one receiving Mortae, she woke. Her body shook. Sweat had dampened her pyjamas and sheets. Knowing sleep was fruitless, she rose half an hour early and opened a textbook. Studying the morning of an exam was common. It was when reality struck, and, gripped with panic, she double-checked her notes.

The alarm, hardwired into the house, sounded at seven. She opened her closet to retrieve her exercise clothes—black stretchy pants and a breathable red shirt. Years ago, Ami had shown Breel the different-colour exercise outfits each of her family members wore. Ami's was a light purple. When Breel asked her parents why they didn't upgrade, Duknum had said it was a meaningless way to spend points.

Breel and Criba were the first in the living room. Criba approached Breel wordlessly and placed her hands on Breel's shoulders. Her eyelids drooped. "I couldn't sleep at all. Promise me. Promise me you'll never draw again."

Breel blinked away her own tears at the sight of her mother's welling eyes. "I promise."

Criba sighed and lowered her hands. "Breel, please don't think that you can get away with it once you're in your own house. I worry enough about you when you're living here, let alone once you move out."

"I said I promise."

Criba shook her head. "How can I believe that? You've promised before, too."

"I didn't have two warnings before."

"This is a real promise this time?"

"I promise it's a real promise. Mother, I'm sorry." She hugged Criba's trembling body.

"Okay," Criba said. "You know I understand, right? You know what I'd rather do if I had the choice."

Criba had once said she loved the writing in school and had wanted to be a textbook writer. Writing textbooks sounded uninspired; however, it wasn't like there was anything else to write. Her mother seemed to have accepted her fate well, so perhaps Breel could do the same.

"I just want you as safe and as happy as you can be," Criba said. "If anything happened to you..."

"It won't."

She didn't look convinced. But Breel was serious—she wasn't going to worry her family anymore.

Duknum and Trafis walked in, and moments later, right at seven-fifteen, the TV switched from the news replay to an exercise routine. For the next half hour, they did stretches, jumping jacks, push-ups, planks, and squats, led by a fitness instructor from the Department of Health.

The exercising wasn't too bad. Except for eating, Mortae, and walking to and from school and the Quaddro, it was the only break from working or studying. Today was too intense a workout to hold a conversation, so they worked out in silence.

Afterward, they took turns showering. Once clean, Breel opened her closet to retrieve her uniform for the day. Since it was Friday, three pairs of blouses and pants were hanging. At the end of every Friday, a driver picked up the dirty clothes, delivered them to a drycleaner, and returned them on Sunday—just in time for a fresh wardrobe for Monday. She dressed, finishing the ensemble by buckling her belt and clipping to it her ID card. On the card was her picture and the words *Breel Sorep: Leader of Tomorrow.*

While her family dressed, Breel retrieved a sizable plastic container from the front porch and placed it on the dining room table. Inside were their plates, cups, and cutlery for breakfast. Underneath were four thermoses of coffee and a warming tray. Her parents had ordered eggs and toast, Trafis an omelette, and she pancakes.

Breel had everything at their respective places at the table when her family joined. Her parents wore the Department of Occupation uniform: raspberry-red pants and a black sweater. The collar of their white shirt lay on top of the sweater. Breel had always liked how her mother's secretary stripings—thin white line between thick teal lines—contrasted with the black shirt.

In history class, they learned which uniforms aligned with each department. However, they weren't taught Career Group stripings. Those were learned by seeing one's stripings and reading their ID card or asking their parents.

The room was silent as Breel and Trafis studied. Breel didn't normally study while eating but had no choice after receiving the warning. Whenever Trafis studied at the table, Duknum gave her looks that asked, "Why aren't you studying?" He claimed he gave her the harder time because Trafis tried his best. Breel, Duknum reasoned, could try harder for higher marks. Criba once told Breel being in the same Career Group as Duknum played a role.

"He hopes you get into a better department than us, Breel," she had said.

In terms of prestige, the Department of Occupation was mid-ranking.

"I don't see why that matters," Breel said.

She cocked her head. "Breel, come on."

Breel rolled her eyes. "Yes, yes. Those working in a top department provide society with the most benefit."

"Yes. He wants you to succeed where we didn't."

"Sounds like he should've done better in school," Breel said.

"His marks weren't as high as yours. He only wants you to do the best you can. He knows you aren't as studious as you could be."

Breel shrugged. It wasn't like she was one of those Leaders of Tomorrow who failed classes and so received Mortae because of it. If the only reward for doing five percent better in school meant working in a more prestigious department, it didn't interest her. She told her mother that.

"I know, Breel," she had said, patting her daughter's arm. "And I understand. I just want you to be happy."

How's happiness even possible?

It was bad enough when she had to draw in secret. But now, avoiding Mortae meant never experiencing happiness again.

They left their dishes for a busser from the Department of Food and were out the door by eight forty-five. Breel's parents bid her and Trafis farewell and headed for their bus stop, while Breel and Trafis walked the short distance to school. In over two weeks, Breel would join the Leaders of Today at a bus stop to head to the Governmental Offices.

She'd only ever seen them from the Quaddro, far in the distance at the end of the street. In History of Lexum IX, she learned they were four buildings, nine floors apiece, with a foyer connecting them. The course prompted many questions such as, "How many departments?" and "How many Leaders of Today in each department?" Her teacher said there were twelve departments, and the number of Leaders of Today varied. She refused to answer questions about rumours of secret departments.

I bet she has no idea.

However, some citizens' IDs said *Government Official* or something equally vague without denoting a department. As such, Breel believed the rumours.

There were no lessons on Friday. Being the last day of school, already halved due to a Mortae, they only wrote their weekly tests.

At the end of the day, Breel and Ami left discrete mathematics and headed toward Ami's locker. Ami put an arm around Breel's shoulders. "Now we're outta here!" Ami said.

"Finally!" said Breel.

Together, they skipped down the hall. Skipping inside was prohibited—though not a Mortae offence—but Breel didn't stop Ami from daring to break a minor rule. Leaders of Tomorrow they passed caught Breel's eye. Some shook their heads, tsking. The mouths of others upturned in suppressed smiles.

Probably wishing they had the courage to do the same thing.

After a few seconds, Ami stopped. "Sorry," she said, releasing Breel. "Didn't even notice what I was doing." She smoothed her shirt.

"It's fine," Breel said.

As they walked at a brisk pace, Breel's thoughts drifted to the near future. She had a whole month of no studying to look forward to. An entire month before starting the Department of Expansion courses. Despite the anxiety of learning her assigned department and starting work, she'd looked forward to this month for years. There was the requirement of learning workplace and Leader of Today etiquette, but it wasn't technically a course—just reportedly a lot of reading.

Having finished school was surreal. Next week they'd be writing the Demna Exam in the Lexum Exam Centre. Later that week, they'd be Leaders of Today. Then all their learning would be through the Department of Expansion. Depending upon their Career Group, they'd take at least one class at a time.

There was subdued excitement since the government prohibited cheering in the halls. For most Leaders of Tomorrow, unless they were to work at the school, it was the last time they'd be inside it.

"Are you gonna miss school?" Breel asked Ami.

"Yeah. I like school. And, as you know, I'm good at it." Ami had the highest mark in all her classes. "You?"

Breel shrugged. She'd wait to compare it to work before making such statements. "It's a little scary," Breel said.

"I guess."

"I mean, after next week, we're supposed to know stuff."

Ami flipped her hair. "Yeah, but that's fine. I can't wait to see how great I'll be at work. No reason to be scared. You have good marks."

I guess she's right. I've yet to fail a test, anyway.

She waited for Ami to stuff everything into her backpack, and Breel did the same at her locker. For the last time, she closed the door with a clang.

Because of the Mortae after lunch, Leaders of Tomorrow ate at home, so Breel and Ami hugged goodbye at the school entrance.

Breel had imagined this moment for a few years. She had pictured herself holding in her emotions as she saw Ami for the last time, except for occasionally crossing paths at Mortae, followed by a long walk home in which she'd reflect upon their years together.

But no emotion welled inside her—only indifference. Yes, she was sad to be leaving Ami. However, she would no longer be around someone who considered themselves smarter and a better citizen than everyone else.

"See you at the Demna if I don't see you at Mortae," Ami said.

As Ami walked away, a weight—one that had been undetectable during twelve years of school—lifted. It was freeing—and a revelation.

Never again will I befriend someone like Ami.

Not seeing Trafis, Breel headed home. As she approached 5 Chrysanthemum Lane, a driver from the Department of Households dropped a box onto the porch and drove to the next house to deliver lunch to the Leader of Tomorrow living there. The box was smaller than usual, as her parents would eat at work.

Breel walked into the house with the box. Trafis was already at the dining room table, grammar book in hand. He closed it.

"I didn't want to ask anything in front of our parents," he said, "but why'd you do it, Breel? Why risk Mortae?"

"I thought I was careful." As she opened the box, she described how and where she'd hidden her drawing notebook.

"Maybe you were, but it's not worth it."

Breel passed Trafis his boxed chicken sandwich. "If there was only one thing you enjoy doing, wouldn't you want to do it?"

Trafis frowned. "If it's illegal, of course not. Please tell me you won't draw again."

Breel set her lunch on the table before responding. "You know me." She lowered her gaze. "I'm terrified of Mortae."

"Really? Then why..." He groaned. "Wow, Breel. That makes no sense. Terrified of Mortae, yet you draw all the time."

Why did Trafis have to bring this up? She sat and opened her lunch.

"I was careful and only had one warning," she said.

"Now two warnings. Get caught again and Mortae."

She picked up her chicken sandwich. As usual, it was almost too thick to get her jaws around it. "Can we talk about something else?"

"Fine." He bit his sandwich and cringed. "Ugh. I hate when they add mayonnaise. Know anything about this Mortae?"

Of course that was his chosen topic. "I heard it's a Leader of Tomorrow."

"Me, too." His voice was but a whisper.

The government never revealed the identity of the Vucapi and the reason for their Mortae until the event itself. However, rumours always spread when someone disappeared. If the government announced a Mortae the next day, the logical conclusion was they were the Vucapi awaiting Mortae in jail. However, no one knew for sure until President Tatem revealed their identity and crime at the Mortae.

Chapter Five

The Mortae was at one, so at twelve forty, Breel and Trafis walked down their street along with other Leaders of Tomorrow. Most of the Leaders of Today would come from the Governmental Offices by bus, so the street was quiet.

Breel could find her way to and from school, Ami's, and the Quaddro. Five years ago, she knew the route to Famut's where those who lived alone resided. Soon, she'd need to learn new routes to and from her new home.

Mortae occurred on a raised platform closer to the north end of the Quaddro. A glass wall in front of the centre and stage right of the platform barricaded it from the crowd—seemingly just to protect President Tatem. No glass protected the Vucapi on stage left. Behind the platform was a wall with a door. The enclosed room held the Vucapi until President Tatem revealed their identity.

In front of the platform were three roped-off sections, each consecutively bigger than the last, separated by space to walk from one side of the Quaddro to the other. The entrances to the sections were on the west and east side of the Quaddro.

Closest to the platform was the Platinum section. It was for a select thousand or so citizens who earned Platinum access for varying lengths of time by providing societal benefits above and beyond the norm. The citizen who alerted authorities to the crimes of the Vucapi always received Platinum access for that Vucapi's Mortae. The Vucapi's immediate family members did too, albeit as punishment for not reporting or realizing the Vucapi's crimes.

Breel and Trafis entered via the north side, walked around the platform on its east side, and waited in line for the middle section—Silver. Approximately one third of citizens had Silver access. It was for citizens with above-average track records—though what this meant practically speaking was unknown.

Leaders of Tomorrow had the same access as their parent in the lowest section. Breel's family had been in Silver—with one exception. Five years ago, for a few Mortae, Duknum had had Platinum access—close enough to the platform to know the Vucapi's eye colour. What her father had done to get it was a mystery.

At the next Mortae, Breel would be in Bronze among other new Leaders of Today. The government expected them to advance to Silver within six months and achieve Platinum access a few times in their lives. She'd need to leave earlier as a Leader of Today as even the line into the Silver section, around half the size as Bronze, took ten minutes to reach the two DOE officers scanning IDs.

The size of the crowd suggested most of the twenty-five thousand citizens of Lexum were in the Quaddro. Normally, Breel would find and join her parents, but space from her father was preferable before the Demna Exam. She led Trafis to a spot near the middle of the Silver section.

"Breel, what're you doing?" Trafis asked.

He was a few feet ahead, waving her over to close the gap within Silver. Breel followed since it was the law for citizens to be as close to the platform they could get within the confines of their section.

Once situated, Trafis stared at the man in front of him, who was wearing crimson pants, a white dress shirt, and a navy-blue sweater—the Department of Education uniform. His Career Group stripings were unfamiliar. Others nodded at the man with respect.

Breel rolled her eyes. *Why do people give such reverential looks to citizens in that department? Give me a break...*

"How were your weekly exams and last day of school?"

Duknum's baritone voice sounded above the din of conversation. Along with her mother, he stood behind Breel and Trafis.

"They were fine," she said.

"Good. Trafis?"

"Went well, I think."

"You think."

He turned back to Breel. "Week after next, you could be in the office beside mine."

He grinned. Breel faked a smile in return. He never told Breel whether he had requested this arrangement. During the last few years, she had asked as many people as she dared whether the government granted such requests; none had heard of them being accepted. Of course, that didn't mean it didn't happen. Anxiety clawed at her stomach every time she thought about how soon she'd learn her department.

Criba stepped between Breel and Duknum. She was like a chihuahua among mastiffs—Breel could've rested her arm on her mother's head.

"I can't believe our daughter's done with school," she said.

Duknum nodded. "Now all that schooling will pay off. You'll have an immense amount of knowledge from which Lexum will benefit."

She was saved from responding when Tanry approached her father. "Hello, Duknum," Tanry said in greeting while shaking hands.

Tanry and Duknum had gone to school together. However, the law "every citizen of Lexum shall keep interactions with nonfamilial citizens outside of their department's section to a minimum" meant citizens usually only saw each other at a Mortae or on a bus. There were events to improve camaraderie and learn from others with relevant experiences and skills; however, they were only within one's own department. All other gatherings required permission, except for family or private gatherings of one's Career Group in their departmental section. The government prohibited other gatherings due to lack, and potentially detriment, of societal benefit.

"Oh, hello, Tanry." Duknum's eyes glanced down at his coffee-brown pants and salmon-coloured sweater.

"I see," Tanry said.

Duknum had always been cordial with Tanry. However, the government had just granted him Silver access after a six-month demotion to Bronze. Duknum had assumed he did something wrong. He also didn't like associating with a fellow programmer in the lowest prestige department—the Department of Sanitation.

Tanry moved elsewhere as a Department of Logistics man approached the platform's lectern. His russet-brown sweater blended into the platform; however, the sun made his ruby-red pants appear to shimmer. Breel was close enough that he wasn't a dot, but the television screens on either side of the platform provided a better view. A pop echoed throughout the Quaddro as he tapped the microphone. The chatter ceased.

"Welcome to this afternoon's Mortae!" His voice boomed the word "Mortae." Cheers erupted. He held up his hands to quiet the crowd. "All citizens are accounted for except for one hundred and twenty Leaders of Today and forty-seven Leaders of Tomorrow approved for leaves of absence because of sickness. We're broadcasting the feed live to their televisions. As everyone else is present, please help me welcome the one, the only, President Hargam Tatem!"

Chants of "President Tatem! President Tatem!" filled the air.

Then, after a moment, the door on the platform opened and President Tatem, sandwiched between his four personal security officers—dressed identically to DOE officers—walked through the doorway. He stepped in front of the microphone. Two of his security stood beside him, facing the crowd. The other two were farther back, looking out at either side of the platform.

Every DOE officer was armed with a tranquilizer dart gun, rather than a lethal weapon. The exception was President Tatem's personal security—they each had a .45 calibre pistol.

Like he needs security. No one was going to attack President Tatem. It was impossible with the glass wall between him and the crowd.

President Tatem lifted the microphone half a foot. Rays of sunshine bounced off his hair, overshadowing his sparkling crystal-blue eyes. Wrinkles showed his age. It made little sense that he continued working when he forced everyone else to retire June of the year they turned sixty.

"Good afternoon, Leaders of Today and Tomorrow!" His voice carried throughout the Quaddro with ease. He paused for the cheering to die down and adjusted his ash-gray suit, his cherry-red tie having escaped in the wind, whipping across his shoulder.

After buttoning his suit jacket, he continued. "Mortae is a cornerstone of our society. The pinnacle of punishment for those who put individual benefit, whether it be for themselves or someone else, above societal benefit. We call these people Vucapi, because once someone breaks our laws, once they engage in actions that benefit an individual rather than society, they are no longer citizens of Lexum. A true citizen always puts societal benefit first."

He spoke slower than most and enunciated every word. Breel had never heard him stammer, use unnecessary words, or even use contractions.

The crowd cheered. President Tatem smoothed his hair even though it was so slicked back with gel not a single strand could move.

"Some of you know today's Vucapi. If so, it doesn't matter whether you considered him an upstanding citizen. He is a citizen no longer. The DOE warned the Vucapi twice for pursuing his interest in writing stories, yet he did it a third time—Mortae is his punishment."

Breel's stomach dropped. Since only Leaders of Tomorrow received warnings, the rumours were correct. Her father's eyes landed on her.

Breel looked away from him. *Oh, I'm in for another lecture...*

"Is this acceptable behaviour for someone who will become a brick-layer?" President Tatem asked.

"No!" the crowd shouted as one. President Tatem and the crowd punched the air with their fists in time, the crowd pulsating. Breel joined because there was no choice in the matter. DOE patrolled the sections, eyeing anyone who didn't participate.

"Does this behaviour benefit society?"

"No!" Air punch.

"Should we condone this behaviour?"

"No!" Air punch.

"What should we do with the Vucapi?"

"Mortae!" Air punch.

"Say it again!"

"Mortae!" Air punch.

"And a third time!"

"MORTAE!" Air punch.

The amped-up crowd was sickening. The noise only increased when the door behind the platform opened. DOE officers flanked a twelve-year-old, his hands bound. The camera zoomed in to show his torn uniform, matted hair, and streaming tears. It'd been months since a Vucapi was so young.

His feet planted, the DOE officers dragged him across the platform and onto a bench on stage left of the platform. The officers stood on either side of the Vucapi, pinning him by placing their hands on his shoulders. The lack of glass on this side of the platform meant an unspoiled view.

"This is Erup Ripam," said President Tatem, microphone popping. Breel imagined spittle flying as he spoke.

The "Mortae! Mortae!" chant continued. The crowd raised their arms as they punched the air in time.

Breel shuddered, and bile burned her throat. *He's just a kid!*

"Breel!" Duknum yelled her name in her ear.

She had inadvertently stopped participating. Having no choice, she joined in. However, she only mouthed the word "Mortae," refusing to audibly chant the word.

"Mortae! Mortae!" the crowd said.

Ahead, a toddler plugged his ears. The boy's mother removed them and said something to him. Moments later, he began punching the air with his fists, wildly out of sync with the crowd.

"The Deliverer!" said President Tatem.

As the crowd cheered, the toddler covered his ears again. Nearby, a baby cried.

President Tatem pointed to the doorway from which a figure in a caramel-coloured lab coat, its hem an inch from the ground, appeared. The coat had to have been custom made to accommodate his broad shoulders. Over his head was a deep hood, hiding his face from the crowd.

"Probably to protect his identity from angered citizens," Famut had said when Breel asked about it.

While his identity was a mystery, it was common knowledge he'd been performing the job for nearly as long as Mortae existed.

The roar of the crowd intensified. The Deliverer stood behind Erup to avoid blocking the crowd's view. He retrieved a needle from his lab coat, movements slow and purposeful to garner excitement, anticipation.

As the Deliverer removed the safety cap from the needle, the crowd quieted for the Vucapi's plea.

"Please no! I'm only a Leader of Tomorrow! I'll be good, I promise!"

"Mortae!" the crowd shouted before falling silent.

The Deliverer outstretched his arm so Erup would see the five-inch needle.

"No!" Erup cried. "Mommy, help me! Please help me! Mommy!" Erup flailed on the bench, limbs windmilling.

The officers' grip kept him on the bench. Erup's voice turned soprano, words no longer comprehensible.

The Deliverer raised Erup's arm and bent it at the elbow, grasping his wrist. As an officer helped keep Erup still, the Deliverer held the needle above Erup's arm.

"Let the deed be done!" President Tatem said.

There was a high-pitched scream from the Platinum section. "No! No! Not my son! Stop, I'll do anything!"

Breel pictured the nearby officers restraining her. Perhaps throwing her to the ground, then picking her up, forcing her to watch. The Deliverer waited for the drama to play out.

Duknum caught Breel's eye. He shifted closer to his wife, squeezing her shoulder during the chanting reprieve.

What the... Breel couldn't take her eyes off her parents. She'd attended every Mortae with them and couldn't recall any in which her father had done this. *What's going on?*

The crowd cheered again, and Breel returned her attention to the television screens. The DOE must have quieted Erup's mother, as the Deliverer was bringing the needle closer to her son's arm. After a few seconds, no doubt an age to Erup, the needle pierced his skin. He cried as it dug further and further, and the Deliverer pressed the plunger.

Chapter Six

The Deliverer replaced the safety cap and returned the needle to his pocket. The officers released Erup. He pitched forward, falling headfirst onto the platform, arm dangling over the edge.

Breel glanced down to avoid the screens as the cameras panned to his parents.

I'm despicable...

However, another voice told her, *You had no choice. If you didn't do it, you'd be the next Vucapi.*

Did Erup's parents believe their son's actions justified Mortae? If they were Hargamites, it was possible. They may have even talked to him about writing, begging him to stop.

Just like my parents...

Breel's knees weakened as President Tatem waited for the cheering to dissipate. What Erup's parents were experiencing was what her own parents and Trafis would experience if she continued drawing. Thankfully, that wasn't going to happen. She didn't want the government forcing her family to watch her Mortae because she didn't heed their warnings.

It was a minute later when the crowd quieted enough for President Tatem to speak. "Another citizen turned Vucapi because of the false belief that individual benefit trumps societal benefit. Forty-nine years ago, citizens unable to afford the luxuries of the rich fought against this belief. They fought for a Lexum where 'societal benefit trumps individual benefit' and every citizen provides value to Lexum. They fought for a Lexum that gives equal treatment to all citizens. They fought for a Lexum in which everyone receives an education, not just those who can afford it. They fought for a Lexum in which everyone contributes. Thanks to these efforts, everyone has the same quality and standard of life. Everyone receives the education they need to pursue a career matching their aptitudes and skills. This happens because we know 'societal benefit trumps individual benefit.'

"Make no mistake. Mortae is the punishment for actions that favour individual benefit. Mortae is the punishment for causing disruption. Mortae is the punishment for disregarding others. All actions must be within the law and selfless. They need to better society.

"If you see anyone disregarding our laws—even if you *suspect* it— your duty is to report them. There is no punishment for those who report other citizens—only reward. So, follow the lead of the citizens who reported Erup and inform our officers of anyone you suspect. Here ends today's Mortae."

President Tatem turned away from the microphone. His security surrounded him as he exited through the doorway. The cacophony of conversation filled the Quaddro as the crowd filed out, starting with the Platinum section.

"What did we learn from today's Mortae?" Duknum asked.

"'Societal benefit trumps individual benefit,'" Trafis said.

Breel groaned. Sometimes it was difficult having a model citizen as a sibling. He was oblivious to the glaring moral holes in Lexum's ways of doing things. But whenever Breel spoke to him about it, he walked away.

"Oh, Breel," said Criba. "I can't believe this is your last Mortae with us."

"Not for long," Duknum said. "She'll get back into Silver."

Breel met her mother's eye. Criba smiled, rolling her eyes at her husband's statement. *At least someone understands it's doubtful I'll return to Silver.*

Once home, Breel headed to her room. The moment she entered it, her fingers itched to grip a pencil—to draw.

Drawing had been her escape.

An escape from the grip of President Tatem and all the laws he created.

An escape from the constant studying.

An escape from her entire life.

Drawing meant visiting the past, a transport to fifty years ago—before President Tatem mandated the massive changes. When she drew, she was in control of her life.

After her first warning, she had vowed to stop. It wasn't worth the risk. But one day, while sitting on her bed, textbook on her lap, the paper and pencil on her desk had caught her eye.

They were alluring.

They called her name.

Whispering, pleading, convincing.

One moment, she was completing an algebra problem, and the next she was sitting at her desk with a number two pencil scratching across a piece of paper.

She was only ever truly happy when drawing. Why deprive herself of that? The rational side of her brain had screamed no. *Don't do it! Mortae! Danger!* But it had been too tempting. After all, Famut had said Leaders of Tomorrow were supposed to try new things.

Oh, to have lived fifty years ago! To draw whenever and wherever she wanted—between classes, in the backyard, or even in the Quaddro. To have fellow citizens walk by and comment on her realistic portraits. To have them ask her to draw them.

When Breel started drawing, she drew everything. Her bedroom, her house, the school, the Quaddro. But portraits interested her the most. Portraits of her parents, Trafis, Famut, Ami, and her teachers. Each time she saw her subject, she'd mentally compare them to her latest portrait, make note of what to fix, and draw a new one. Having her hobby was like living fifty or more years ago—when pictures were ubiquitous and everyone had them posted on the internet and printed at home.

The internet still existed, but only for work. Likewise, pictures only existed in textbooks, training manuals, and on the IDs everyone wore.

Long ago, Breel had risked telling Famut about her drawing. He outlined concern after concern: being caught, falling grades, Mortae... But not once did he tell her to stop. Instead, he assisted Breel in devising rules to decrease the risk of anyone discovering her hobby, such as only drawing in her bedroom and not drawing the day the housekeeper came by.

His encouragement showed Breel how important it was to express individuality. But he was clear that even more critical was being careful. There was no mistaking the risk.

Swallowing her grief over drawing, she pulled a textbook toward her. However, she'd only read one paragraph when a knock sounded.

Breel turned to find her parents standing in the doorway.

"We'd like to come in," her father said.

"I want to study."

"This is important." He sat on the edge of her bed. Criba's eyes were closed, and she placed a hand on the wall as if to steady herself. Breel squirmed in her seat and avoided her father's gaze.

"Today was one of many Mortae you've attended," he said.

"Many" was an understatement. There were dozens per year. Frequency varied and was often in groups with several Vucapi within a week or two, sometimes at the same Mortae, followed by a dry period. Many were Leaders of Tomorrow like Erup, who received one warning too many. It was rare for Leaders of Today to fail at being good citizens.

"How many more must you witness before learning disobedience will lead you to being the Vucapi? You're out of warnings as a Leader of Tomorrow, and even if you weren't, you'll receive no warnings as a Leader of Today. From now on, doing anything illegal is automatic Mortae."

Breel stared at the ground to avoid glaring at her father. "I told you I won't draw anymore."

"I had to be sure. President Tatem's a good man. That's why he gives Leaders of Tomorrow leeway. Given the resources used to educate citizens, the last thing he wants is to end lives. But anyone who disrupts Lexum is a risk and liability. We cannot return to the old ways because we'd never have enough people working. That's why Mortae is necessary."

"I understand."

She truly did understand her parents' fear. But the reasons for Mortae being "necessary"? She didn't understand those at all.

Ridiculous circumstances made one Mortae particularly memorable. It had been a dark night that teemed rain, the water nearly overflowing the curbs. Even though the Vucapi, a driver from the Department of Utilities, had expressed concern because of the lack of visibility, his Career Group Head ordered him to drive a lineman to a downed powerline. He hit an unseen bump. There was a scream. He pulled over to investigate—he'd run over a toddler. The driver, lineman, and toddler's mother didn't know first aid, and the doctor arrived too late.

The driver paid for the incident with Mortae even though his Head had forced him to drive despite his concerns. If the government taught first aid to all Career Groups, the child might have survived.

Due to the Leader of Tomorrow curfew, the mother had broken the law by allowing her child to be outside. She said her child ran out of the house when his father opened the door, but that wasn't good enough for the Department of Enforcement. She, too, paid for the incident with Mortae. President Tatem used the event to reinforce the importance of the curfew.

When Breel had expressed her anger at this Mortae, Duknum had scolded her for questioning President Tatem and the DOE, saying the driver and mother should've been more careful. He had said that receiving Mortae for such actions ensured everyone knew carelessness would not go unpunished.

While that was the most ridiculous Mortae, every Mortae was ridiculous. Erup should not have lost his life just because the government prohibited bricklayers from writing.

"I hope you understand," Duknum said. "You have great potential if you put society first. Don't be selfish."

Gritting her teeth at the word "selfish," she nodded. "I said I promise."

Duknum looked back at Criba. Breel followed his gaze and frowned. Tears flowed down Criba's face, and her chest rose and fell rapidly. It tore Breel's heart.

"Oh, Criba," said Duknum.

He leapt to his feet and pulled his wife close. She burst into tears. Breel stared, jaw slack, as he rubbed Criba's back and whispered something in her ear.

Well, this is awkward.

It seemed rude to return to studying, so she waited for this rare display to end. She stared at the floor. Criba was worried, but this was another level. *What's this even about? Does it have anything to do with his touching her at Mortae?*

Finally, a minute or two later, Criba extracted herself. "I'm sorry," she said, drying her eyes.

Duknum shook his head. "You have nothing to apologize about." He put an arm around her shoulders and guided her to Breel's bed.

I had no idea my father was so sensitive!

Her parents sat across from her as if they were newlyweds and not the largely affectionless—not so affectionless?—people Breel knew.

Criba spoke in a shaky voice. "You getting your first warning scared me. This second one terrifies me because... because... Duknum?"

He rubbed her arm. "When your mother was eight, her older sister got in trouble for the third time and received Mortae."

Breel blinked. "What?"

She never told me she had a sister!

"She wasn't nice to me," Criba said, staring at her lap. "My parents favoured her and blamed me for her death." Tears welled in her eyes, but she blinked them away.

"I'm sorry," Breel said. There didn't seem to be anything else to say. "Did she draw?"

"No," Duknum said. "What she did isn't relevant. And obviously, her Mortae wasn't your mother's fault. Thankfully, your mother's largely gotten over the difficulty of seeing Mortae. However, she's terrified of once again seeing the Mortae of someone she loves."

So, her mother had a secret sister, witnessed her Mortae, and understandably had issues because of it. No doubt they were finally telling Breel about this in a last-ditch effort to get her to conform. But what was there to say? Breel had already said she wouldn't draw again.

"Your mother's too reserved to take a hard line with you," Duknum said. "But believe me when I say my hard lines come from both of us."

"I know that," Breel said.

At least I think I do.

Criba finally looked at Breel through swollen eyes. "Please don't tell anyone. The only people I've told are your father's family and now you."

"I won't," Breel vowed. "And I promise, I won't draw. I understand the severity."

Apparently satisfied, her parents left, arms around each other.

Breel sat stunned. *How does she carry all that inside her?* Her mother was so strong. Breel ached thinking about all the worry she caused her.

Then there was her father. For some reason, he'd never shown his children that side of himself. She finally believed her mother when she'd once said Breel's father and his family gave her everything her birth family lacked.

Until that moment, Breel'd never considered her parents to have much of a relationship. Sure, they worked in the same section, married, and had children. But they never seemed to do anything alone together to develop their relationship. Not that there was much time or opportunity to do so—other than in bed at night, heading to and from work, and sitting alone together at departmental events.

I guess that must be enough.

Needing to study, Breel pushed thoughts of her parents out of her head and opened a textbook even though all she wanted to do was draw. However, the need for self-protection, and keeping her promise to her parents, was larger.

Perhaps this was for the best. Had the DOE not scared her into submission, she would've continued drawing after becoming a Leader of Today. At some point, that would've led to Mortae and her death would've ruined her mother.

It wasn't long before supper arrived—a turkey dinner to celebrate the end of school. There was plenty of meat, dressing, vegetables, bread, and gravy to go around. Dessert was an apple pie. Trafis studied during supper, as he had his final exams for grade eleven on Monday. No one commented on Breel's lack of a textbook.

Their food delivery included meal request cards for the next week. The two or three options for breakfast, lunch, and supper rotated monthly with occasional special meals. Everyone having their favourite meals meant they marked their choices within seconds and left the cards on the table for a busser to collect when clearing the table.

Since it was nearly seven, they congregated in the living room, Breel and Trafis on one couch and their parents on the other—the second one courtesy of Lexum Catalog points. Minutes later, the TV volume increased, as was its default on the hour. A couple of instruments—violins, according to Breel's History of Lexum I teacher—played an upbeat thirty-second tune leading into the news. Most of the thirty minutes replayed the Mortae. Breel grimaced as, for a second time, Erup's mother screamed. Then, Erup pitched forward onto the platform.

Next was news of upcoming changes to the Department of Education's curriculum for certain Career Groups.

Finally, President Tatem gave his daily address. Wearing his suit, he stood behind a microphone in front of his oak desk. It overflowed the edges of the camera.

"Good evening, citizens of Lexum. Congratulations to our Leaders of Tomorrow on finishing another year of school. I know you all studied hard, doing your best to become Leaders of Today with maximized utility to benefit society.

"Forty-nine years ago, selfish endeavours were the way of life. The rich bribed themselves into better university programs, better careers. Often, they were not qualified for these careers and so society suffered. They rarely took the jobs society needed filled. When they could not get a job they wanted, many preferred engaging in hobbies instead of working the so-called undesirable jobs. You know the horror stories of incompetent doctors performing surgeries because, instead of continuing education, they played sports or games or created pointless art."

Breel rolled her eyes. *Doesn't he ever have anything new to say?*

Not for the first time, Breel imagined people she knew and drew them in her mind. But, as usual, the government put the TVs on such a high volume that any attempt to tune him out was in vain.

"We vowed to change all that," said President Tatem. "To put an end to such selfishness. To 'embrace the collective.' To ensure every citizen benefits Lexum by doing what they are best at. By studying hard and maximizing your utility, you have done your part in this. And Lexum thanks you."

He was all smiles as he spoke and looked directly into the camera—into the soul of the citizens of Lexum. A shiver zapped Breel's spine.

"We have among us Leaders of Tomorrow who, in eleven days, will be Leaders of Today. To those Leaders: tonight, we celebrated the end of your schooling with a special dinner. Next week you will write your Demna Exam. Thanks to Nito Test improvements and upgraded curricula, not only has there been no failing grade in the Demna Exam in over twenty-five years, but scores are significantly higher than in the past. I trust this year's exam writers will continue that trend. When you receive your marks, you will also learn your assigned department. What a glorious time! You will soon fulfill your societal duty by working. Doing this is your way of paying Lexum tenfold what the government spent on the education generously given to you."

President Tatem ran his hand over his hair. "You will learn more in your Congratulations Package, and we've planned exciting events including departmental meet-and-greet dinners. These intra-departmental monthly events foster a community in which you will learn from each other.

"Normally my remarks are longer, but I do not want to keep our Leaders of Tomorrow from studying. Let all your actions be of benefit to society and 'embrace the collective.' Until tomorrow, goodnight."

The news ended at quarter to eight instead of the usual eight. Trafis was halfway to his bedroom before the television volume had even lowered.

"You heard President Tatem, Breel," Duknum said.

"I know, but I was wondering what sort of intra-departmental events there are?"

Even Trafis stopped to listen.

"They're one evening a month," Duknum said. "Could be anything. There are also seminars led by someone sharing what they've learned through Department of Expansion courses."

Because apparently taking your own courses isn't enough.

"Can you pick what you want to learn through the Department of Expansion?"

"Within reason. It must apply to your Career Group, and your Head needs to approve."

Translation: no.

Typical.

She dragged herself to her bedroom and returned to studying.

Chapter Seven

The days were long in the week leading up to the Demna Exam. The only breaks Breel had were to eat and watch the news. As morbid as it sounded, even attending a Mortae would've been a welcome change of pace.

She and her classmates didn't know details about the practical exam, beyond logistics, as it was illegal to speak of them. However, creating a program was likely, so Breel spent a lot of time programming. Occasionally, she studied the less exciting parts of the curriculum.

When Trafis had finished his exams for the year, he continued bringing textbooks to the table to study for his Demna Exam during his month-long school break. Breel also started bringing a textbook to every meal to appease her parents. Several times a day, her father checked her room to ensure she was studying.

Finally, the first day of the Demna Exam arrived. Sleep had been elusive. Anxiety gnawed at her stomach. However, it was more due to anticipation about her assigned department than the exam itself. Breel exercised and showered in a daze, not fully waking until eating her eggs.

For the first time, she took the bus with her parents. The driver instructed her to scan her ID card when boarding. With the not-quite Leaders of Today on the bus, most seats were full.

Sitting across the aisle from her parents, Breel stared out the window as they passed identical houses and streets.

I wonder which classes' exams I'll write first? Not that it matters…

They headed west toward the Quaddro and turned south to go around it. The Governmental Offices were in the distance. A few minutes later, with the offices still in the distance, the bus stopped.

"Lexum Exam Centre," the driver announced.

Breel stood, gripping the back of the seat in front of her until her shaky legs could bear her weight. The Demna Exam was causing more anxiety than she'd thought. As she passed her parents, Criba smiled. Duknum remained stoic but patted her arm.

"Do well," they said in unison.

"We know you will, Breel," Criba added.

She and the other Leaders of Tomorrow disembarked and followed a wide pathway to the building. It was one-storey, its frontage covering half a block with glass walls and a high ceiling.

More buses arrived. Those in academic streams were in their late teens. Those who had less information to learn for their Career Group were as young as ten. They formed lines in front of three sets of double doors. The only sound was the near-continuous beeping as the DOE scanned IDs of everyone who entered. Breel spotted Curia from her discrete mathematics class. Breel smiled at her, and Curia waved back. Ami wasn't in sight, but that was just as well.

The last thing I need right now is Ami being annoying.

Inside, greeting everyone, was a prominent wall-to-ceiling poster of a baby sitting on grass that read, *Every citizen of Lexum depends upon you.* Breel averted her eyes as she checked into the QRS desk to pick up her exam folder and Confidentiality Statement. On the far side was the cavernous exam room with rows upon rows of desks cramped together.

Every footfall echoed as the Leaders of Tomorrow walked to their desks. Breel settled into one near the middle of the room. From this new vantage point, the gap between the desks, around five feet, appeared spacious, like islands in an archipelago. The desks themselves were bigger than those in the classrooms.

The exam started at nine. They had eight hours, not including a lunch break, to finish. Breel flipped opened her folder. Inside were eight exams, one package for each set of like classes, including history and English.

Might as well get the worst one over with. Breel opened the history exam.

The first question read: *Walls surround Lexum. Explain why these walls are necessary. Include at least three security features of the walls in your answer.*

She wrote: *The walls keep citizens safe from the dangerous animals and environment outside.* Breel didn't comment on not knowing the type of animals and why they were dangerous. They had only learned a plethora of dangerous, carnivorous animals were likely to eat anyone venturing outside the walls because of inadequate food sources.

"Not true," Famut had said. "That's a scare tactic."

She was uncertain whether he had lied to ease her fears or if he had known the truth.

Breel finished her answer by outlining the security features of the walls: the DOE guards, two permanently locked gates, and a stash of weapons within the walls to defend Lexum, if needed.

Years ago, Leaders of Tomorrow had taken a field trip to the gate. Breel had bounced on the bus seat as she'd imagined all the trees and animals on the other side.

Unlike the wired backyard fences, which allowed for visibility on all sides, the gate and walls were galvanized steel. The gate towered over her at forty feet high and opened by inserting a foot-long key into an electronic lock.

"It was pointless," she complained to Famut. "I really wanted to see the other side!"

"There's nothing to see anyway," he said. "It's just desert. Not much except the occasional bush."

"How d'you know?"

He had refused to answer.

Breel wanted to vomit at the second question: *What heroic acts did President Tatem engage in forty-nine years ago to save our society from collapse?*

Back then, Lexum had multiple government officials, not a dictator. There was only one lower class seat in the government held by a young future President Tatem. Officials struggled to control the bribery of the upper class. The bribes got them into specific university programs and jobs they perceived as more desirable, leading to underqualified medical doctors, teachers, accountants, and more. Meanwhile, demand was high for janitors, carpenters, and factory workers.

The lower class demanded radical changes, arguing this wouldn't be an issue if they had an equal opportunity to attend postsecondary school and thus be employed in all types of jobs, not just those requiring apprenticeship or no further education. One proposal suggested allowing free education to the lower class, but the upper class protested having to pay for something the lower class received for free.

Nothing changed. Civil war broke out. Government officials were killed until only the future President Tatem remained.

He became president shortly thereafter and equalized all citizens. President Tatem implemented Career Groups based on an aptitude test, so one's background didn't limit them. He abolished currency, as everyone would give to Lexum and receive in return only what they needed. To reduce education costs, citizens would take only the courses needed for their future career.

The upper class protested their loss of power, despite the punishments received for their revolts. Residential break-ins, vandalism, and thievery were common. President Tatem heightened security with the advent of IDs. The internet, widely used to propagate rebellions, was abolished for anything but work-related purposes. Only Leaders of Today and Tomorrow who needed a computer for school or work were permitted one at home. Hardware and software were preprogrammed so citizens could only access what they needed. President Tatem destroyed anything he deemed extraneous and irrelevant to one's Career Group or daily living.

Public executions of rebels eventually turned into Mortae for any citizen who dared break one of the newly formed laws. Within a few years, society was unrecognizable. The changes created better outcomes, because everyone held jobs for which they were qualified and competent.

At least, that was the story told to every Leader of Tomorrow. No doubt President Tatem exaggerated the facts. But Breel wrote her answer, including all she had learned from her history classes.

The next question said: *List the laws of Lexum that every citizen must follow.*

Breel suppressed a laugh. The government enforced its laws starting in infancy, so any citizen could spout them off.

In History of Lexum IV, each law had a dedicated week to learn and discuss its relevance and importance. Breel recalled the three laws: 1) Attend each Mortae, unless otherwise excused due to illness, 2) Be fully engaged in each Mortae, and 3) Keep interactions with nonfamilial citizens outside of one's department to a minimum.

Thank goodness I don't have to describe them or talk about why they're needed!

The following question was similar: *List the laws of Lexum that every citizen of Lexum shall not do.*

The list was so long one could write for years without pause. But in reality, there were four over-arching laws. Citizens shall not: 1) Engage in behaviour that places individual benefit over societal benefit,

2) Devote time to activities that are not associated with one's Career Group, 3) Discuss test- and exam-related content with anyone, and 4) Discuss work-related details with anyone outside of one's Career Group and Department section.

Breel wrote her answers. The only good coming from having such propaganda spewed at her was easy regurgitation on exams.

* * *

When the exam finished at five, Breel dropped her pencil. Her fingers screamed from clutching the stick of graphite for endless hours. She shook her hand to regain feeling in it.

However, the exam had gone well. Even discrete mathematics. *Mr. Gaimster would be proud!*

Walking with the crowd to the doors, Ami called her name. Breel sighed but squeezed past someone to walk beside her.

"Breel, I was looking for you." Ami grinned as if the entire Demna, not just the first day, was over. "What'd you think? Weren't those the easiest exams ever?"

Breel was confident in how she did but wouldn't put the Demna Exam in those terms.

Ami frowned. "Oh, no! You didn't do well?"

"No, I did."

"Oh." Ami's smile returned. "You finished it all?"

"Yeah." *Barely.*

"I even had time to check over some of my answers!"

They headed for the curb to catch their buses. Now that they were out of the building, the chatter increased among the Leaders of Tomorrow. Some looked relieved, and others stood waiting without talking to anyone, staring at the ground.

"That's good," Breel said.

She bit her tongue to avoid saying, *Be quiet, Ami. No one wants to listen to you being obnoxious about exams.*

"I wish we took the same bus to talk more about the exam! Not the content, of course."

I'm glad we're not.

But Breel said, "Yeah, it's too bad."

"Oh, well. You probably have to study, anyway."

Breel frowned at the word "you." "I don't *need* to study. I study because we're supposed to study."

"True. I don't need to study either," Ami said as a delivery van drove past the bus stop.

"My marks are high too, Ami." Breel turned to show her contempt, but the sun caused her to squint, so she dropped her gaze to the road instead.

"Yeah, I know. Why'd you say that?"

"Because it sounded as if you think I'm dumber than you."

"Don't call yourself dumb. Your marks just aren't as high as mine."

She pictured her fist meeting Ami's delicate face. "I didn't call myself dumb."

"Kinda sounded like you did."

Breel clenched her teeth, and this time she didn't care about having to squint.

"Why're you mad?" Ami asked.

Breel swallowed her reaction as she imagined blood spurting across Ami's face. No. She wouldn't risk getting in trouble for an altercation.

"Never mind," Breel said.

Imagining punching Ami was fun, but citizens had received Mortae for fighting. Her most poignant memory of a fight was one that happened four years ago in the school cafeteria. Above the din of conversation had come a scream of anguish when a girl learned her sister had kissed the guy she was interested in and planned to date once allowed as a Leader of Today. The girl grabbed her sister's chair out from under her, and her sister fell onto the floor with a thud and a cry. The girl yanked her sister up by her arm. Fists flew. Leaders of Tomorrow and Today intervened. It ended in a dislocated shoulder, broken tailbone, and broken nose for the sister. It had ended in Mortae for the girl who'd injured a highly valued future surgeon. But the sister had recovered and still became a surgeon.

Breel's bus pulled up, and she boarded without another word.

Chapter Eight

The first day of the Demna Exam was over, but Breel still had most of the computer programming-oriented exams to write.

The news provided her only break. Following the upbeat violin duet was the usual half an hour outlining the day's news, most of which focussed on the Demna. A female reporter spoke as a camera panned the room full of Leaders of Tomorrow.

"I didn't even notice the cameras," Breel said.

Her parents chuckled, and Duknum reached over to pat her leg. "That's my girl. Too busy acing her exams."

"Today," said the reporter, "over one thousand Leaders of Tomorrow wrote day one of the Demna Exam, successful completion of which will turn them into full-fledged Leaders of Today. Next week, we'll have everything from new doctors to janitors, from new glass blowers to teachers, from new tilers to photographers. Today, the Demna Exam's focus was on general knowledge. Day two will cover Career Group-specific knowledge. Day three is a Career Group-specific practical exam."

The only other news was of a chemist discovering a new drug.

Next, President Tatem gave his daily address from his office.

"Citizens of Lexum. Congratulations to those who completed day one of the Demna Exam. I know you did well, so when you become Leaders of Today later this week, you can give back to Lexum like you have always wanted. Whether next week you are delivering meals and supplies, typing on a computer, constructing buildings, or anything in between, every one of you has a crucial role in keeping Lexum functioning. Your entire life has led to this point.

"But being a Leader of Today is also a great responsibility. While you will no longer be under your parents' roof, you will still be under the proverbial roof of Lexum. Everyone under this roof has responsibilities to all citizens, as our every action affects everyone's well-being. Therefore, our actions must benefit society. Do not be fooled into thinking you are independent when you leave your parents' house. Lexum is a wonderful machine, and every one of us is part of that machine. Every part depends upon every other part. If too many parts break, society breaks. The government and all Leaders of Today have put time and energy into teaching you to become competent Leaders of Today. Your friends are counting on you. Your teachers are counting on you. Your parents are counting on you. I'm counting on you. Every citizen of Lexum is counting on you."

Breel tried not to gag as President Tatem sipped his water.

He placed his glass on an unseen surface. "To our other Leaders of Tomorrow: for some of you, in a year from now, you will write your Demna Exam. For others, that is two or more years away. However, it is coming. It is never too soon to study for it. Use this month's break for what it is for—studying for the Demna. Plan your study schedules for the next year or more, collate your notes, and study them. As with all illegal activities, any Leader of Tomorrow found engaging in activities counterproductive to Demna Exam preparation will receive a warning.

"To all citizens: let your every action be of benefit to society. 'Embrace the collective.' Until tomorrow, goodnight."

* * *

Ami was nowhere in sight on day two of the Demna Exam.

Thank goodness. I don't need her to brag about how awesome she did when I messed up part of the programming languages exam.

That particular exam was worrisome, but she faked a smile and said it went just as well as day one. Despite that, a weight had lifted. Somewhat. The written portions of the Demna Exam were over. Just the practical exam remained. Perhaps it'd be creating a database or writing a program to solve mathematical problems or making a macro.

When Breel entered the Lexum Exam Centre for the third and final time, the poster at the door had changed. On it were four Leaders of Today from different departments and Career Groups with the words, *Everything you need to know, the Government of Lexum directly provides.*

At the QRS desk was a box of index cards. The citizen at the desk handed Breel hers, and Breel walked into the exam room. Unlike the first two days, the desks were stacked in the middle of the room and Leaders of Tomorrow congregated along the walls with their Career Groups and one teacher from the Department of Teaching. Breel passed various-sized groups, from one or two Leaders of Tomorrow to two dozen or more.

The Leader of Today with the computer programmers had a clip-board, scanner, and glasses so thick they'd unbalance anyone. Breel didn't recognize her.

"ID, please," Glasses said, holding her scanner toward Breel. Breel scanned her ID, and Glasses marked her clipboard. "We have two others to wait for."

"Hey, Breel," said Sero as he stepped beside her. "Good luck."

"You too."

The other programmers, not being the chattiest bunch, only nodded or exchanged looks of recognition. A couple minutes later, Glasses escorted them into the hall and down a clanging metal stairwell.

"Oh," Sero said in whisper.

They'd never been in a basement before. Its walls and floor were cement, with a seven-foot-high ceiling. There was a faint musty odour.

Breel scrunched her nose. *Ugh, basements are gross.*

Glasses stopped partway down the hall to address the group. "No speaking once we're inside the room." There were a few chuckles, given the lack of conversation already. "Find the seat labelled with your name. Touch nothing until I tell you to start."

Glasses held the door opened for everyone to file in. The room looked exactly like every computer lab they'd ever worked in, with four rows of long tables. Breel found her seat in the second row, an empty chair on either side. In front of her was a computer with dual monitors, an ergonomic keyboard and mouse, and a Confidentiality Statement.

At eight, Glasses clicked her mouse, and instructions appeared on the whiteboard, projected from her monitor. They were to fix—not create—a database. Breel shuddered. Only eight hours to make the database interface user-friendly, add the ability to catch errors, and make the code readable. There was a communal groan.

* * *

Breel's database was a programming feat of the ages. The sloppy interface was now intuitive, and the new error-catching system would stop any error in its tracks. The spaghetti code was now lasagna code with lovely layers and developer comments. When five rolled around, Breel smiled at her accomplishment.

They filed out of the room, shoes scuffling across the cement, and then...

"We're done!"

"Yes! Goodbye school!"

The normally reserved group cheered and high-fived each other, as did other Career Groups leaving their rooms. No one listened to the

Leaders of Today demanding they behave. Breel flew up the stairs and walked through the main floor arm-in-arm with Sero and three other classmates.

Two Leaders of Today blocked the exit, hands on their hips. "We understand your excitement, but this is not appropriate behaviour!" said a middle-aged man with a receding hairline.

His voice, somehow projecting throughout the entire hall, stopped the conversation. Despite that, energy sizzled off the soon-to-be Leaders of Today like an egg cooking in a pan on a Department of Food video.

Once outside, the talking resumed.

"I hope I get to *make* programs," Sero said. "I don't wanna fix someone else's mess."

Breel chuckled at his clever way of saying he despised the practical exam.

An unfamiliar girl: "I hope I'm a nurse at the hospital instead of at school."

A boy from her logic class: "I want a job super high in the government. I wanna know *everything*!"

I just hope I'm not in the Department of Occupation or Enforcement.

* * *

Fifteen minutes later, Breel walked into her bedroom. Now that the Demna Exam was over, for the first time, there was nothing to study. Her increasing anxiety about her future department mauled her high. She welcomed a break from studying, but if only there were something with which to occupy her time and her mind before starting the required reading about etiquette.

She found exactly that. Stacked against the wall were a dozen premade cardboard boxes. On her desk was a roll of clear tape and scissors.

That's why we had that strange lesson on how to pack boxes a few months ago!

Beside the tape and scissors was a sheet of paper with instructions. It said she'd receive her Demna Exam mark Friday morning at ten. That afternoon, a driver would take her and her packed belongings to her new home.

But Breel had all Thursday to pack. She wanted to celebrate, and the best way was by drawing.

No, no... you can't do that.

Breel sank into her bed, blinking back the tears. She'd never draw again.

Chapter Nine

Friday at 8:00 a.m.: For the first time, Breel's parents didn't work. They were exempt, as their daughter was about to become a new Leader of Today.

9:45 a.m.: Duknum paced with his hands clasped behind his back.

9:47 a.m.: Breel uncrossed her legs and shook her foot awake.

9:50 a.m.: Trafis peeked his head into the living room and, instead of returning to his bedroom to study, plopped onto the couch beside their father.

9:51 a.m.: Duknum peered out the window.

9:52 a.m.: He resumed his pacing.

9:54 a.m.: Criba patted Breel's leg. They shared a nervous smile.

9:56 a.m.: An engine purred. Duknum glanced out the window again.

9:57 a.m.: A delivery van pulled into the driveway.

9:58 a.m.: Duknum beat her to the door, opening it before the driver stepped onto the porch.

This was it.

The lifelong wondering was about to end.

Department of Occupation?

Department of Enforcement?

Somewhere else?

Anywhere else. Please...

The driver—from the Department of Teaching—held an oversized manila envelope and an ID scanner.

"I can take that," Duknum said.

"The envelope's addressed to Breel Sorep."

"I'm her father."

"Only Breel Sorep can accept the delivery. Orders from President Tatem."

Duknum stepped back. The man scanned Breel's ID, handed her the envelope, and left without a word.

Breel sat on the couch, surrounded by her family.

"We're proud of you no matter the outcome," Criba said.

"Yes," Duknum said. "But I have no doubt you did amazing."

A bead of sweat ran down Breel's face as she ripped the envelope's seal, which proved difficult due to her shaking hands. She looked inside to find three sheets of paper and a card—her new house key.

That meant she passed. She was officially a Leader of Today.

Some of the tension released from her body. But not all... *What's my department?*

The first page listed her marks. Her lowest was a B-plus in History of Lexum. Not bad! For the practical and most of the computer science exams, she achieved an A plus. Even programming languages, she got an A—*wow, I guess I didn't mess up as bad as I thought*—and discrete mathematics an A-.

"Well?" Duknum said, leaning forward. "Read them out to us."

She did so, even though all she really wanted to do was learn what her department would be. By the time she finished reading out her marks, her parents' faces probably hurt from how much they were smiling.

"Oh, Breel, congratulations," Criba said with a rare hug.

"That's our girl!" said Duknum. "I knew you could do it! Where will you be working?"

Breel removed the next sheet of paper—a letter that said, *Congratulations, Breel Sorep, Leader of Today!* She scanned it, finding in the second paragraph the answer to the question she'd had all her life. Her department was in bold letters, plain as day.

Her heart stopped. Her breath caught in her throat.

"What is it, Breel?" Her father's voice was high.

"It... it says Department of Education."

The smile left Duknum face.

Oh wow, he really did want me to work with him!

However, his disappointment was but a memory moments later. His eyes lit up. "Wow!" he said. "My daughter? The Department of Education?"

Breel read that paragraph again, needing to double-check even for her own sake. "Yes, Department of Education."

"Congratulations!" said Criba. She grasped her husband's arm. "Duknum, our own daughter! In the most prestigious department!"

Breel exhaled. *Thank you for anything but the Department of Occupation.* She leaned back against the couch. Until that moment, she hadn't known how convinced she'd been that she'd end up in her father's department.

But she was Department of Education. Despite her record, the government had placed her in the most prestigious department. Citizens would look at her crimson pants and navy-blue sweater, wishing they had the same uniform or perhaps wondering how she managed such a good placement. It'd take time getting used to citizens like Trafis gawking at her.

Her parents continued to beam at her. Breel's face burned.

"What'll you be doing?" Trafis asked.

Breel read the brief details: "*Duties will include creating and maintaining databases that analyze the Nito Test and determine whether Career Groups require curriculum changes.*"

"Incredible!" Duknum said. "Breel, you'll be single-handedly responsible for the future of new Leaders of Today! What a tremendous privilege and responsibility!"

That was the last thing Breel wanted. "I don't think it'll be single-handedly," she said. "I mean, I'm sure there'll be more than one programmer."

His smile didn't falter. "Yes," he said, "but think about it. Lexum depends upon Leaders of Today working in the Career Group they're meant to work in, the one they're best at. You'll be the person who creates the databases which determine that Career Group! Your work will be integral in deciding whether the classes Career Groups take should change, which of course directly impacts all citizens! I write programs that determine future supply and demand of Career Groups, so our departments work closely together. I suspect you'll have access to my programs, so you know how to code the data import. And then your programs will probably be used by mathematicians to analyze results and decide if someone should be assigned the mathematician or mathematics teacher Career Group, for example."

He said all this very quickly. It was strange hearing her father speak so passionately about his job—he was normally tight-lipped about it, as per the law.

Breel had never thought about where the Department of Education got its data. If all went well, that happened behind-the-scenes. It sounded like he didn't know how it happened, so that was likely the case.

Breel removed the last sheet of paper from the envelope, which said a couple of drivers would pick her up at two to move her to her new home.

The minutes ticked by. Duknum jabbered on about the Department of Education and provided the same advice everyone told Leaders of Tomorrow.

"Make sure you attend all the departmental events."

He said this even though they were mandatory.

"Be sure to remember everything you've learned in school. It all matters."

He said this even though teachers crammed so much knowledge into their heads that it was impossible to forget the information anytime soon.

Eventually, Breel pretended to watch the repeated news. Her father got the hint and retreated to the master bedroom to work on a Department of Expansion assignment.

Lunch came with an unexpected cake. It had three layers with chocolate frosting and the words *Congratulations, Leader of Today* in white frosting.

Impersonal, but better than nothing.

After lunch, Breel visited Trafis in his bedroom and sat on the edge of his bed. His desk was invisible underneath his books.

"What is it?" he asked, turning in his chair.

"Thought we should talk, since these are my last hours before moving out."

"Oh. Okay." He put his feet on his bed, crossing his ankles. "How d'you feel about it?"

"To be honest, I never thought much about moving out. It was always about where I'd work and what I'd do."

"Bet you're glad it's not the Department of Occupation."

"Uh-huh."

Trafis shook his head. "Can't believe you'll be at the Department of Education. I wonder about Ami."

"Me, too. I'll probably see her on Monday's orientation."

He grinned. "She'll be so jealous if she's not in your department."

The Department of Education had been Ami's lifelong dream, of course. Being anywhere else would devastate her.

Trafis sighed. "It's gonna be so weird without you here."

She nodded. He'd be lonely without her. They rarely talked at home since evenings and weekends were for studying; however, they always had the walk to and from school. Being younger, he'd never done that walk alone.

"We'll visit each other lots," she said.

"I want to see your new place!"

"It's gonna be the same, just smaller."

Standard houses only differed in size and number of bedrooms. One adult had one bedroom. Two adults had one bedroom, but the rooms were larger. Two adults and a child had an additional bedroom and even more spacious common areas. There were five-bedroom houses, but the government permitted few people to have three, let alone four, children. With her record as a Leader of Tomorrow, Breel assumed the government wouldn't even allow her to have one child. However, it was a possibility that they'd make an exception because of her likelihood of producing intelligent offspring of high societal benefit.

But Breel wasn't sure if she wanted children. Famut never had them. One day, when Breel was twelve years old, he told her and Trafis he didn't want to bring children into their society.

"But, Uncle Famut," Trafis had said, "even if you wanted kids, you can't have kids 'cause you aren't married."

The government only allowed married citizens to bear children. Apparently, forty-nine years ago, anyone could. But President Tatem convinced the populace that preventing pregnancy except through geneticists and a petri dish was the best course of action.

"Some day," Famut had said.

"Why haven't you asked Centia to marry you?" Breel had asked.

"Ree, we're just taking it slow. We don't want to rush."

Yet Famut had dated Centia, who also worked at the Department of Health, longer than Breel could remember. They'd only met her a handful of times. Famut said Centia was shy with little desire to go through the effort of getting special permission to visit from the

Department of Enforcement.

"If we lived in Intercludae, would our parents, Trafis, and I see her more?" Breel had asked one evening at her uncle's house.

"Of course," Famut had said. "In Intercludae, there wouldn't be rules about who you can and can't visit."

"And no rules about what I do in the evening after school?" Breel asked, thinking about drawing.

"Yes. In Intercludae, everyone can do whatever they want."

"But what about other people?" Trafis asked.

"In Intercludae, we'd still think about others. But we'd think about ourselves, too. Sometimes you need to put yourself first."

Trafis gasped, hands on his mouth.

Famut patted his arm. "It's okay. Intercludae's a story. Just my way of having fun, get you thinking for yourselves."

"Since you don't wanna have kids, are we like your kids?" Breel asked.

"You're definitely like my kids."

Duknum had sat her and Trafis down a few weeks later to tell them Famut had disappeared and, he assumed, was dead. Until Mr. Progrio, he was the only person Breel personally knew who disappeared.

Talking with Trafis, it occurred to Breel that, being a single person, her house would be the same dimensions as Famut's had been.

"I'm visiting you whether you like it or not," Trafis said.

"Of course you can visit. I'll need visitors! It'll be so boring living alone. I don't know how Uncle Famut did it."

Trafis shrugged. "Everyone does it eventually. Guess you'll find out soon enough. Well, I better get studying."

Breel rolled her eyes. It was the government's fault for making Trafis believe studying for an exam a year away was more important than talking with his sister who was about to move out. But arguing was pointless.

"Okay. Happy studying."

And happy not studying to me.

Chapter Ten

Breel's entire family hugged her before she left.

"Goodbye and good luck," Criba said.

"She'll be fine," said Duknum.

The two drivers—wearing taupe pants and blood-red sweaters—were from the Department of Households. They'd already closed the van's back door, Breel's boxes tucked inside. With a deep breath, she walked down the driveway of the house that'd always been home—until now.

Breel got into the backseat, surrounded by her boxes. The driver behind the wheel knew where he was going but didn't tell Breel. He turned down Chrysanthemum Lane, driving west toward the Quaddro.

It was surreal. Done with school. Being a Leader of Today rather than a Leader of Tomorrow. Leaving home for her own house. Sitting in a vehicle other than a bus for the first time.

The farther the van drove, the more her stomach tightened. The life she knew was over. Surely not having to study for exams, only working on assignments for courses, meant her new life would be better.

The two-lane road was devoid of traffic other than the occasional delivery van. Everyone else was at school or work. It appeared she was the only new Leader of Today on Chrysanthemum Lane.

The van headed south, parallel to the Quaddro, then west again. Finally, it turned onto an unfamiliar street. Breel missed the street sign. All the houses looked like Chrysanthemum Lane—except smaller. It seemed this street was for single-person families.

The van turned down another street. Low-hanging tree branches blocked the sign. "What street is this?" she asked. But, as expected, neither driver replied. Their job was to move her. It wasn't to answer questions.

She'd be ready for a street sign at the next turn. But the next turn was into a driveway. Her driveway. Breel stiffened as the van parked. Stopped on her driveway. In front of her house. On an unknown street. Her stomach flipped and flopped. Suddenly, the van was too warm.

She exited the vehicle and observed her new house. The only differences from her old house were the smaller size, the house number of 37, and the white chrysanthemums. Someday it'd seem like her house, but it didn't yet. It was just some random smaller house the government forced her to live in.

The drivers followed Breel to the door, each carrying a box. She swiped her new key against the scanner. Nothing. As her stomach knotted, a metallic whirring filled the air. The door unlocked. At least one knot disentangled as Breel walked inside.

Everything looked the same as her old house, albeit half the size. She walked through the living room, with a couch and TV on low, to the dining room. A package of papers was on the table. The cover said:

CONGRATULATIONS PACKAGE

Breel Sorep

Department of Education

Computer Programmer

She flipped through the dozen or so pages. It listed rules, expectations for the weekend, and instructions for Monday.

Great, more rules.

Behind the stapled package was a thick envelope. She tossed everything back onto the table to read later.

The drivers retrieved more boxes, and Breel walked down the short hall to the bedroom and bathroom. Four boxes were already there.

It was like her old bedroom, only slightly bigger. There was the same bed and dresser. The bookcase had two more shelves to accommodate Department of Expansion coursework. Inside the closet were eight Department of Education uniforms. The desk was a few inches wider with a desktop computer. Beside the keyboard was a stack of thick books. She read the spines: *Workplace Etiquette, Socializing Dos and Don'ts for Leaders of Today,* and *How to Maximize Your Utility as a Leader of Today.*

Breel groaned. *These books are each at least five hundred pages long!*

On top of the books was an instruction sheet: "Dear new Leader of Today: You probably already know much of this information from your parents and other Leaders of Today. However, there is still much to learn. I expect you to finish reading these books within the next month—before you start the Department of Expansion courses. There is no test. However, these are rules you must follow. Remember to embrace the collective. President Tatem."

Breel shivered. *That's a lot of information to absorb...*

"That's all the boxes," said one driver.

"Thanks," said Breel.

He held out a hand. "I need your old house key."

"Oh. Okay."

She extracted it from behind her ID card and handed it to him.

Next, he extended the scanner. "Just need to scan your ID."

"Again? Okay."

After the scanner beeped, the driver studied the screen as if he hadn't confirmed her identity only thirty minutes ago.

After the drivers left, the momentous occasion became real. She was alone in a house. Her house. For the first time.

"WAHOO!" she yelled.

She kicked off her shoes, leaving them sprawled in the hallway.

She jumped on her bed until the blankets were on the ground and left them where they lay.

She tore open her boxes, finding an empty notebook and a pencil. Halfway to the desk, she stopped. Reaching for them was an automatic reaction. The words of the DOE officer echoed in her mind: *If you're caught engaging in any other unlawful activities, drawing or otherwise, it means Mortae.*

"But I'm alone," she said to herself.

There were no parents to breathe down her neck. But, without a doubt, housekeepers would keep a close eye on her. Thanks to the snooping housekeeper who turned her in, she'd never draw again.

* * *

Breel read through the Congratulations Package during supper.

The first page said her address was 37 Crescent Road. She was to catch the 8:45 a.m. bus each morning at the corner of Crescent and Main Street.

Every day, her breakfast would arrive by 8:20 a.m., lunch by 12:15 p.m. (on weekends), and supper by 6:15 p.m. The housekeeper would come weekdays at 2:00 p.m., and a driver would pick up her clothes for washing each Wednesday (a change from Friday) and return them on Friday.

As a Leader of Today, she had an email address for work and governmental correspondence. It reinforced that using email for personal reasons would be met with swift punishment—Mortae always an option.

The next page outlined changes for Leaders of Today: no warnings; other than generalities, no talking about their work other than to their section's Career Group and Career Group Head; and viewing Mortae would start in the Bronze section.

Next, she read about the forms of general remuneration. There was one's assigned department that, depending upon the Career Group, was based on school grades. There were many others as well: the section from which one watched Mortae, more variety in meals on one's weekly order cards, and appetizer and dessert options on days other than special occasions.

Work also had forms of remuneration such as better work assignments or a promotion to Career Group Head, Assistant to the Director, or Department Director. Reportedly, promotions had additional perks. Finally, citizens were remunerated with points to purchase items from the Lexum Catalog.

A rush of energy swept through Breel at the words "Lexum Catalog". Leaders of Tomorrow didn't accumulate points, and Breel's father never allowed her and Trafis to view the Lexum Catalog. Points accumulated in certain ways, and Leaders of Today received monthly statements via email. Some ways to gain points were well-known: job performance reviews, school performance of one's children, reporting illegal activity to the DOE. But no one knew them all.

A thin white envelope on the table caught Breel's eye.

Could it be...? A burst of adrenaline tore through her.

Without reading the rest of the Congratulations Package, she tore the envelope open. Inside were two booklets. Her eyes lit up as they landed on the first—the Lexum Catalog. It was twenty pages and smaller than a standard-size sheet of paper, but the cover was glossy and inviting. There were many options such as expanded meals for a year, a bigger bed, prettier sheets, improved furniture, a personal vegetable or flower garden tended by a gardener. Breel's parents had taken advantage of more meal options, a queen-size bed instead of a double, and a second couch. She wasn't sure what else, if anything, they'd bought with their points.

The second booklet said *Department of Expansion: Computer Programmer Career Group.* Inside were a list of mandatory and elective courses, such as niche programming techniques and general learning about the government and History of Lexum.

After setting the booklets aside—with plans to thoroughly review and fantasize about the Lexum Catalog later—she returned to the Congratulations Package. The third page listed instructions for her first day of work. She was to catch her bus, disembark at the Governmental Offices, and follow the signs to the Orientation Session.

The last few pages outlined her schedule during her first week: Monday: 8:00 a.m. to 12:00 p.m.—Government of Lexum Orientation. 1:00 p.m. to 5:00 p.m.—Department of Education Orientation. 5:00 p.m. to 9:00 p.m.—Department of Education meet-and-greet.

Tuesday through Friday she had job shadowing all day, the only break being a Department of Education lunch-and-learn from twelve to one.

Breel frowned. *What's a lunch-and-learn? What's job shadowing? Doesn't sound much like programming to me...*

Pushing the confusion aside, she read the last page, which reiterated everything President Tatem had said on the news the previous night. It concluded by telling her to start reading the *Workplace Etiquette* book.

Having nothing else to do, she the followed instructions and started reading about how to conduct herself at work.

Chapter Eleven

The first strange thing about Monday morning was having the bath-room to herself. No more scheduling wake-ups.

The second was exercising alone and being able to take a longer shower.

The third was putting on crimson dress pants and a navy-blue sweater overtop a blouse—not to mention now having Career Group stripings.

The fourth strange thing was walking down an unfamiliar street. Well, except for the smaller houses and white instead of red flowers, Crescent Road was identical to Chrysanthemum Lane. But the people differed. There were no Leaders of Tomorrow, and everyone walked by themselves.

The fifth was walking to a bus stop to get to work rather than walking to school without taking a bus.

The sixth was standing at the bus stop as other citizens noted her Department of Education uniform. A middle-aged man, from the Department of Transportation, given his coral pants and onyx sweater, looked her up and down.

"New to the Department of Education, eh?" His low, gravelly voice grated on the ears.

"Yep." Breel tried to ignore his stare.

"Working there was always my dream," said Onyx Sweater. "But the government had other things in mind."

Breel flashed a small smile as the bus rumbled up the street. It stopped a couple of blocks away for another group of citizens to board.

"You must be so happy," he said. "Department of Education. You really get to benefit Lexum in that department."

By this point, the entire bus stop was listening. There was nowhere for Breel to hide.

When Breel said nothing, he asked, "What career stripings are those?"

"Computer programmer." She didn't recognize Onyx Sweater's stripings either and was curious but didn't ask, as that'd just invite further conversation.

"Fancy computers, eh? Never used one."

The bus rumbled up, and the doors opened. The man boarded with the others, so Breel hung back to avoid him. As per her parents, Leaders of Today had favourite seats, and she didn't want to sit in one of them. She followed the last person on and scanned her ID card. Her stomach clenched as she imagined the scanner not accepting it.

But the familiar and, in that moment, comforting *beep* sounded. She was indeed a Leader of Today. Breel made her way down the aisle. Onyx Sweater was three-quarters down, so she settled into a seat closer to the driver.

The bus stopped five times on its way to the Governmental Offices. At the second stop, a woman wearing black pants and a sunshine-yellow sweater stood in the aisle beside Breel. "You're in my seat."

"Sorry," said Breel.

She moved to the empty seat across the aisle. Challenging the woman wasn't a good idea, especially not on her first day of work. Besides, arguing with someone who worked at the DOE, whatever her Career Group, wasn't smart.

At the next stop was a familiar smiling face and blonde hair. Ami boarded with her head high even though she wasn't wearing the same uniform as Breel. Instead, her uniform matched that of the rude woman, but with the mathematician thin-thick-thin patterned mint-green stripe combination on her arm.

Breel laughed aloud but stopped herself short. For once, she had beaten Ami. However, she had but a moment to get her satisfaction in check. She took a few deep breaths and wiped the smile off her face.

"Hey," Breel said as Ami approached.

Ami's face lit up, and she stopped. "Breel!" Her jaw dropped. "No way! No way! *You* got Department of Education?"

"What's that mean?" Breel asked even though she didn't particularly care to hear the answer.

"Really, Breel? You don't exactly have the best record. And my marks were always higher."

"Please take your seat," said the driver.

Ami sat, causing the seat to bounce.

"It's not fair!" she said. "I should've gotten Department of Education!"

Breel rolled her eyes. "But we're in different Career Groups so weren't competing against each other. I'm sorry you didn't get the department you wanted so much but—"

"You never cared about your department as long as it wasn't Occupation or the DOE."

Ami crossed her arms. If they weren't on the bus, Breel could picture her stomping the ground like a tantruming toddler.

"Can't you at least be happy for me?" Breel asked.

"Obviously, I'm happy for you." But she'd snapped her words.

"You're not really showing it."

"Oh, calm down, Breel. I'm working in the DOE now. I can't have a squabble on a bus."

You started it. She rolled her eyes as Ami smoothed her sweater.

Wanting to appease Ami though, she said, "At least the DOE's still prestigious."

"I guess. I mean, it took a bit to get over the shock and disappointment. Obviously, my marks were excellent, my lowest was an A-. I was surprised to get a mark so low. But I guess someone else got better marks than me. Or the Department of Education doesn't need mathematicians right now. But that's unfair. You get it and I don't just because of demand? I worked hard for it, but instead I get the DOE."

Breel said nothing. It was safer not to answer. The bus rumbled past a nondescript industrial building that took up half a block.

Ami sighed. "But you're right. At least it's the DOE. Like you said, it's still prestigious. My job description was vague, though. Something about analyzing Vucapi data. But maybe I'll learn things about Mortae!" For the first time, she was her characteristic enthusiastic self. "Wouldn't that be cool? Maybe I get to determine who's likely to break the law! Maybe I can create algorithms to predict lawbreakers! Are you excited for our first day? I sure am."

Either Ami had truly gotten over the DOE shock, or she was putting on a good show about her feelings for her job.

"I guess," said Breel. But her stomach wriggled as she said it. More than anything, Breel wanted the day to be over or, at least, to get away from Ami.

Minutes later, the bus stopped in front of the centre Governmental Offices. It was wider than the Lexum Exam Centre, with at least half a dozen doors. Connected to each corner of the foyer was a different nine-floor building.

Breel followed the crowd inside. The first room was a foyer. Its marble floors glistened; shoes squeaked. The walls were sterile white. Instead of doors leading to the adjacent buildings, each corner had four elevators, two on each side. Most people headed to an elevator.

On both sides of the foyer was an enormous poster of President Tatem sitting at his desk. The one on the left said, *Every citizen of Lexum depends upon you.* The right poster read, *President Tatem devotes his life to the citizens of Lexum—do you?*

Straight ahead was another room. Above the entrance hung a white banner with dark block letters that said, "Welcome New Leaders of Today." Breel followed the crowd into a spacious antechamber with sign-in tables reminiscent of the Demna. A photographer at the QRS table scanned Breel's ID and took her picture in front of a white wall.

"Your new ID will be delivered to your department later today," said the photographer. "Please take a seat in the auditorium."

Breel searched for Ami because, though angry at her, there was comfort in sitting with someone she knew. Ami was already walking toward the auditorium. Breel hurried after her.

She gasped when she walked into the twenty-thousand-seat room. It was far larger than even the Lexum Exam Centre. There were dozens of rows of seats in a U shape facing the stage. The seats were in three sections, each separated by a stairwell. A gigantic screen hung on the wall behind the stage.

They descended a long staircase to the front, where three hundred or so were already sitting. Steps echoed throughout the room.

Breel caught up to Ami halfway down the staircase. "Want to sit together?"

"Okay."

They found seats in the second row. The girl Breel sat beside wore a Department of Occupation uniform. Breel didn't recognize the Career Group stripings, so figured the girl probably wouldn't work with her father.

Everyone trickled into the cavernous auditorium. Some chattered in hushed voices. The younger Leaders of Today huddled together among their Career Groups. More than one cried, comforted by their friends.

Breel ached for them. *I couldn't imagine working at that age and living with four other young Leaders of Today.* They had to wait until turning seventeen to live in their own house.

At eight, the same man who opened every Mortae walked onto the stage. The drone of conversation decreased. "Welcome, Leaders of Today!" he said.

The new Leaders of Today cheered. He held up a hand, cutting them short. "Today is a glorious day—the advent of your work for the Government of Lexum!"

His enthusiasm, his smile, was nauseating. His proximity made it even worse than at Mortae.

"But I know I'm not the person you want to hear from. Put your hands together for our esteemed President Hargam Tatem!"

Cheers erupted.

"Ooh!" Ami said. Her clapping hands were a blur. "I've only ever seen him at Mortae!"

When President Tatem and his four personal DOE officers appeared from backstage, the crowd stood. Ami was among the first to burst out of her seat. There were some catcalls ("I love you, President Tatem!" and "Marry me!") amongst the cheers, shrieks, and squeals of delight. Breel had no choice but to follow as everyone rose to their feet.

Unless they'd been in the Platinum section, it was the closest they'd been to President Tatem. He grinned, taking it all in. His sparkling blue eyes were even more alluring in person. Breel caught herself staring into them but blinked and looked away.

No, don't get sucked in.

"He's soooo handsome," Ami said, head tilted as she stared and clapped.

Breel rolled her eyes. Why Ami liked an old guy was a mystery. The only thing going for him were his eyes. However, many textbooks referred to him as "handsome," so Ami's attraction was cultural and, given the reaction of the girls in the room, typical. But while Breel could admit he'd been handsome in his younger years, she wouldn't have ever considered him a looker.

It was at least a minute before others started sitting. Breel waited until at least half the crowd had returned to their seats before doing so herself. Ami was one of the last to remain standing.

"Thank you all for that magnificent welcome," President Tatem said, light bouncing off his teeth and hair. "But that is, in fact, my job. Welcome to the Departmental Offices. Today is the happiest day of your life, because you go from Leader of Tomorrow to Leader of Today. From now on, Lexum will benefit fully from all you've learned over the past ten to seventeen years, depending on your Career Group. Finally, you will be giving back."

Breel zoned out as he droned on, taking ten minutes to reiterate what he said ad nauseam every day on the news: how everyone depended upon them, that they had an immense responsibility to society, and so on.

He left to cheers and calls for him to come back. It took a couple minutes for the Department of Logistics man to quiet the crowd. Next, each of the twelve Department Directors spoke. Some, such as the Department of Teaching, gave detailed information. But after years of being instructed by teachers, there was little to learn. Others, such as the Department of Logistics, said little more than, "We coordinate schedules and organize and open events."

After the Director of Utilities finished, the Logistics man took the microphone again. "This ends the Government of Lexum Orientation. Lunch will be in the antechamber until one. Around that time, someone from your department will collect you for your departmental orientation."

Everyone filed out of the auditorium to find stacks of food containers where they had signed in. Long tables had been set up in the middle of the room where some were already eating.

"Eat together?" Breel asked Ami.

Ami shrugged, which Breel took as agreement. She retrieved her lunch from the QRS table and joined Ami. They ate in silence for a few minutes, Breel with her chicken club sandwich and Ami with her chicken salad.

"I hope we get to see President Tatem every day," Ami said, her head tilted again.

"I doubt it," Breel said. "I imagine he's busy."

Other than at Mortae and the seven o'clock news, he never made appearances.

"Yeah, I guess. But it's super nice of him to talk to us." Ami finished her salad in a hurry and studied her shirt.

"What're you doing?" Breel asked as a boy wearing a DOE uniform with officer stripings sat across from them.

Ami picked something off her cuff and flicked it onto the floor. "I need to look good on my first day."

Understandable, but picking fluffs off a new sweater was overboard.

"You look great," said the boy. He thumped his chest "Name's Matus. DOE officer."

Ami smiled. "Ami. Mathematician."

Matus frowned. "Borrrring."

"Hey!"

"What about you?" he asked Breel. His jaw dropped. "Department of Education?"

Breel sat straighter and breathed in deeply. "Yep. I'm Breel. Computer programmer."

He pretended to gag. "Ugh. Just as bad."

"You're not a very nice person," Ami said.

Matus tutted. "I wouldn't tell me that. You wouldn't want me to arrest you on the first day, would you?"

Ami stopped. She didn't even go on about her high marks.

Breel glanced at the others at their table, all of whom were ignoring everyone else as they ate. None were the Department of Education. She turned to check the tables on their side of the room.

"What're you doing?" Ami asked.

Having no luck, Breel returned to her sandwich. "Seeing if there's anyone else from my department."

Before she could check the other side of the room, an amplified voice said, "Department of Utilities? If you're with the Department of Utilities, come over here."

All conversation stopped. Near the door, a short, balding, middle-aged man in a peach-coloured sweater and pebble-gray pants waved from behind a microphone. Well over fifty Leaders of Today from ages ten to seventeen joined him, many still holding their lunches. As each filed out of the room, the man cross-referenced their IDs with a clipboard and led them out of the room.

While they left, conversation and the tinkling of silverware filled the room again as everyone scrambled to finish their food.

A couple of minutes later was the Department of Teaching's turn. "I'm only taking the teachers," said the young woman at the microphone. "Teachers only, please!"

Nearly thirty Leaders of Today left with her.

Next, over one hundred Leaders of Today, including a huddle of ten-year-olds, left for the Department of Housekeeping.

Five minutes and two departments later, the Department of Education was called.

Chapter Twelve

Conversation stopped.

"Just the Department of Education computer programmer," said the voice at the microphone.

Breel walked to the man at the microphone, every eye on her. Although, he was not exactly a man—he was hardly older than Breel. His eyes... It was like President Tatem staring at her. He didn't smile; however, at least he wasn't frowning. His gaze was more trance-like.

Breel showed her ID card. He reviewed it, sandy hair flopping in front of his face.

"Um... I'm Breel Sorep," she said.

He brushed back his hair. "Breel."

"Yeah."

He smiled, his eyes sparkling. His grin wasn't creepy like President Tatem's or nauseating and over-the-top, like the man who opened Mortae and their orientation. It was genuine and friendly. "Wow. Breel Sorep. Hello. Nice to meet you." He pumped her hand five times.

"Nice to meet you, too."

"I'm Cafrec Masna. Ready to go?"

"Aren't there others?" She glanced around the room. But no one was walking toward them.

"Just you. My—our—boss got permission for me to pick you up separately from the rest. Works better for some Career Groups."

Breel dared another glance around the room. Some had returned to their lunches or talking to tablemates, but many eyes were still on her.

Cafrec led her to the first bank of elevators on the right side of the empty foyer.

"This foyer and auditorium are the first floor of the centre building," Cafrec said. "The elevators take you to one of the four buildings where the departments are. From the foyer, each elevator only goes to specific floors to help with traffic flow. The Department of Education is floors six to eight of the southeast building. Unless we have special permission, we're not allowed on any other floors."

He motioned to a bank of elevators, two on each side of the southeast corner.

"We're on floor eight, so we take the last one." He tapped the doors of the fourth elevator. "However, we'll start at floor six, which is elevator three."

On either side of the group of four elevators was a number panel. He selected 6 and the button lit up, fascinating Breel. It'd be her first elevator ride, and it was all she could do to wait for the elevator to arrive.

Cafrec grinned, hair flopping yet again. "I bet you have lots of questions."

"Yeah."

He looked at her through his unruly hair. "I was in your position last year, so fire away. I know what it's like."

"Am I really the only computer programmer for the Department of Education?"

"Yep. I was too, last year. Means we both achieved the highest Demna marks in our Career Group."

The highest marks in her Career Group... Breel let that sink in. *I never expected that!*

She thought of Ami. "My best friend, a mathematician, gets even better marks than me and got Department of Enforcement. Are you saying she'd be in the Department of Education if there were an opening?"

"If she achieved higher marks than other mathematicians, yes." The elevator chimed, and the doors opened. "After you."

The doors revealed a stainless-steel box with mirrors on two sides and a door on the opposite sides. Taking a deep breath, she walked in.

"Are you claustrophobic?" Cafrec asked as the doors closed.

"No."

"That's good. I know someone who is, and he has a hard time with the elevators."

The doors clanged shut. A moment later, the floor shuddered. Gravity pushed her body downward as the elevator forced her to rise against it.

She looked at Cafrec to get her mind off the uncomfortable sensation. He was quite handsome, putting a younger President Tatem to shame. He had long lashes and a prominent brow, but it was his eyes and particularly his smile which did it for Breel—they lit up his entire face.

I bet Ami's jealous Cafrec isn't her colleague.

Cafrec pointed to a scanner beside the door. "This is for access to the restricted ninth floor."

"For the secretive departments?"

"That's my guess."

He leaned against the side with his arms crossed and foot planted against the wall. He caught Breel's eye via the mirror. She looked away, cursing herself for being so awkward.

"I'm really excited you're here, Breel." She could only smile, because she certainly couldn't say the same. "It's natural to be nervous. I'm your mentor. I show you around and you shadow me as I work. Oh, and I'm your escort to our departmental events."

Her heart fluttered. "You are?"

Cafrec grinned, eyes twinkling. It was strange to see such eyes that weren't full of malicious delight. "Yeah. I mean, if you'd like. Feel free to ditch me."

"I could use the help."

"You'll be in excellent hands. I'm quite popular."

He grinned. *Is he teasing me?* She didn't ask.

Another chime, a lurch, and the doors opposite from the ones they'd entered opened. Breel exhaled, not realizing she'd been holding her breath. She decided she didn't like elevators.

They stepped into a room with a U-shaped mahogany desk which comfortably sat a man—typing on his computer—and two women—both on the phone. To the right was a bullpen with three rows of six cubicles. All eighteen occupants were typing.

"Each floor has a foyer with the offices along the exterior walls," Cafrec said. "A hallway wraps around the entire floor."

"It's a giant square?"

"More or less. Each floor has its own secretaries." He motioned to the desk and, pointing to the bullpen, said, "These are some of our curriculum developers."

Cafrec led her down the hall, pointing out various offices for the curricular editors, exam writers, exam editors, and the Heads of each of those Career Groups. Every office door was closed. Every so often, there was another bullpen rather than an office. Cafrec explained that approximately half of Career Groups had an office.

"Please tell me I get an office," Breel said.

She shuddered just thinking about working out in the open, surrounded by others, for hours each day.

He winked. "You'll find out."

They circled back to the elevators and headed to floor seven, which looked identical to six.

"Our interdepartmental liaisons are half of floor seven," Cafrec said.

"What's an interdepartmental liaison?" Breel asked as they walked past a bullpen.

"In our department, they work with the liaisons in the Departments of Occupation and Health and perhaps others to obtain data from those departments. The inputs of the programs we write are from those data."

Floor seven also housed data entry clerks who inputted marks and other school-related information and exam preppers who printed and organized tests and exams. One of the preppers looked to be twelve.

"Is that all they do every day?" Breel asked once they were back in the elevator. "Print and organize exam packages?"

"They do other stuff too. Not sure what, though. But yeah, that's their main job."

Yikes, that sounds boring.

The elevator chimed for floor eight. Cafrec grinned. "Welcome to the nerd floor. Home to computer programmers and mathematicians. There's also the offices of the Director of the Department of Education and Assistant to the Director of the Department of Education."

"That's a mouthful."

Cafrec laughed. Some of the tension in Breel's shoulders released.

The floor was identical to the others. They walked down the hall and around the corner, stopping partway. Cafrec extended an arm to an office door.

"In you go."

The nameplate read *Computer Programmers—Cafrec Masna and Breel Sorep.* She breathed a sigh of relief. Spending her life in a cubicle would've been dreadful.

Each of the far corners had a L-shaped desk with a computer and dual monitors. Papers cluttered one desk. Beside each was a cabinet with a shelf above it. Of course, on the wall in front of each desk, in perfect view while at the computer, was a poster of President Tatem with the words, *Embrace the collective means working hard all day, every day.* Along the far wall was an east-facing window. Rows and rows of houses were visible and, beyond them, trees lining the perimeter of Lexum. Being in the middle of Lexum, the trees and lack of proximity to the wall blocked the view of whatever lay beyond.

"Welcome to our office," Cafrec said.

"Just for when you're my mentor?" she asked.

"Forever. We're stuck together." He grinned.

"Oh." She hadn't expected sharing an office. However, anything was better than the bullpen.

Cafrec sat at his desk. Facing Breel, he tilted his chair back and crossed his arms. "Is there a problem with that?"

"No. I just... well, I didn't know what to expect, to be honest."

"We're the only ones in our role, so that's why we're together."

She sat down. Her chair was comfy, at least, with a headrest and armrests. "We're the only computer programmers?"

"Oh no, lots of us in the Dep of Ed. We're just the only ones writing programs which determine Career Groups and their classes. Oh, your new ID card is on your desk."

Breel picked it up. The picture wasn't too bad. She was smiling, at least. It was strange seeing herself in a different uniform and reading "Leader of Today—Department of Education—Computer Programmer" rather than "Leader of Tomorrow—Computer Programmer." She replaced her old ID.

"What time is it?" she asked. "My orientation starts at one."

Cafrec pointed to himself with both thumbs. "I'm your orientation. By request of our boss. Most Career Groups have a formal one, but I guess he thought it makes sense to give you your own. A little odd, since I did the formal one last year. But whatever, I guess. We'll talk for a bit, then you'll meet with the Department Heads. Don't expect to learn much, though. Even within the department it isn't clear what everyone does."

Breel shrugged. She'd expected nothing less from Lexum.

"You won't even learn much from the other computer programmers. I don't even know how many of us are in the department. I guess around two dozen based on how many attend the seminars, but not everyone is required to attend every single one. I mostly work with the Head of Computer Programmers, you now, and our Career Group's secretary. We work on the intranet, the information we need already completed by someone in this or another department. To avoid mistakes, and you definitely don't want mistakes, we usually work in pairs or groups. I check your work and you check mine. When it's error-free, we mark it as complete, which signals to whoever uses our programs that it's ready to go. Deadlines are tight."

If they were working together, at least Cafrec seemed nice. *For now... Anyone can be nice for the first few hours.*

"Ask me some of your questions," Cafrec said.

"Okay. Was it hard going from a Leader of Tomorrow to a Leader of Today?"

"A little. Well, a lot. It was weird. Really weird. Living alone was hardest for me just because it was so different. For others I know, it was losing the cushion of warnings."

Breel nodded. The fear of having no warnings was all too fresh.

"Oh?" His eyes twinkled as he leaned forward. "Do tell."

Breel shrank back. "Tell what?"

"The warnings you received."

Her face flushed. "Oh. Um... no. That's fine."

"Fair enough. Well, we should get to it."

Chapter Thirteen

Cafrec showed Breel the supply room, where she loaded up with new pens, pencils, writing pads, sticky notes, paper clips, and a calculator. Back at their desks, they chatted until nearly two, Cafrec explaining the computer system and office procedures.

"They don't teach Leaders of Tomorrow Lexbase," Cafrec said. "But you should be able to navigate it easily enough."

Lexbase was the government's database software. Breel's father worked with it daily.

"Privileges are massively strict," said Cafrec. "We only see what we need for our jobs."

"I can imagine."

He grinned yet again. "Oh, Breel, I'm looking forward to working together. My last officemate was a real grouch."

"What happened to him?"

"He retired."

In June of the year Leaders of Today turned sixty, right before new ones started working, they retired and moved into a retirement home. Visitors were allowed once per week, but only if the retiree and visitors were in good standing. Visitations occurred in a central room near the entrance of the retirement home—visitors couldn't go anywhere else in the building.

Breel and her family had visited her grandparents every week when they were alive. Duknum would always ask his parents how they were doing, and the answer was always the same: "We're fine, Duknum." There was never embellishment. Not even her father knew what they experienced in the retirement home.

Breel had complained about it to Famut once. "I don't want to live there one day!"

"Me neither," he said. "Maybe it won't be around once you're that age though. It's likely President Tatem's way of keeping those who remember the pre–civil war days locked up. It'd have been impossible for everyone to agree with his changes. Those who didn't were killed. Anyone who survived and was above a certain age ended up in the retirement home with little ability to influence anyone."

Even at her young age, Breel had been impressed, albeit disgusted, at the lengths to which President Tatem went to control the populace.

I bet that place doesn't make Cafrec's previous officemate any less grouchy.

"You're to meet with our Head now," Cafrec said.

"What's he like?"

"Really strict. But he's fine if you do your work right and on time. Just don't ask many questions."

Breel frowned. "He doesn't like questions?"

"Not if he thinks you should know the answer, or you're asking something that you're not allowed to know. So, bring me all your questions. The other thing he doesn't tolerate is lateness." He jumped to his feet. "Bring your old ID. He'll turn it in."

Breel followed Cafrec down the empty hallway, stopping at the third door. The nameplate read, *Head of Computer Programmers—Samit Tucap.*

Samit's office was twice the size of theirs. His desk faced into the room, allowing him to both look out the window and at the door. The oak desk—a less elaborate version of President Tatem's—dwarfed the computer and dual monitors. He had so much paperwork, the reddish-orange top was only visible from the sides.

Samit stared at his monitor, hands flying across the keyboard. "One moment," he said in a pleasant baritone.

When he looked up, he smiled at Breel. Like Cafrec, his was genuine. *Maybe he won't be so bad.*

"You must be Breel," he said.

"Yes. Nice to meet you."

"Get to your work, Cafrec," he said. "I'll make sure Breel gets to her next meeting. Who's it with?"

"Head of Secretaries."

The moment Cafrec left, Breel's insides felt jumpy. She eyed the door, wishing she could've gone with him. Apparently, Cafrec had calmed her. Never having had a boss before, she wasn't sure of protocol or etiquette—if the *Workplace Etiquette* book explained it, she'd yet to get to that section—so she stayed near the door.

"Do you have your old ID?"

Breel handed over her card, and he placed it on his desk.

"Have a seat, Breel." He motioned to two armchairs across from his desk. She sat in the closest one.

Samit turned his monitors, which had been blocking his view of her, and leaned forward, folding his hands on the desk. "My name is Samit Tucap. However, you're to address me as Mr. Tucap or sir."

"Yes, sir."

Cafrec had called him strict. Intimidating seemed a better way to put it. For all she knew, Mr. Tucap's smile had been a figment of her stunted imagination. He had a no-nonsense air about him.

He nodded, light reflecting off his bald head. "You learn fast. Good. The rules here are simple. Do your work, do it right, and learn from everyone else to increase your knowledge and utility to Lexum. Do this, and one day the government may promote you to my job, once I'm retired, of course, or perhaps even the Director of the Department of Education."

Breel smiled, pretending that interested her. Mr. Tucap spoke at a faster pace than most yet still managed to enunciate his words. His eyes never left her as he spoke, as if he were reading her. She shrank against the chair, an involuntary reaction.

He explained how there were two to four computer programmers per unit within the department. They administered databases and wrote and updated codes. Breel and Cafrec's programs assisted with the Nito Test and curriculum decisions. Other computer programmers wrote code to mark exams or speak to parts of Lexbase used in other departments.

"What other departments do we work with?" Breel asked.

"All that concerns you is we get data from other departments. You're not an interdepartmental liaison, so you don't need to know those details." His response was robotic.

"Yes, sir."

Oops… I need to save all my questions for Cafrec.

Mr. Tucap continued. "This is how it practically works. Each computer programmer section has a weekly standing meeting with me. Yours is Fridays at two. With few exceptions, and I'll let you know if there is one, you're to finish your assigned work by then. We'll discuss it, then I'll give you your work for the next week. Of course, this week is different, as you'll shadow Cafrec. On Friday, I'll give you your own work for next week. Have I been clear? Or are there questions?"

Translation: *do you dare ask a question and insinuate I haven't been clear?* She had many questions. However, she said, "None, sir."

"Good. Finally, we work in the prestigious Department of Education. I expect all my staff to behave and work accordingly. I won't tolerate sloppiness or laziness. Anything less than your best is not benefitting Lexum."

Breel stopped herself from rolling her eyes. "Yes, sir."

"Your next appointment is with the Head of Secretaries a few doors down on the right. You'll see the nameplate on the door."

He readjusted his monitors. Realizing he was dismissing her, Breel stood. Halfway to the door, he called her name.

"Yes, sir?" she said, turning.

He didn't speak right away, as if he were unsure if he should. But then he said, back to his initial friendlier tone, "I went to school with your uncle."

She gasped. "Famut?"

"Yes. We saw little of each other come the higher grades, but always spoke when our paths crossed. He was a good man."

Why is he bringing this up? She was bursting to know and to ask for anecdotes about Famut; however, she didn't dare ask questions. "Thank you, sir."

He smiled.

He should smile more often; he doesn't look intimidating when he smiles.

"It's good to have you here, Breel. You're in good hands with Cafrec. I'll see you Friday."

* * *

For the next couple of hours, Breel travelled to each Head's office as they explained their section. Except... no one had much to say.

The Head of Secretaries told her he was the Head of the Department of Education's secretaries—as if that wasn't obvious. But he was more open to questions than Mr. Tucap, so she asked what the secretaries did and what tasks she could ask them to do for her.

He looked at Breel as if she'd just admitted she didn't know the alphabet. "They're not your secretaries. Why would they do things for you?"

So it went with every Head, telling Breel things obvious to even a young Leader of Tomorrow. Many quoted President Tatem, saying how proud she must be to finally benefit society. She asked questions to those more open to them; however, they never gave in and divulged more than intended. Breel stopped asking after a while. She'd save her questions for Cafrec.

* * *

Breel knocked on her closed office door shortly after four.

"Come in," said Cafrec.

She entered, and he turned in his chair, waving. "No need to knock. It's your office, too."

"Oh, okay." She closed the door and sat at her desk. "Why does everyone close their doors?"

"Because opened doors invite distraction, which invites conversations, which causes decreased productivity. That's what President Tatem says."

Should've guessed it was something like that.

He leaned forward, hands clasped on his lap. "How'd it go?"

"I dunno."

"Uh-oh. Not up to your standards?"

"No."

"Yeah, mine wasn't either." He didn't explain.

There was so much to ask. Her gut told her she could trust Cafrec, but was her gut trustworthy? He said she could bring questions to him, but maybe she shouldn't bring *all* questions. Best to start with something innocuous.

"The Heads were vague in their descriptions. Does that become clearer with time?"

Cafrec laughed. "The only thing that becomes clearer is we're not supposed to know anything unless it crosses our desk. Even then, we aren't told more than what's needed."

"It seems weird."

Cafrec crossed his ankles. "As in you'd think they'd want people working together? That it'd help us to learn from each other?"

"Yeah, exactly." Her muscles relaxed. It seemed Cafrec was of the same opinion.

"They only want citizens learning from their own Career Group. Even in our near-daily luncheon seminars, we only learn technical things. Never anything specifically job-related."

"But why can't we learn from other Career Groups?"

"What can I learn from a mathematician?" He rolled his eyes. "Or a secretary?" He nodded. "Or a curriculum writer?" He nodded even more.

Breel cocked her head. "So... you're saying there's nothing we can learn from anyone other than programmers?"

"Exactly. I have nothing to learn from anyone else." But he nodded so vigorously his head nearly flew off his neck.

Cafrec's eyes went right through her, as if transporting a message straight to her soul.

He's saying he doesn't agree with his words. She nodded her understanding.

"Any other questions?"

Perhaps he'd be less cryptic outside the Governmental Offices, but Breel figured she might as well ask. "Mr. Tucap said he'll assign me work on Friday. Will it be a lot? Does he expect me to know what I'm doing then?"

"Of course not. You'll receive less work than me at first. But after a month or two, you'll be getting approximately an equal amount."

"I'll know what I'm doing by then?"

He laughed. "Nah. I mean, in some ways, yeah. But it takes a while."

Realizing she was tapping her fingers on the arm of her chair, she moved her hand between her legs. "But… what if I suck?"

"Not possible, Breel! If you suck, you wouldn't be in this department, right?"

"Yeah, I guess." He had a point, but it didn't assuage her anxiety.

"Don't worry. I'll make sure you don't suck. That's my job as a mentor."

His grin helped her feel a little better.

Chapter Fourteen

Breel spent the last hour of the day reading an overflowing three-inch Lexbase binder. As Cafrec had said, the software was like what she used in school, but she still needed to become acquainted with the interface, coding, and datasets. Thankfully, the differences were minimal, so the task wouldn't be too difficult.

Shortly before five, Cafrec started putting his desk back to order. "Today we have the event, of course," he said, "but normally the buses leave at five fifteen. With the busy elevators, it's best to leave right at five."

Breel marked her page with a sticky note and closed the binder. She stood to leave with Cafrec, but he shook his head. "You need to declutter your desk for the cleaners."

She placed the binder on her shelf, and she and Cafrec joined the steady stream of other Department of Education staff walking to the elevators. Given the number of people, the quietness, with only the occasional greeting, was striking. Only a few smiled at Breel and welcomed her.

It took five minutes to get onto a half-full elevator. When it was impossible for anyone else to squeeze inside, they descended. When the doors opened, the people closest to them stumbled out.

The windows at the end of the hall overlooked the lawn at the entrance, but there were no exterior doors and no auditorium. Clearly, it wasn't the first floor. Everyone headed to several open doors, leading to other rooms, along the walls across from the elevators.

"Breel," said Cafrec as he squeezed her elbow. "You're blocking the way."

She was standing immediately outside the elevator, impeding traffic flow. "Oh. Sorry." She stepped out of the traffic flow, Cafrec with her. He grinned. Breel's heart skipped a beat.

"All events are on floor two of the main building," Cafrec said as they walked across the hall. "Each department has a dedicated room."

They entered theirs, eyes taking a moment to adjust to the dim lighting. It was full of round tables: two-seaters, four-seaters, all the way up to ten. There was enough room for hundreds of people. Some Leaders of Today were at a table, others in line at one of two crescent-shaped bars, both on opposite ends of the room.

Cafrec pointed to the bars. "Drinks are at the bar. Everyone's allowed two alcoholic drinks. The buffet is always at the ends of the room, too." He pointed to a long table with a white tablecloth. There was no food on it yet. An identical table was on the other side as well.

"And these are for people to socialize?" She spoke louder to account for the growing volume of conversation, a far cry from the near-silence a few moments ago.

"In theory."

"What happens in reality?"

"People eat and talk with their Career Group or section. Most leave as soon as allowed at eight."

It now made sense why Breel's parents arrived home from every event at eight fifteen.

They joined the drink line. A dozen bartenders meant they waited only a couple of minutes before one scanned Cafrec's ID.

"The usual?" he asked.

Cafrec nodded, and the bartender filled a glass with amber liquid from a tap.

The bartender scanned Breel's card. "For you?"

"Uh... same."

A few moments later, she and Cafrec, drinks in hand, scanned the room for a seat.

"What is this anyway?" Breel asked, pointing to her glass.

"Beer."

"Oh."

Beer wasn't a foreign word, but Leaders of Tomorrow were prohibited from drinking it. In fact, obtaining it was impossible, since the government only allowed alcohol at department events.

Breel took a sip, making a face at the strong, bitter taste. Cafrec laughed, his own beer spilling over, splatters narrowly missing his shoes. "You'll get used to it." He drank to prove it before examining the room of filling tables.

"Who'd you normally sit with?" Breel asked.

"My officemate." He grinned.

Her heart pounded against her ribcage. "You mean you don't want to sit with others?"

He frowned. "You want to?"

"No." Breel paused. Had that retort been too quick? "I mean, I just don't want you to feel obligated to sit with me."

Wow, I sound like an idiot.

"As your mentor, it's my job to attend the event with you. And even if it weren't, I'd still do it. It's not nice to be here alone. Anyway, like I said, people usually sit with their section's Career Group, and that means you. Come on, I see an empty table."

Cafrec led her through the maze of tables and Leaders of Today walking to the bar. He selected a two-seater in the middle of the room. It hit Breel that for at least three hours, it'd just be her and Cafrec.

That's what it'll be every day at work.

"Do you like these events?" Breel asked.

He made a face. "Not so far. At my first one, my mentor sat with a few other computer programmers. They'd gotten to know each other from the seminars. All of them are old grouches. They even make Mr. Tucap seem young, and he's gotta be at least forty-five. But I tagged along because what else was I to do? For three hours I listened to them whine about their wives and kids.

"I tried talking with others, but no one seemed very interested. Really the only reason to talk to people outside your own Career Group is for romantic reasons."

"Romantic reasons?"

Breel's heart fluttered. *Is that really what he said?*

"Yeah. That's another reason for these events. It's practically the only way to meet someone."

That was true. Only bus rides and before and after Mortae gave other opportunities.

He laughed. "Sometimes there are singles events, but they're awkward."

"I'd imagine so."

She sipped her beer and involuntarily grimaced. The tables around them were all occupied, and the number of people at the bars was dwindling. The event would start soon.

"My parents met at an event," Cafrec said. "They work for the Department of Health."

"Mine are at the Department of Occupation."

"Uh-huh. See? They met at something like this."

As he sipped his drink, Breel tried to figure him out. Was he coming on to her? Or was he impressing upon her the government's control on all its citizens? Not that she'd mind the former. Cafrec was handsome with incredible eyes, President Tatem-like though they were. He had a beautiful smile and, unlike most other Leaders of Today she had met, was friendly.

The government expected approved citizens to have their first child by twenty-five. Those who didn't—and were preapproved—received a visit from someone at the fertility clinic who described the process and encouraged them to procreate. But that was years away. No need to worry yet about whether the government wanted someone like her to procreate or about Cafrec's intentions.

Changing the topic, she asked, "Is the food good at these events?"

His eyes lit up. "Oh, it's amazing! Best food ever. And the variety! They take a lot of the menu options, including ones you need to buy with points and ones not available anywhere else, and put them all on the table."

"Wow." She grinned, fantasizing about the upcoming feast.

"Be prepared to see new food all at the same time. It's incredible! I recommend everything. Especially the desserts."

Breel laughed.

Cafrec rested his elbows on the table, chin on his interlaced fingers. "Breel, how come I've never seen you before?"

"I dunno. I wondered the same."

"You'd think we'd have seen each other at school. I'm only a year older than you."

A young woman at the next table glanced at them, and Breel looked away. *She better not be listening to our conversation!*

"Guess our paths just never crossed," Breel said.

"Yeah. Did you like school?"

"It was okay. I mean, school itself I liked. The studying part? That was hard."

He leaned back with a groan. "I hear you. I hated hitting the books. Most of my studying was doing practical stuff. Writing programs and whatnot. I could do that all day."

"Then you're lucky that's your job."

"True, true. Unfortunately, the Department of Expansion courses are like being in school."

"How's that going?"

He drank before answering. "Better than school. No tests. Just assignments and lots of reading. But still..."

"What're you taking?"

"Just finishing the first course. It's a year long and mandatory for everyone. It's about the Governmental Offices. Covers stuff like how the departments interrelate and the role of each department."

"Oh! You'll learn useful information."

He snorted. "Yeah, right. It's useless. Everyone's course varies based on their department and Career Group. It's all things that would've been helpful to know earlier."

Breel groaned. Classic Lexum. "Pointless then."

"Very."

Even though he stopped talking, Cafrec's eyes didn't leave her. When most people would break eye contact, he didn't, apparently unaware of the awkwardness. Breel's brain raced for something to say. "Cafrec?"

"Yeah?"

"When you started working, did you find lots of people... um..." She struggled to find the right word.

"Unfriendly?"

She nodded. It could only be a good sign that he finished her sentence.

"I did. It was a shock. A symptom of the *only talk if it's necessary to complete your work* culture. Socializing is supposed to happen at these events, not at work. But, as you can see, people clique up. You'd think they'd come over to get to know you. But they don't. I mean, some do... sort of. But only to say hello, not to talk."

"It's just so weird. Is that a Department of Education thing?"

"No. It's an every-department thing."

Chapter Fifteen

At twenty past five, the event still had not started. However, Breel didn't mind—talking to Cafrec was enjoyable.

Cafrec said, "Since my entire family works at the Department of Health, they were shocked that I got into the Department of Education."

"Were your parents upset?" Breel asked.

"Are you kidding? They were thrilled that I got into the most prestigious department. How about yours?"

"My father's a programmer, too. He was happy I got into where I did, but always hoped we'd be colleagues at the Department of Occupation."

"I'm guessing you're glad that didn't happen."

"Yeah."

Cafrec nodded. "Normal to not want the same department as your parents, I think."

Before she could fully express her relief, there was the echoing noise of someone speaking into a microphone. It was five thirty on the dot, and the Director of the Department of Education gave some remarks and gave a brief speech, officially welcoming Breel and the other new Leaders of Today to the department. As a new Leader of Today, she and those at their tables could take their food first, followed by the Director, their Assistants, the Heads, then everyone else. His speech was just a few minutes long—a far cry from the lengthy ones of President Tatem.

Cafrec wasn't joking about the buffet. Everything seemed to be on offer, including food she'd only ever heard about. Cafrec told her what each was as they filled their plates. Roast beef. Duck. Shrimp. Vegetable kebobs. Cranberry cheese ball. Lobster ravioli. So many unfamiliar foods she was eager to try.

When they returned to their table, Cafrec laughed so hard at the sight of her plate he nearly fell off his chair. "It's piled twice as high as mine, and I eat a lot." Before Breel could explain she took a bit of everything, he added, "But last year mine was even higher than yours."

She paced herself through her plate during the next hour and was only halfway when Cafrec got up for dessert. He returned with two plates, placing one in front of Breel.

"There you go," he said. "Just in case they run out."

Breel couldn't take her eye off the desserts. There were five tiny slices of cake, six squares, and a small bowl of ice cream. It looked heavenly. "Thanks!"

"I also put them on a normal-sized plate instead of those tiny things." He motioned to the next table, upon which were four dessert plates so small only three tiny desserts—four, if you didn't mind them touching—could fit on each.

"One of everything," he said. "Just try to resist eating it before finishing your mound of food."

"The mound is good, but yeah... it might be a challenge."

"Then allow me..." He pulled her dessert plate toward himself. "Now you can't reach it."

Breel laughed. She couldn't remember a time when she'd laughed so much with someone. Cafrec was new enough that he hadn't grown grouchy and unfriendly and had an enjoyable carefree attitude—or at least, that was how he portrayed himself.

Breel polished off both plates as they talked, speaking about their childhoods, school experiences, the departments in which their friends ended up—though Breel only knew about Ami—and the transition from Leader of Tomorrow to Today. Whether by accident or design, Cafrec asked nothing that elicited an opinion of the government.

The only interruption was when the news played at seven, albeit for only fifteen minutes instead of the usual thirty minutes during event nights ("we don't want our new Leaders of Today to miss out on socializing with their colleagues," said President Tatem).

In time, the room was less than a quarter full. Most remaining were heading for the door.

"Where is everyone?" Breel asked, having missed the mass exodus.

"It's after eight."

Breel glanced at her watch, and her jaw dropped. It was approaching nine. "Oh no!"

Cafrec laughed. "Relax. You live alone. You don't answer to your parents anymore. But Leaders of Today have a nine-thirty curfew, so we should get going."

She followed Cafrec to the elevators, and he pushed the button to go down. "The last buses left shortly after eight, so we'll have to walk. But most of Lexum is within a twenty- or twenty-five-minute walk from here."

Walking meant being outside in the dark. Due to the early Leader of Tomorrow curfew, that was something Breel had never done. Even worse, she'd yet to learn how to get to her house. She bit her lip. "Walk? Oh."

He gave her a sideways glance as the elevator chimed. "What's wrong with walking?"

She followed him into the small space, staring at the floor to avoid looking at him. "Um... well... I know how to get to my bus stop but..."

"You don't know how to get home."

He said it so matter-of-fact, without judgment. "Oh, thank goodness you understand. I was afraid you'd think I'm an idiot."

"Are you kidding?" he asked, exiting the elevator. "If you were an idiot, you wouldn't be in the Department of Education."

Streams of light shone through the windows onto the floor, but the foyer was mostly in shadow. The posters were unreadable, at least.

"I get it," Cafrec said. "The first Mortae after I started working? It took me an hour to find my way home. After fifteen minutes, I finally asked for directions. Twenty minutes later, I found my street but scanned my ID at every house because I couldn't remember the number. I was at the tenth house when a DOE officer came by."

"Oh no!"

"Yeah, I was nervous. She scanned my ID, saw I was a new Leader of Today, and escorted me home. Not the first time she needed to do that."

They walked across the grass to the sidewalk. A DOE officer standing near the entrance narrowed his eyes and folded his arms.

"Aw, he's just jealous we're having fun and he's on duty," Cafrec said.

Since the sun had long set, the streetlights were on. It was rather unsettling, especially when lost. The darkness was unfamiliar and eerie. The moon—which Breel knew was sometimes bright—was covered by clouds, so only the streetlights illuminated their surroundings.

They were in the non-residential part of Lexum. While many worked in the Governmental Offices, numerous Career Groups were elsewhere, such as the kitchens or farms. Across from the Governmental Offices were creamy white buildings. Each was three floors, one hundred metres long, and completely square. The first floor had no windows; the second- and third-floor windows were only four-feet square. The roofs were flat. The average citizen knew that at least one section of the Department of Food resided there. The common belief was these buildings held the kitchens.

"What street do you live on?" Cafrec asked as they approached the sidewalk.

"Um... Crescent. Why?"

"What kind of mentor would I be if you wander around by yourself in the dark? I think Crescent's this way." He pointed northwest.

"Oh, okay. Thanks." While having Cafrec escort her was embarrassing, she didn't protest. A DOE officer catching her alone after curfew was far worse.

Then it hit her. For the first time, a guy was walking her home. *I doubt Ami's being walked home!*

"Do you walk in the dark like this often?" she asked. Talking helped quell her fears of the surroundings and not finding home in time.

"Nah," Cafrec said. "I always take the bus after the events. But that's fine. I'm glad to have someone to talk to at them."

As three-bedroom homes replaced the identical white buildings, streetlights became more ubiquitous, and the darkness wasn't as bad. Three others were on their way home too, each by themselves. One, walking at a brisk clip, was a heavy stepper, each footfall echoing in the quiet night.

"I bet these events have been boring," Breel said.

"A snooze fest." Cafrec pointed to the next street. "We're turning down here."

The street was deserted. Breel craned her neck to read the street sign, but they'd already passed it, and the sign was in shadow. She'd need to pay attention to avoid getting lost next time.

They walked past a few houses and another side street (Lexum Avenue). Someone in bright yellow caught Breel's eye and held up a hand.

"Just where're you two going?" The DOE officer's voice echoed.

The neon career stripings on their bumblebee uniforms are even visible in the dark!

"Oh, boy," Cafrec muttered. "We just left our department's event.

Today was her first day, and since it's dark, I'm walking her home."

The man, at least half a foot taller than Cafrec, placed his hands on his hips, feet wide. He studied their faces and unhooked a scanner from his belt. "IDs." Cafrec already had his out. The officer scanned their IDs in turn. "Seems like that holds up," he said, staring at the screen. "You understand the curfew?"

"Of course," Cafrec said. "We'll be home by then."

"Be sure you are." The officer ambled down the street.

"I bet he's gonna knock on my door right at nine thirty," Cafrec said, stepping up the pace.

"Probably. You seem to know how to deal with him."

"Let's just say I had a few run-ins during my Leader of Tomorrow years."

Breel slowed, intrigued. "What do you mean?"

"Don't slow down. I need to be there when he knocks on my door."

"Right, sorry." She resumed the fast pace.

"I did some things not everyone appreciates. Here's Crescent. Which house number?"

"Thirty-seven." *I can't believe I remembered.* "What things did you do?"

"Just... things."

"Okay, sorry. We just met. Too much."

"Well, yeah. But mostly I just..." Now it was Cafrec who stopped. He faced Breel, who paused midstride. He spoke in a whisper. "I want to tell you. Just not on the sidewalk."

"Oh. You trust me with that information?"

"Yeah. I mean, you practically said you've received warnings. If you had warnings, it's safe to tell you the warnings I had. It's others I don't trust. Just like I don't trust whether they have audio bugs in the offices."

He had been purposely discordant when saying he had nothing to learn from other Career Groups! Breel didn't push. After all, someone could leave their house and approach them in the dark without notice at any moment.

Cafrec peered at the closest house. "That's fifty-nine." Breel followed him to the next one. "Fifty-seven. Just down here then."

"You can go," Breel said. "It's not far."

"Oh, that's fine. I've got time before that officer comes knocking."

A couple of minutes later, they were at her driveway. Cafrec viewed it from the sidewalk. "Nice place. Looks like mine." The corners of his mouth were upturned in a suppressed smile.

"Don't you mean exactly the same?"

"Hmm." He observed the lawn. "Well, I think that blade of grass is bent the other direction on my lawn."

"Is that so?"

"It is." He grinned, then said, serious once more, "You remember how to get to our office?"

"Floor eight?"

"That's the one. Last elevator in the southeast corner."

"Thanks for walking me home."

"You're welcome, Breel."

He didn't move. His blue eyes gazed at her, causing her stomach to flip and flop. Despite the awkwardness, part of her wanted him to never avert his gaze. Her mind raced for something to talk about so he'd stay longer.

Remembering the DOE officer, though, and how it was nearly nine thirty, she bade him goodnight.

Chapter Sixteen

Breel tossed and turned in bed. It wasn't being a new Leader of Today, her new job, or the intimidating Mr. Tucap that kept her awake. It was Cafrec.

Breel had never experienced immediate feelings for a guy—until now. Certainly, there'd been guys she liked, and she'd discussed them with Ami many times over the years. But Ami had always been the one to like boys the second she laid eyes on them.

I actually kinda wish I could talk to Ami about it.

Though, of course, that conversation would lead Ami to say annoying things, so no, it was best that their paths didn't cross.

Breel fell asleep after midnight. It was as if no time had passed when her alarm jolted her awake.

Going through the morning routine without having to wait for anyone and exercising and eating breakfast alone continued feeling strange. As much as she was glad to have independence from her parents, something was missing. Exercising alone was lonely. Eating alone was worse. The house felt monstrous in size for a single person. But every new Leader of Today experienced living alone, even those who started in group homes, so it was simply an adjustment.

This time, Breel paid attention to the bus route. Once she arrived at the Governmental Offices, she was certain she could walk herself home when needed.

She followed the crowd to the elevators. The ones on the right side of the southeast corner had long lines, so she waited in the shortest one which was for the elevator second on the left.

"Breel!"

She turned at the sound of her parents' voices. They were standing a few feet away, so she moved back to join them. They waved, Criba so much it was a wonder her hand didn't fly off.

"How was your first day?" they asked in unison.

"It was good." *Thanks to Cafrec.*

"You're smiling! Good to see."

"Are you planning on getting up there today?" A gruff-voiced man behind them pointed to the elevator. They were holding up the line.

"Sorry," Duknum said. He placed his hands on Breel's shoulders. "Our daughter just started yesterday. Department of Education."

"Uh-huh." The man rolled his eyes and walked past them, effectively butting in line.

Breel started toward the elevator. "Wait, Breel," Duknum said. "Which floor are you on?"

"Floor eight. What about you two?"

"Four. You're in the wrong line."

Right—Cafrec said the elevators went to specific floors. She bid her parents goodbye and joined the correct line. A few minutes later, she was on floor eight. The man and woman getting off with her didn't speak.

"Good morning," Breel said to the three secretaries as she walked by their desk.

They stared at Breel with dazed sixpressions. *I guess people aren't used to that.*

Cafrec was in their office, peering out the window. He turned when she entered, and his eyes lit up. "Breel!"

Breel smiled, grateful to be working with someone personable. The trick would be to not become jaded like the others.

"Morning, Cafrec."

"How was the rest of your night?" He slumped into his chair. His sandy hair flopped into his face. He pushed back the errant strands.

"It was fine," she lied, thinking of her lack of sleep. "Yours?"

"Good, good. Shall we get started?"

All morning Cafrec showed her various computer systems and databases and what their job entailed. It didn't appear difficult. He also showed her how email worked, since she now had access to it as a Leader of Today.

"Do I have food on my face or something?" Cafrec asked after an hour.

"No. What do you mean?"

"You keep looking at me rather than at my monitors."

Her face burned. She turned away. "Oh. Sorry. I just..." She scrambled for an excuse. "It's natural to look at someone when they talk, you know?"

"Sure. Makes sense."

Shortly before noon, they left for the lunch-and-learn.

"It's called a Department of Education lunch-and-learn," Cafrec said. "However, like today, it's almost always just for each Career Group. Basically, we eat lunch and listen to a seminar."

"Should I take notes?"

"Nah. I mean, you can, but we rarely do. The presentation's available on the intranet."

They joined the other programmers in a room with a conference table. They picked up their boxed lunches from a second table near the door before sitting halfway down the long table.

Right at noon, Mr. Tucap stood at the front. "I'm presenting today's seminar," he said. He turned on the projector, and the words *New Features* appeared on the white screen. "I'll discuss the Lexbase features going live on Monday. Depending upon your role, you'll need to account for some or all of them in the databases you program."

How pointless! Breel barely even knew how to use Lexbase. She glanced at the rest of the room. The nineteen other programmers sat angled toward Mr. Tucap, some staring intently. A couple were in their early twenties, but most appeared to be closer to Mr. Tucap's age. A handful had gray hair and aged faces—mere years, if that, away from retirement.

The hour dragged. Breel struggled to pay attention. Mr. Tucap repeated himself several times and spent much of the presentation reading his slides, most of which had paragraphs of small text. He held questions to the end; however, he ran out of time for them.

"What'd you think?" Cafrec asked when they returned to their office.

"My lunch was good."

"I presume you're really just referring to your soup and salad."

"Yeah."

"Sometimes the seminars are fine. Other times... not so much." He didn't elaborate.

During the afternoon, Cafrec had Lexbase code modifications to make and gave some of them to Breel. "I think I covered all, or at least most, of what you need to know. But ask if you have questions. I don't bite." He grinned and turned to his computer.

Throughout the day, she asked an inordinate number of questions, but Cafrec remained patient. When she finally finished modifying the code he'd given her right before five, she suppressed the urge to bounce in her seat with excitement.

"Sorry for the zillions of questions," she said as they shut down their computers.

"Nah, don't worry about it. That's what I'm here for."

A few minutes later, they were part of the crowd making their way to the bus stops.

"Which bus is yours?" Cafrec asked.

"This one." Breel pointed to the *#5 bus* sign.

"I'm number eight on the other side of the road. Good job today."

"Oh? Thanks."

"You sound surprised."

"I asked a lot of questions."

"Obviously, you did. You just started using Lexbase."

She nodded. Neither moved as Leaders of Today walked around them to their buses. Breel glanced away as Cafrec stared.

"I guess I should cross the road before it's filled with too many buses," he said.

He ran across the empty street. When he got to his stop, he waved. Breel waved back.

Chapter Seventeen

The rest of the workweek was like Tuesday. Cafrec showed her another aspect of their job, she read the binder, attended a lunch seminar, and completed a task from Cafrec.

Whenever she wasn't thinking about work or her new life or reading the dreadful etiquette books, she thought about Cafrec. His sparkling crystal-blue eyes, his smile that lit up his face, his friendliness, which was a stark contrast to everyone else she met.

It was good, in a way. Cafrec gave her something to obsess over and get her mind off drawing. Often when at home in the evening, struggling through the dry textbooks, thoughts of drawing plagued her. But she persisted in her unwillingness to give in. Drawing wasn't worth the risk of Mortae.

In the evening, she'd close her eyes and imagine drawing Cafrec. His long lashes, stunning eyes, and oval face. The prominent ridges of his eyebrows. The sandy brown of his thick hair and its tendency to flop everywhere. Picturing this was the closest thing to drawing she could do.

However, evenings were long. Eating supper wasn't the same without having her family to discuss the day. She couldn't talk to Trafis about rumours at school. While it was nice to be alone and more independent—or at least as much as that was possible in Lexum—she missed their conversations and togetherness. Her stomach felt like an empty pit whenever she thought about it.

Friday differed from the rest of the week, as they had their meeting with Mr. Tucap. Papers still hid his desk's surface. Cafrec updated their boss on what he'd been teaching Breel.

"Very good," Mr. Tucap said. "Now, I want you to put everything aside to focus on something new."

He handed them each a binder with a good one hundred and fifty pages inside. The front was blank.

"Like with everything else, this assignment is confidential," said Mr. Tucap.

"Yes, sir," Cafrec said, and Breel nodded.

Cafrec opened his binder, so Breel did the same. The title *Lex Code* stared up at her. She thumbed through the first fifty pages. Lex Code was a programming language—one she'd never heard about.

"Lex Code was widely used decades ago, pre–civil war," said Mr. Tucap. "There's talk of using it again. Therefore, you're to learn it over the next two weeks. Cafrec, I know you did this last year, but you're to brush up on it. I've updated the content, so ensure you thoroughly study the example code."

"Yes, sir," he said.

Breel shut the binder. Learning an obsolete language that may or may not come back into use was senseless. It wasn't exactly what she had in mind for her first task from her boss.

"Is there a problem, Breel?" Mr. Tucap's tone was challenging.

"No, sir."

"Good. I expect you to complete your first assignment in a manner befitting someone working in the Department of Education. Look behind the binder's last tab for instructions and assignments to complete by our next meeting."

"Yes, sir."

"You may go. Have a good weekend and see you next week." He

started typing before they even left the room, his hands a blur over the keyboard.

Back in their office, Breel dropped the binder onto her desk with a thud. "It's like we're back in school!"

Cafrec laughed and leaned back in his chair. "At least you didn't have to read this last year, too."

"True. Have you ever seen Lex Code used?"

"Never. I think it's his way of assessing our skills, seeing if we're good enough for the Department of Education."

"But they've assessed our skills for years!"

He shrugged. "I don't think there's any other way to look at it."

"I guess. What happens if we're not good enough?"

Cafrec gave her a pointed look.

Ah. Mortae...

* * *

There were a couple of hours left to review the Lex Code binder. Breel was reading a boring synthesis of technical information when Cafrec gasped.

"Turn to page forty-one," he said. "You're not going to believe this..."

She found the page. On it was an example of *if* statement code. The first line jumped out:

```
If ( FirstName = "Breel" or FirstName = "Cafrec" )
```

"What?" she said, head cocked.

"Our names weren't here last year," Cafrec said, tapping his binder.

"They weren't?"

"No. I would've remembered that."

Breel frowned. "Well, he said he updated it. I guess the updates were to personalize it."

Cafrec snorted. "Mr. Tucap? Yeah, right. He's not that personable or creative."

Footsteps outside the door drew Breel's attention away from Cafrec. She expected a knock, but there wasn't one. She turned back to Cafrec. He looked at his monitor and slammed his hand on the desk.

"Shoot!" he said. "It's nearly five. We need to get going. I guess this *if* statement's a mystery for Monday."

They cleared their desks. Cafrec's interest in why their names were in the *if* statement was puzzling. Mr. Tucap said he'd updated the binder, so the only logical explanation was he wanted to make going through it more interesting. *He's making a big deal out of nothing.*

"Weekend plans?" Cafrec asked as they put their things away.

"Beyond those textbooks, not sure."

"Oh man, the etiquette textbooks are horrendous. I fell asleep reading the *Workplace Etiquette* one." Breel laughed. "Maybe I'll see you at the Mortae?"

President Tatem had announced the Saturday Mortae during the Thursday news. It wasn't on the usual Friday since orientation of the new Leaders of Today already took up enough labour time.

"I'll be in the Bronze section," said Breel.

She rolled her eyes. *Obviously. Don't be so stupid.*

Chapter Eighteen

The next morning, she half-expected to see Cafrec at her door to escort her to Mortae. But he wasn't there. It was a weird thing to escort someone to, but nonetheless disappointing.

She arrived at the bus stop five minutes early. Unless there was a medical exception, the government considered missing the first Mortae as a Leader of Today an act of rebellion—one that could mean your own Mortae. It was doubtful the government would give her leeway, so she didn't dare chance missing the bus.

As her stop filled with people, most eyes landed on her and another woman, noting their Department of Education uniforms, before returning to their conversations.

"Hi."

Breel startled at the voice, inches from her ear. And there was Cafrec, standing beside her. Her heart skipped a beat, and she smiled like a dork.

"Hey!" she said.

Breel groaned. *I sound too happy for someone going to a Mortae.*

"I thought I should take your bus," Cafrec said. "Wouldn't want you to get lost again." He winked.

Breel blushed. Then her face burned more when she realized she'd blushed. Her heart raced. "Thanks. But I thought we couldn't take other buses?"

"You can if there's room. I'll risk it."

"Good to know. Um... how're you?"

"Good. You?"

"Fine."

A woman ahead of them turned in their direction. She opened her mouth, noticed their uniforms, and walked away. Apparently, Breel sounded as awkward to the woman as she did to herself. If only she had experience with boys other than Trafis and the mostly socially inept, shy boys in her classes.

"You're different from most of the boys I went to school with." Breel wasn't sure why she said it. The words just slipped out.

"Yeah? How d'you mean?"

"Well... you talk, for one."

Cafrec laughed so hard, more than just the same woman stared. He ignored them. "I know what you mean. Most of my classmates would rather read a textbook or stare at zillion lines of code than talk to—*gasp!*—people."

"Yeah," said Breel. "Despite having every class with them, the only friends I made were Leaders of Tomorrow from other Career Groups."

Cafrec nodded as the crowd returned to their own conversations. "I hear you. I had a couple of friends in my Career Group, but not many. That's why I'm glad you're my officemate. I was hoping for someone who can hold a conversation."

The bus pulled up, and they boarded, mere inches of space between them in their seats. Breel's heart had yet to return to a normal rhythm.

"Have you heard anything about today's Mortae?" Cafrec asked.

"Nothing." It wasn't like she'd had an opportunity, anyway. School clearly offered far more chances to hear such information.

"Me neither," he said.

The bus ride was shorter than what Breel had as a Leader of Tomorrow. Mere minutes after boarding, they joined the line at the Quaddro.

Breel spotted Mr. Gaimster heading to the Silver line.

"What is it?" Cafrec asked.

"Oh, nothing. Just saw the teacher I had for advanced discrete mathematics."

"Oh, Mr. Gaimster! He's a cool dude." Then, in a serious voice, Cafrec said, "I hope this Mortae isn't like the last one."

Breel shuddered at the thought. But experiencing any Mortae, no matter who it was for, wasn't something she wanted to do alone.

She was in luck, as Cafrec was still in Bronze. Though Breel was curious, she didn't dare ask the inappropriate question of whether he'd yet to attain Silver as a Leader of Today.

They moved up as close to the platform as possible from within the Bronze section. The images on the screens were much smaller than the Silver section, thanks to being so much farther back.

As they waited for it to start, Cafrec was quiet. Something on the ground had caught his attention. Or perhaps he was staring into space.

At nine, the usual nameless man tapped the microphone. "Welcome to this morning's Mortae!"

Cheers rang throughout the Quaddro. He announced that one hundred and six citizens of Lexum were exempt from the Mortae. "And now," he said, "please welcome our beloved President Hargam Tatem!"

As he took the stage with his security, Breel glanced at Cafrec. He faced the direction of the nearest screen, which projected an image of the platform. However, his eyes looked at the ground, not at the screen.

President Tatem greeted the crowd. "Good morning, Leaders of Today and Tomorrow!" More cheers and clapping.

Breel dared a sideways glance at Cafrec. He was clapping, but his hands came just short of touching.

The cheers died down, and President Tatem extolled the benefits of

Mortae. Cafrec and Breel exchanged glances. His face was pale, his lips pursed. However, he managed a small smile. Breel couldn't muster the will to smile back.

"Some of you know today's Vucapi," President Tatem said. "If so, it does not matter whether you considered her an upstanding citizen. She is a citizen of Lexum no longer. Today's Vucapi is a geneticist."

Breel gasped. Had this unfortunate woman worked with Famut? Depending upon her age, it was possible.

President Tatem continued. "Since we only want the best possible progeny, we prevent pregnancy through hormones in the food supply. As you know, only approved couples can have children with the help of a geneticist. These couples come to the clinic to have their eggs extracted and provide a sperm sample. Geneticists fertilize the eggs with the sperm and transfer the embryos into the woman."

President Tatem said all this matter-of-factly. Then his eyes flashed, and he raised his voice. "But this geneticist genetically modified your sex cells! She wanted you to produce Leaders of Tomorrow who go against the grain, disobeying the rules of Lexum."

The crowd roared.

"Is he serious?"

"Can't be! It can't be!"

"Death to the geneticist!"

Above the din of people expressing their surprise and disgust came the chant of "Mortae! Mortae! Mortae!"

Again, Cafrec didn't join. He stared at the screen, jaw slack.

"Cafrec! Cafrec! You're going to get in trouble." Breel tapped his arm, and he looked at her with eyes so wide they nearly burst from their sockets. "Cafrec, you need to chant."

He raised shaky arms and moved them, completely off the beat. He didn't say the accompanying "Mortae!" chant. His chest rose and fell as if he'd just run the perimeter of the Quaddro.

He knows the Vucapi. It was the only explanation.

Breel couldn't imagine witnessing the Mortae of someone she knew. Her poor mother... and now Cafrec... She wanted to say something but was at a loss for words.

"Is this acceptable behaviour for a Leader of Today?" President Tatem asked.

"No!" The crowd punched the air as they screamed the word.

"Does this behaviour benefit society?"

"No!" Air punch.

"Should we condone this behaviour?" President Tatem shouted.

"No!" Air punch.

"What should we do with this individual?"

"Mortae!" Air punch.

"Say it again!"

"Mortae!" Air punch.

"And a third time!"

"MORTAE!" Air punch.

Breel resisted the urge to cover her ears. It was the loudest Mortae crowd in Breel's memory.

The cameras zoomed closer as a DOE officer and the Vucapi emerged from the room behind the platform. Unlike most, the DOE didn't drag or carry her across the platform—she walked. Rather uniquely, there was a gag in her mouth. Her red hair was matted to her head. She sat on the bench, without a DOE officer forcing her onto it.

Something flew across the stage and hit the Vucapi's arm. It wasn't the first time this had happened. Like then, President Tatem didn't stop it from happening—it was undoubtedly why the glass barrier ended before the Vucapi's bench. Citizens were encouraged to throw objects at them.

Citizens threw more objects, one hitting the woman right in her face. She flinched each time something made its mark but didn't move.

"This is Centia Masna," President Tatem said, effectively stopping the object-throwing to get on with the main event.

Breel gasped. The name of Famut's geneticist girlfriend was Centia. She'd been a redhead. There was no question—this woman was Famut's girlfriend. First, Famut "disappeared," and now his girlfriend was being punished with Mortae. Surely, that couldn't be coincidence.

President Tatem said Centia had been playing with genes. But Famut had never believed what President Tatem told the crowd about the Vucapi, so Breel didn't believe what he said about Centia.

Maybe, like Uncle Famut, Centia's also anti-government and believes we should have more choice and freedom. That must be what got her into trouble.

If that were the case, then President Tatem was even more likely to lie—to give any excuse to kill her.

Breel's gaze returned to Cafrec. He had a hand over his mouth, eyes shut. Tears rolled down his cheeks. Suddenly, it hit her—his name was Cafrec Masna. No wonder Cafrec reacted as he did.

The "Mortae! Mortae!" chant grew louder. Leaders of Today and Tomorrow pounded the air with their fists with each chant. Breel stepped closer to Cafrec and, seeing no patrolling DOE officers, put an arm around him. His warm body shook against hers.

"Cafrec, we have to participate."

The words were like poison. Breel raised her arm and punched the air in time with everyone else. Cafrec did the same, though only extending his arm partway. *No one better see and report us...*

"The Deliverer!" said President Tatem.

The chanting intensified as the burly Deliverer emerged, wearing his usual hooded lab coat. He approached Centia, extracted a needle from his pocket, and, slow as ever, brought it to her arm.

They held Centia in place even though she sat still. She remained perfectly upright, staring past the crowd with her head held high.

The needle plunged into her arm, and the DOE released her. For a moment, she didn't move. Then, as if in slow motion, she fell forward, somersaulting onto the platform before hitting the ground.

137

Chapter Nineteen

Breel turned to Cafrec as everyone left the Quaddro. He stared at the ground. "Cafrec, I'm so sorry. Who is she?"

"My cousin."

That was all he'd say, but Breel understood. She didn't tell him about Centia's relationship with her uncle. It was probably the last thing he wanted to hear.

As the Bronze section was twice the size of Silver, it took twenty minutes to leave the Quaddro. Once on the bus, they sat side by side, Cafrec's shoulders slumped.

"I just realized this isn't your bus," Breel said as it pulled away.

"Oh, yeah."

He disembarked with her a few minutes later. Breel waited until everyone left before saying, "I'm so sorry, Cafrec."

"I can walk you home."

It wasn't what Breel had expected. but she agreed. *He probably doesn't want to be alone.*

They ambled down Crescent Road in silence. Breel wasn't even capable of thinking about how Cafrec was once again walking her home. Her thoughts were plagued with the knowledge that someone else—Cafrec's cousin, Famut's girlfriend—had lost her life. Maybe Centia had genetically modified sex cells and maybe she hadn't, but that wasn't a reason to kill somebody.

All too soon, they arrived at house 37. Cafrec followed her up the driveway, stopping at the foot of the porch. "What're you doing the rest of the day?" he asked. "Reading those thick, dry books, I guess?" He was far from his cheery self.

"Yeah, try to, anyway." She shuddered. "How about you?"

"I really don't have plans. I mean, obviously studying for my course." He rolled his eyes.

Breel's feet stepped closer, as if independent of her brain.

"We can talk," Breel said. "If you want to. Doesn't have to be about the Mortae."

"Sure." His agreement was immediate.

They sat on the edge of her porch. She kept more space between them than there'd been on the bus, despite preferring less. "So... um..." She wasn't sure what to say.

Cafrec rescued her. "Planning on seeing your family at all?"

"Tomorrow."

"Looking forward to it?"

"Yeah, mostly."

"Mostly?"

"My father will grill me about programming and our department." Other than that, she really wanted to see them all. Until now, she'd never gone more than half a day without her family.

Cafrec angled himself to face her. "Like what you do all day?"

"Yeah."

"And your colleagues?"

"Probably."

"And your officemate?" He managed a smile.

Breel laughed and immediately regretted it. *What am I, thirteen?*

"I didn't know it was a funny question," he said.

Breel said nothing, not trusting herself to speak and unsure how to explain herself. She took interest in her black standard-issue shoes.

"Cafrec, will you be okay?"

He brought up his knees, arms resting on them. "Yeah." He stared into the abyss.

The white chrysanthemums waved in the wind. Breel breathed in their earthy scent.

"I just wanted to say…" said Cafrec. He trailed off.

"Yes?" Breel asked.

Cafrec lowered his voice and said, "I feel the same."

"About what?"

"Mortae." His voice was barely a whisper. He blinked away tears. "I could tell you… you know… weren't into it. And I know it wasn't just for my benefit. I noticed even before he said who it was…" He trailed off.

Adrenaline surged inside Breel. Cafrec shared her views! Once again, she'd have someone to talk to about it. However, this was concerning. Had Cafrec only noticed because he shared her views? Or was her behaviour so obvious anyone could clue in to her beliefs?

"Me too, about you," she said. "Even before. Did you know Centia well?"

He straightened his legs as a delivery van drove by. "Not really. I mean, I saw her once or twice a year at family stuff. She was my father's cousin, you see. But she stopped coming a few years ago. I think she was distraught and couldn't bear to be around the family."

"Why? What happened? I mean, if you don't mind telling me."

"Her boyfriend died. Well, he disappeared, but we assume he died." Breel gasped. "Yeah. It sounded suspicious, like the other disappearances. I met him a number of times when he got permission to see her family. He seemed to really care about me. He was easy to like."

Breel burst with excitement once more. *Should I tell him?*

No. This was about him talking about his cousin. She didn't want to intrude on his recollections. Her relation to Centia's boyfriend was irrelevant for the moment.

"I got the sense he was anti-President Tatem," Cafrec said. "The family figured the government quieted him. They went on about how he deserved it, that his actions were suspect. Most told Centia she was better off. The lack of support caused her to stop coming to family events. I missed them both. Her boyfriend would sit me down and tell me all these interesting things."

Interesting things... Had Famut told him about Intercludae? Something niggled at Breel, begging her to tell him. Taking a deep breath, she said, "Her boyfriend, Famut, is my uncle. I mean, was my uncle."

His jaw dropped. "No."

"Yeah, Famut Sorep."

He was silent, chewing his lip thoughtfully. A strong breeze blew the fresh chrysanthemum scent their way. Finally, he said, "Breel, we need to talk where people can't walk by and hear us."

"Come inside."

"Are you sure?"

"Yeah."

They went in. She poured two glasses of water from the bathroom tap and joined Cafrec in the living room.

"Have a seat," she said, motioning to the couch.

"Thanks," he said, taking the proffered glass. "Um... I don't think the living room is best." He motioned to the television.

"Dining room?"

He nodded, and they sat next to each other at her table. "That's better," he said. "I suspect they have cameras, or perhaps even audio equipment, in living rooms. How else do they determine whether everyone watches the news?" It sounded like Famut had also told Cafrec about his suspicions of surveillance tactics. "There's more I can say, and it's fitting to say it today after they killed Centia. Can I trust you?"

He used the term *killed* rather than *punished*. Famut's influence was clear.

"You can trust me," Breel said.

He folded his hands and placed them on the table. "I believe you, especially after observing you at Mortae. After Famut died, Centia told me the whole thing. Swore me to secrecy, but she said I needed to know."

He wasn't making any sense. "Know what?"

He downed half the glass before responding. "Said if things worked out how she and Famut planned, one day I'd have an officemate named Breel, and we'd escape Lexum to help their cause."

Leaving Lexum was a dream. But Breel frowned. It was lunacy. How could Centia predict the future? "I don't understand."

"I take it Famut never told you I'd likely be your officemate?"

"No. He never mentioned you."

Cafrec's brow furrowed. "Centia said when it was time, she'd give us instructions."

"But..."

"She's gone, I know. She told me that one day she may be a Mortae victim."

Mortae victim. Again, it was Famut's terminology. Or perhaps Famut had been using Centia's word.

"How'd she know?" Breel asked.

"I'm not sure what happened, but clearly, she was doing illegal things. Maybe the government's accusation was right. Who knows."

Breel's mind spun. Cafrec's cousin had dated Famut. Centia had told Cafrec they'd be officemates. *Seems too coincidental to not be true.* But how would Centia know this?

Cafrec said, "Centia told me if she died, between us we'd have enough clues to leave Lexum."

"But I know nothing! How do we do that? And leave Lexum? Where would we go? There's nothing out there except a dangerous desert."

Cafrec held up a finger, silencing her. "You could imagine my shock when you started as my officemate, proving Centia's prediction correct. I considered telling you then or on our walk home, but I didn't want to overwhelm you."

"Yeah. Good call." That day had already been overwhelming.

"I visited Centia on Tuesday night and told her you're my officemate. She asked if you and I could walk by her house on Saturday after supper. You know, to get around your needing approval since you're not family, we'd meet her by chance. I agreed, though I didn't know how to invite you. I mean... that's just a weird thing to do."

Breel nodded. What had Centia been planning to tell them? Cafrec never got to invite her for that walk, but, if he had, would she have agreed? That was an easy answer. Of course—if only to have more time with him.

"That's why I asked what you're doing this weekend," he said. "I also planned to invite you when I met you at the bus stop. I figured the invitation may be appealing, to give you a break from those dry books."

Breel's heart fell. *He doesn't like me...*

Swallowing her feelings, she said, "But you didn't invite me."

Oh, geesh, hopefully that didn't sound as depressing to him as it did to me.

"No, I chickened out."

Breel exhaled, relieved he didn't mention her tone. "And it's too late to see her."

Cafrec stared at the table for a time. "Breel, there's something going on. Centia and Famut went to all this trouble to give us—well, me—information. They both knew something was going on. We need to figure it out. Finish what they started."

There was a sinking feeling in Breel's stomach. "But they were killed for it."

Cafrec glanced at the wall to blink away fresh tears. "I'm willing to take the risk. Whatever they did, they did it for a long time. Centia went undetected for five years after your uncle "disappeared." She's a painstakingly organized and careful person, so trust me when I say her breadcrumbs would've been well thought out."

Breel frowned. "But what breadcrumbs? What information did they give us?"

"We need to figure that out. Because I'm tired of restrictions." He gesticulated while he spoke. "I'm tired of fearing death over breaking some ridiculous, minuscule rule. I'm tired of the government forcing me to watch Mortae. I'm tired of pretending to be excited when people die. If I don't do something, I'm just as bad as President Tatem and everyone else who goes along with it."

Famut had certainly made sure Breel agreed with that. However, despite agreeing with Cafrec in principle, it was risky. "We'd be putting our lives in danger," she said.

"Breel, I can't live like this anymore. I just can't. Centia and Famut started something, and I trust them. I want to finish it. They said things are different out there, that we can do what we want. We'd be beyond President Tatem's rule."

As he spoke, Breel's stomach constricted. Neither choice was good. Finish Famut and Centia's work and chance Mortae. Or continue living a life she didn't choose. *But isn't this what you've always wanted? To do what you desire instead of what President Tatem dictates?*

It was impossible to know what'd be in store if she agreed. Without Famut and Centia, discovering what they had been up to seemed unlikely. Searching for others who knew seemed just as impossible, and perhaps even riskier.

"I understand your hesitation," Cafrec said. "I don't want to rush you."

She took a drink, her arm shaking. Status quo meant continuing to hide her true self and working in an unfriendly environment. Her father said Department of Expansion courses were rigorous. Even worse, she could no longer draw. Get caught drawing—Mortae. That would be her life for... for what? The rest of her life. Her entire life would be this. What kind of life was that?

Forging ahead with Cafrec in finding the clues Famut and Centia supposedly left them was the only other option. And then what? What had they started that needed finishing?

It was appealing to use this as an excuse to meet with Cafrec outside of work. It wasn't something to fear, since they were in the same Career Group and therefore allowed to visit each other socially. Together, they could have an amazing journey. For once, she'd choose her own path. They'd leave Lexum and never return. Few knew what lay beyond Lexum, but it had to be better than this. She'd be able to draw anytime she wanted without repercussions. She could hone her craft, perhaps become an illustrator!

Or, they'd have a short journey ending in Mortae. Breel shuddered. The thought of being another Centia was terrifying.

But Breel wasn't happy, and Famut had said he always wanted her to be happy. Clearly, he intended for her to do this. She'd be happier outside Lexum, since it was the only opportunity to draw, to do what *she* wanted. Perhaps they'd even discover what happened to Famut.

But...

I promised my parents...

You only promised your parents you wouldn't draw.

Yes, but it implied that I wouldn't do anything to jeopardize my safety.

Mother said she only wants you to be happy. Going with Cafrec will give you the opportunity for happiness.

But you may "disappear" like Uncle Famut or Mr. Progrio or be killed in

Mortae... and your mother will be forced to witness another family member die.

Breel sighed. "Cafrec, I... I really want to. But it's hard..."

"I know," he said.

She thought about how long Centia lasted in Lexum after Famut. Cafrec was right—if she was careful enough to last that long, surely she would ensure things would be as safe as possible for Breel and Cafrec.

Breel's heart screamed at her to agree, to tell Cafrec that she'd join him. But her brain screamed back. *But your family! Your promise!*

But I'm a Leader of Today. I need to make my own decisions.

"You don't need to decide tonight," Cafrec said.

Breel nodded, then grimaced. Keeping her promise to her parents versus fulfilling her own happiness. *What an impossible decision...*

"Is there anything else you want me to tell you?" he asked.

"Okay. Where's the guarantee? You've been convinced for years. But what convinced you?"

"Centia and Famut did, with their absolute certainty. How adamant they were that my life would be so much better out there than in here. The way they glowed when they talked about it... Centia was usually very reserved, but sometimes she'd get so excited talking about things she could hardly sit still. She was like that when she told me about how one day we'd meet and escape together. She went on about all the work they've put into this and how hard it is to wait for us to leave."

Famut had wanted her to escape... He had filled her imagination with dreams of the fictional Intercludae to inspire her. *This is my chance. I can leave and never return. I could even draw.* The one person she trusted the most wanted her to follow Cafrec's lead.

Famut was the person she looked up to more than anyone else. She had to do it for him and for herself. If everything went to plan, it would work out and she would do her best to help her family escape, too. But if not... *may my parents and Trafis forgive me...*

"I'm in," she said.

Cafrec grinned. "You're sure?"

"Yes. Clearly, Uncle Famut wanted me to do this, and I'd be lying if I said escaping isn't something I've fantasized about all my life. Maybe someone out there knows what happened to my uncle. Plus, I..." She lowered her voice. "I really want my freedom. My parents won't be happy, especially since I promised I'd keep myself safe. But my mother will understand, because she also would prefer another Career Group. I think my father is too law-abiding to understand but maybe... one day. I feel awful that I'll hurt them, but I'll do it."

Cafrec grinned. "Oh, I'm glad. I was afraid it'd take days to convince you."

Breel shook her head. "Uncle Famut's involved. He wanted me to do it, and you said they would've thought it out well."

He rubbed his hands. "Good. Why don't I come over tomorrow after supper and we can talk about it more?"

"Okay."

Was I too energetic?

"I should go," he said. "But before I do, you understand we can't talk about this to anyone, right? Not even your family?"

"Well, duh. Of course I know that."

Cafrec left a couple minutes later. When Breel closed the door, despite her quivering insides, she grinned at the thought of finally, perhaps, discovering what had happened to Famut.

Chapter Twenty

Breel's mind spun as she ate her Sunday lunch. She'd have expected her thoughts to be on what she'd agreed to do, the excitement and fear of leaving Lexum, the possibility of finally being able to draw unhampered, or how Cafrec was coming over Sunday evening for further discussions.

But Cafrec wasn't interested in her. He only walked her home Monday night to tell her what Centia and Famut had told him and invite her to Centia's. Breel tried not to think about it. After all, they clearly had something important to do. Even if she couldn't date him, at least she could be around him.

The trick would be not giving something away when visiting her family. Perhaps her father grilling her about her first week of work and the Department of Education would keep them occupied enough for discussion not to lead to Famut, as it sometimes did. But there wasn't much hope for a non-Famut discussion, given Centia's death.

After lunch, Breel left to visit her family. Since she wasn't on an official trip deemed far enough to warrant a bus ride, she had to walk the thirty minutes—though the thirty minutes turned into fifty, as she didn't know the way. But she knew how to get to the Quaddro from her house and from the Quaddro to her parents' house, so she took a detour to the Quaddro.

Finally, Breel stepped onto her parents' porch. As Leaders of Today could still enter their parents' homes, she waved her ID card and the usual *beep* sounded, followed by the lock disengaging.

Her parents were sitting on one couch and Trafis on the other, talking. They smiled at Breel. "Well?" Duknum asked as Trafis leaned forward.

"Hey, everyone," Breel said, sitting in her usual spot beside Trafis.

"Nice to see that you're smiling," Criba said. "We're relieved to see you doing well."

"Yeah. It's going fine."

Duknum frowned. "Just fine? Did your first week go well?"

"Is the Department of Education all it's cracked up to be?" Trafis asked.

"Are you doing okay as a Leader of Today?" asked Criba. Worry lines formed on her forehead.

They fired these questions in such quick succession, it took a moment to parse them. "Yes, I'm not sure yet, and yes."

Duknum cocked his head. "Huh?"

"Yes, my first week went well. I'm not sure if the Department of Education is all it's cracked up to be, and yes, I'm doing okay."

"Good," said Criba. "I found it hard, at first."

Breel nodded. *I doubt anyone finds it a breeze.*

"How many Leaders of Today are in your department?" Duknum asked. "How many computer programmers? What sort of work do you do in general?"

"Sorry, I'm not allowed to say."

Lying was the easy way out. Besides, it very well could be true. The government swore certain Leaders of Today to silence more than others, and that could include those in the Department of Education.

Thankfully, the lie had its effect, and talk turned to her house, coworkers, and so on. "The Head of Computer Programmers is intimidating. My officemate is nice, but everyone else is standoffish. People don't seem to enjoy talking with one another."

"You're there to work, not talk," Duknum said. "That's what those events are for."

It was a typical response.

* * *

The visit was one long interrogation, so when the time came to head home for supper, it was a relief.

Thankfully, Breel's family only mentioned Famut once. As suspected, it was during talk of the Mortae. "Hadn't that Centia woman been dating Famut?" Duknum asked. Breel and Trafis said she had, and that was that.

Trafis offered to walk her home.

"How's studying?" Breel asked as they walked. Her parents had focussed so much on her, she hadn't gotten the chance to ask.

"That's what I wanted to talk to you about. I didn't tell you before, but a few weeks ago, right before final exams, we taught for the first time."

"What!" Breel said. "How come you didn't say anything? And how'd it go?"

Trafis' face reddened. "I... I didn't want to talk about it. You see..." He slowed, playing with his ID hanging from his belt. "I hated it!" he cried in anguish.

Breel's heart broke. "I wasn't a fan of programming the first time I did it."

His eyes widened. "You weren't?"

"No."

He considered that for a moment and returned to their normal walking pace. "But you like it now?"

"I don't hate it."

"But you'd rather do something else."

It was a statement, not a question. Was she really having this conversation with Trafis? He'd never talked about such things. He always diligently accepted his lot as a future English teacher.

"What're you trying to tell me?" she asked.

He glanced around, like Cafrec had, before speaking in a low voice. Breel leaned in. "I don't wanna be an English teacher, or *any* teacher for that matter. I know I have no choice but—"

"But it sucks."

"Yeah."

"And if you had a choice?"

He shrugged. "I dunno. I dunno what I'd rather do. I just don't wanna teach."

That wasn't surprising. Despite Famut's asking, Trafis had never considered other options.

They stopped at a traffic light, waiting for a line of delivery vans. "What happened when you taught?" Breel asked.

"I was teaching grade one and just kept repeating myself and forgetting what I was saying. They stopped paying attention. I hate talking in front of kids. I felt so awkward and uncomfortable."

"They don't teach you tricks for getting more comfortable?"

"Next semester when we take public speaking."

Practical skills sounded far too important to wait to the very end of schooling. Not wanting him to think he was a lost cause, she said, "I'm sure it'll all work out. You'll get more comfortable the more you teach and develop those other skills. It'll work out. They wouldn't assign you as an English teacher if they didn't think you had it in you."

"I guess. I knew you were the one person I could tell. Anyway, thanks for listening."

The light turned green, and they crossed the empty street.

"How's it really going, Breel?"

"It's fine."

An automatic response. But she paused to take stock of everything. Despite her unfriendly colleagues, her job was okay. Cafrec made it better, of course. Living alone wasn't easy, and though there were the etiquette textbooks to read, they were too dry to keep her attention for long.

"Fine for real?" Cafrec asked.

She led the way onto Crescent Road. "Yeah. I mean, it's an adjustment, but it's fine."

"I'm glad you're happy."

I wouldn't go that far...

"Have you spoken to Ami?" he asked.

"She got the Department of Enforcement."

Trafis snorted.

"What's that mean?" Breel asked.

He said nothing as they walked past a woman from the Department of Households on a riding lawnmower. The smell of freshly cut grass was strong, and Breel inhaled deeply as Trafis sneezed.

Once they were past the woman and the roar of the engine, he said, "It sounds about right, that's all. Not sure why you're her friend. Like, does she know you draw? I mean, used to draw? Please tell me you're still not drawing!"

"No, not after what happened. And no, I never told her I draw."

"Clearly, you don't trust her enough to know."

Now Breel was silent as they walked past a man from the Department of Households. He swept grass clippings from the sidewalk back onto the lawns.

Once they were out of earshot, Breel said, "I wouldn't trust anyone with that information. You, Mother, and Father only know because they caught me."

"I guess. I'm only saying Ami sees herself as a model citizen."

"True."

"If she had anything against you, she wouldn't hesitate to stab you in the back to score points with the government."

"I know." Breel was grateful when they arrived at her house and Trafis could stop talking about it. "Here it is."

Trafis looked it up and down. "Yep, looks like ours, only smaller."

"Wanna come in for a minute?"

"I better not. Father would wonder what took so long, and I don't want to lie about our conversation. I need to keep my clean record."

To most anyone else, Breel would've thought, *Good luck.* But not to Trafis, as falling in line was second nature to him. His floundering would turn into flourishing. He'd finish his last year of school confident and ready to serve the government and its citizens as a Leader of Today.

"It was nice to see you, Breel."

"You, too. Good luck with school. Things'll get better. You'll see."

He shrugged. "I hope so."

She smiled her encouragement. "They will."

"Good luck at work."

"Thanks. I'm glad you're my brother."

"Same. Well, my sister, that is."

He left, sneezing once on her driveway ("I hate grass cutting day," he muttered), and she picked up her food from the porch and stepped inside.

Chapter Twenty-One

Even though it wouldn't make Cafrec arrive sooner, Breel shovelled her chicken breast, rice, and vegetables into her mouth. Afterward, she watched the news. As Cafrec had suggested, a form of surveillance through the television probably let the government know who didn't watch it. Likely one reason for the televisions always being on.

Her interest was piqued when President Tatem spoke about Centia. He didn't do it with his characteristic grin. Instead, his lips curled. He spoke louder than usual, his words deliberate.

"I want all citizens of Lexum to know that we take seriously the disgraceful actions of Centia Masna. Many of you are rightfully concerned that what she did affected your children. We are investigating this.

"Regardless of how her actions affect individuals, there is an enormous effect on Lexum. She deliberately manipulated our processes and safeguards so women birth children who fit certain criteria, thereby advancing her own agenda.

"This is despicable. Her selfish actions were a direction violation of embracing the collective. These Leaders of Tomorrow may not be capable of reaching their full potential, negatively affecting all citizens of Lexum. This is yet another reason societal benefit must always trump individual benefit."

He sipped water while smoothing his slicked-back hair with his other hand.

No one's ever had such a love affair with their hair.

When President Tatem's gaze returned to the camera, he had his usual grin, eyes boring into his viewers. Breel shivered as if coming inside from a frigid walk. President Tatem spewed more propaganda. When the news ended, she hightailed it out of the living room, fists clenched. Why did everyone make such events an excuse to explain how the government's sick laws and views were right?

Her standard-issue watch said it was seven thirty-five. Not knowing where Cafrec lived, she was uncertain how long it'd take him to arrive. Breel chided herself for overthinking this. Cafrec didn't feel the same about her, so there was no point in dwelling on him. They were just two coworkers leaving Lexum together.

While waiting, she read the *Workplace Etiquette* textbook. The author explained for one twenty-page chapter the reason for the closed-door policy in all departments. Breel's eyes glazed over, but she persevered. The alternative was thinking about her plan to go against her promise to her parents. Not wanting to focus on that or experience the associated pain in her stomach, she kept reading the book.

He arrived precisely at eight fifteen. Breel sat at her table. Cafrec stood beside the other chair, shaking his head.

"Can you believe Tater?" he said.

Breel smiled. "That's what Uncle Famut called him."

"That's where I got it from. I hate how the government interprets every unlawful action as putting oneself ahead of society." He gestured like an octopus. "I don't know what Centia was doing or why, but what makes them think it was a bad thing? In fact, I don't even believe them."

"I'm not sure I do either," Breel said. "Uncle Famut never did."

"Yeah," Cafrec said. "Maybe they had something against her, maybe they didn't. But she wasn't messing around with eggs and sperm." He slammed his palm on the table. "Ouch." He shook his hand. "I mean, let's say she really was experimenting with sex cells. Why do it? She must've had a reason. Everyone knows couples need the fertility clinic to conceive. Maybe she learned something. But what would that be, and why affect eggs and sperm?"

Breel shrugged. "I don't know."

"Whatever Centia did would've been for a reason," Cafrec said, sitting down. "It would've been for far more than her own benefit. But I just don't see what eggs and sperm have to do with anything. Anyway, sorry, I'm done."

"It's okay." Breel certainly understood needing to vent. "I only met Centia a few times, but I agree. Whatever she did, she did it for a reason. Have you talked to your family about what happened to her?"

He forced a laugh. "No way. They're such Hargamites that if it were allowed, they would've been standing side by side with him at Mortae agreeing with his every word."

Breel shook her head. "Hard to believe you're related."

Cafrec stretched his legs. "Right? I think it would've been different if they weren't suspicious about your uncle. But they figured she must be like him and anti-government. Guilty by association, I guess."

"She must've covered her tracks well given what your family's like."

"Yeah. It must've been a lot of work. I'm sure Tater has lots of ways to sniff out citizens, and there would've been some good stuff on her. Without a doubt, my family would've reported her in the past, but I guess the government had nothing on her. Who knows if they were the ones to report her this time, though. Maybe it was because the government caught her doing something." He sighed. "I dunno... maybe she really was experimenting with eggs and sperm. So, Breel, how d'you break the law?"

Breel froze. "What?"

He leaned forward, elbows on the table and head in his hands. "You said you've had warnings. What'd you do?"

CHAPTER TWENTY-ONE

It wasn't a question people generally asked. "Um... what'd I do? Uh..."

He frowned and leaned back. "I told you everything Centia and Famut told me. For all I knew, you were pretending to be like me. Maybe the government planted you to come into my good graces, gather information, and feed it back to Tater."

"Sounds like something only someone who's doing that would think of." She didn't believe it, but the words tumbled out.

His brow furrowed. "Are you saying I'm a spy?"

"Are you saying *I'm* a spy?"

As soon as she spoke, he grinned to show he was kidding. "But in all seriousness," he said, "telling you all this was a risk. I saw your reaction at Mortae and know we have the same beliefs, but it's still risky. And you knew it was fine after seeing my reaction at Mortae. There's no harm in telling me how you got your warnings."

He was right. "It's just ingrained in me to keep it quiet, that's all. Okay..." She took a deep breath. "I draw."

"Oh! Cool." His face lit up. "Where're your drawings?"

"Confiscated by the DOE. Twice."

He frowned. "Oh. I'm sorry. Wanna know my warnings? It's only fair." Cafrec leaned forward with a smile.

"Of course I do."

"Now," he started, "it's been a while since my last warning. After what happened to your uncle and with Centia removing herself from the family, I had to be careful. Because I wasn't careful before that. I'd been to many Mortae, obviously, but it finally hit home when we learned Famut disappeared. My family, like many others, assume disappearances mean the government killed someone in private. It took his supposed disappearance for me to come to my senses."

He pushed the hair out of his eyes and said, "A few years before, I was in History of Lexum VIII class. You remember learning about all the supposedly wonderful things Tater's done for Lexum?"

"Oh, yes."

History classes were propaganda classes. They learned what life was like before Lexum elected President Tatem as their leader. How people only focussed on making money to buy things and impress others. How everyone only cared about themselves. How President Tatem had a vision—a vision that would eliminate the need for money and the need to impress others. One that would give everyone equal opportunity to rise to their potential. History classes villainized currency and selfishness. It promoted the current reality as the only solution. Around History of Lexum VI, Leaders of Tomorrow were supposed to be convinced, if they weren't already.

"It started convincing me," Cafrec said, his face reddening. "However, Centia explained how things aren't right. She and Famut talked to me, challenging what I learned in class. Not in a pushy way, mind you. They just didn't want me falling victim to the lies and propaganda."

"Uncle Famut did the same with me."

Breel'd had long walks with Famut and Trafis. During them, Famut would ask how their classes were going, always most interested in history. When they told him what they were learning, he'd ask, "What do you think? Do you think that's right? What would you do if you were President Tatem?" It was through these questions, and gently challenging all they learned, that he had influenced Breel's beliefs.

Cafrec spoke quieter. "When I was thirteen, in a class's notes, I referred to President Tatem as Hargam. I couldn't convince my teacher I wanted to save time by writing his first name instead of President Tatem. He said if I used the acronym PT, he wouldn't have called the DOE. The DOE and my parents came. The DOE gave me a warning. My parents believed I was innocent. My father yelled, saying how dare she insinuate I'm not a good citizen. Oh, Breel... it was terrifying. Famut and Centia—shortly before he disappeared—impressed upon me the importance of being invisible. They promised me that one day the time would be right. Until then, I had to follow the laws and learn everything I could or else Mortae.

"But then, in my second to last year of school, I put an X through President Tatem's name in a history test. Seemed innocuous enough. Not to my teacher. She demanded I explain myself and didn't believe it was coincidence that my X happened to be on his name. I got my second warning. My parents weren't on my side that time."

"So, you obeyed."

"Yes. I was a good little Leader of Tomorrow. Not that I had any choice."

"I think many Leaders of Tomorrow receive one warning," Breel said.

"Most, I'm sure."

"And as for two warnings, well..." Breel trailed off.

"I honestly don't think many get two. Most Leaders of Tomorrow I knew were Hargamites, practically worshipping him."

That was true. One warning was common when innocently doing something illegal. But the severe admonishments and threat of Mortae forced most into submission. And, as Cafrec said, most considered President Tatem saint like. They'd never deliberately disobey him.

Ami came to mind, and Breel briefly told Cafrec about her. "At orientation, she gushed about him, going on about how handsome he is and how awesome it is to see him so close up."

Cafrec rolled his eyes. "Do girls really think he's handsome?"

"Yeah. For some reason. Looking at him makes me want to vomit."

"That's too bad, since we look at his stupid face every single day. On all those posters in the foyer, on the news, at Mortae. Those creepy eyes..." He shuddered, then checked his watch. "It's after nine. I need to go."

It was disappointing, despite having known their time would be short.

Of course, such feelings were ridiculous, since they'd see each other the next morning. She followed him to the door.

"I think we should do this tomorrow night, too," she said.

Do I sound casual and innocent?

"Okay," said Cafrec.

"Really?" Her heart swelled.

"Yeah, of course. We have a lot to discuss. And, I mean, I'm sure you want a break from the tedious rulebooks. Not like you have the Department of Expansion courses yet, which, honestly, are refreshing after the first month of learning rules."

Breel agreed. The books were awful. Not just dry, but overly detailed about the inanest subjects. There was no need explain how to listen to a seminar when she'd been listening to teachers in a classroom for years.

"But what about you? You're in those courses."

He shrugged. "It's fine."

Either my father's wrong and the courses are a breeze, or Cafrec doesn't care about doing well in them.

Either way, Breel was grateful. It meant more time with Cafrec.

Chapter Twenty-Two

The moment Breel walked into the office the next morning, Cafrec approached her. "Look at this," he said. "Read the whole thing."

He held out his open binder, pointing to an *if* statement. It was the same one he had showed her on Friday. Breel set the binder on her desk and leaned over to read it.

```
If ( FirstName = "Breel" or FirstName = "Cafrec" )
    CreateLocal (
        AddressDirectionQuaddro = "North";
        CrawlThrough = "WallPipe"
    )
Else
    CreateLocal (
        AddressDirectionQuaddro = "Other";
        CrawlThrough = "N/A"
    )
End if
```

Breel frowned. Cafrec's eyes were piercing, jumping between her and the binder. *Why is he so worked up?*

"That's weird," she said. "But okay... It creates a local variable. Something about the direction north and crawling through a wall pipe? Again, I'd say Mr. Tucap is just having fun making up weird examples."

Cafrec tapped his finger beside the subsequent *if* statement. "Keep reading." Breel turned back to the binder.

```
If ( AddressDirectionQuaddro = "Other" )
    CreateLocal (
        Destination = "Not found"
    )
Else if ( AddressDirectionQuaddro = "North" )
    CreateLocal (
        Destination = "Fantastical Place"
    )
End if
```

Breel gasped. Fantastical place... Famut referred to Intercludae as a fantastical place. Could it really be? Her jaw dropped.

"You know about Intercludae?" she asked Cafrec.

"Famut's fantastical place, yes, of course! But isn't the example referring to it more interesting than me knowing about it?"

He was right. Cafrec had known Famut, so it wasn't difficult to believe he knew about Intercludae. But Mr. Tucap? Sure, he and Famut had been friends, but Intercludae was a children's tale.

"I don't understand," she said, sitting to quell her shaking legs.

"I got here early, walking instead of taking the bus, to look at it further. I think it's directions to Intercludae."

"But it's fantastical," she said. Cafrec looked at her pointedly. "Isn't it?"

"Maybe it's not."

Breel's body vibrated. *Intercludae... is real?* Considering what had just happened to Centia, Intercludae being referenced in the binder seemed too coincidental. "We should ask Mr. Tucap where these examples are from."

"I agree," he said.

Cafrec logged into his computer, showing Breel the meeting scheduling system as he looked at Mr. Tucap's calendar. He booked a meeting for ten. While waiting, Breel found another *if* statement.

```
If ( FirstName = "Breel" or FirstName = "Cafrec" )
    CreateLocal (
        Time = "Night"
    );
    CreateGlobal (
        MilesWalk = "ChrysanthemumHouseNum"
    )
Else
    CreateLocal (
        Time = "Day"
    );
    CreateGlobal (
        MilesWalk = "None"
    )
End if
```

"I think you're right. I think it *is* directions," she said.

Cafrec rolled his chair beside hers and set his binder on Breel's desk. He smelled like the standard-issue vanilla shampoo.

"Look," she said, "the first *if* statement is saying if it's us, we walk north of the Quaddro and crawl through a pipe in the wall."

"I remember being told about drainage pipes in the walls," Cafrec said. He read the code further. "I suppose the *else* portion is saying don't go in any other direction."

"And the second *if* statement says that there's no destination if we go any direction but north. However, if we go north, our destination is Intercludae."

"Crawl through a pipe..." Cafrec tapped his finger on the desk.

"Intercludae is somewhere outside Lexum," Breel said.

Cafrec peered over his binder, guiding his finger along while he read. "And then the next example says to go at night and... what's this Chrysanthemum house num?"

"I lived on Chrysanthemum Lane as a Leader of Tomorrow. I think it's referencing the house number, which is house five. It must mean that once we leave the pipe, we walk five miles at night."

Cafrec's hair fell in his face. "I think you're right," he said, pushing it back. "And the second section is telling us not to walk in the daytime." Cafrec leaned back. "Wow... okay..."

"Cafrec, what're the odds of Mr. Tucap giving us these examples days after Centia wanted to meet with us and then... Mortae?"

"Not high. Not high." His finger tapped his lips. He stared at the desk.

"It must've been on purpose."

Her heart fluttered. Intercludae.... Was it truly an actual place? Even though she'd spoken with Cafrec about leaving Lexum on the weekend, part of her hadn't really believed it was doable. But if the example was real, not only did Intercludae exist, but it seemed to be their destination. That meant others were already in Intercludae, so finding their way was achievable. The possibility of finding out about Famut and of drawing again was thrilling. Wanting to know more, she read the next example:

```
If ( AddressDirectionQuaddro = "North" and MilesWalk =
ChrysanthemumLaneHouseNumber )
    CreateJSON (
        MilesWalk = ChrysanthemumHouseNum;
        BuildingNumberEnter = Calculate (
        ChrysanthemumHouseNum ^ 2 );
        Entrance = "Refrigerator"
    )
Else
    CreateLocal (
        MilesWalk = "Error"
    )
End if
```

She read the code, carefully reviewing the JSON, or JavaScript Object

Notation. "It's using the global variables from previous examples."

"Yeah, it is," Cafrec said.

She hadn't meant to say it aloud. According to the code, they were to walk five miles, enter building number 25, and come across a refrigerator for an entrance. She'd only seen refrigerators in food production pictures and videos.

"How's a refrigerator an entrance?" Cafrec asked, stealing the words right from her mouth.

But it was time to see Mr. Tucap, so that discussion would have to wait. Binders in hand, they left their office. Another Leader of Today around their age walked past as if they were invisible.

Moments later, Mr. Tucap greeted them with a stiff nod.

"Morning, sir," they said in unison.

Mr. Tucap leaned back in his chair, one foot on the edge of his desk, hands clasped on his lap. He eyed them one at a time, apparently waiting for them to start.

Cafrec took a deep breath and said, "Sir, we were wondering about the examples."

Each word was deliberate. Mr. Tucap made him nervous, not that Breel could blame him.

"Interesting, aren't they?" their boss said.

Breel and Cafrec exchanged glances. It wasn't the response they expected. "You could say that," Cafrec said.

Mr. Tucap put his foot on the floor and held up a finger. He turned to his monitor, and his hands flew across the keyboard. After a moment, Mr. Tucap pushed his keyboard out of the way, turned his monitors, and leaned forward, folding his hands on the desk.

"Okay, kids, listen up. There's no audio surveillance in the offices because that's a security risk. There's video, though the quality is purposely too low to read lips, papers, or monitors. Homes are a different story. There's more surveillance equipment than you can imagine. Your discussions over the weekend? Let's just say it's a good thing I'm a skilled hacker and programmer. I'm not the Head of Computer Programmers in the most prestigious department for nothing."

Breel's jaw dropped. "I... I don't understand, sir," she said.

He held up a hand, silencing her. "Just listen. Careful where you discuss all this. Not here, as you never know who may walk by your office. Whatever you do, stop discussing it inside your houses—I can't be hacking into the system all the time to plant fake surveillance feeds. The safest place is your backyard. But speak quietly, barely above a whisper."

Breel glanced at Cafrec, but this time he didn't look back. He stared at Mr. Tucap, open mouthed, eyes wide.

Mr. Tucap continued. "Breel, I told you I went to school with Famut. I also knew Centia, albeit only electronically. She contacted me the other day, fearing for her life, thinking she'd failed in bringing you two to, well, you know where. She begged me to act. That's what the coded instructions are about. Not my best coding, I'll admit, but I had little time to whip them up. The contents are too dangerous to discuss aloud. Follow the instructions to learn what you need to do. Just as important is to complete the assignments to learn Lex Code."

"But, sir—" Cafrec said, finding his voice.

Mr. Tucap held up a hand. "I told you not to speak, Cafrec. After what's happened, you need to get there soon. Don't delay."

"Like... today?" Breel asked.

"This week. Learn Lex Code first."

"Why's Lex Code so important?" she asked.

Mr. Tucap pursed his lips. One too many interruptions. But he wasn't being fair, not wanting them to speak. He wiped his glistening brow. He hadn't been sweating the other day. "I don't know exactly, as I'm not privy to everything. My task is to ensure you learn Lex Code and, after

Centia contacted me, ensure you get to... well, you know where. Meet with me at the end of each day to hand in your completed assignments. After work on Friday, follow the instructions in the examples."

He dismissed them. It took Breel's legs a moment to find the strength to stand. Centia trying to talk to them, Mr. Tucap being on their side, coded messages... and Intercludae being an actual place. It was surreal.

"Coming, Breel?" Cafrec asked.

He was already standing at the door. Breel followed him out of the office, grateful that she didn't have to do this alone.

Chapter Twenty-Three

That evening, President Tatem took advantage of a slow news day to reinforce, yet again, that he would not tolerate behaviours like those of Centia Masna. When Cafrec arrived shortly after, he started ranting about it, but Breel silenced him, wanting to first ensure neighbours couldn't overhear.

Breel's backyard was identical to, albeit smaller, than her parents'. There was a ten-by-ten-foot patio—a solid concrete mass made of crushed stones that'd shred the feet of anyone walking on it barefoot. Beyond the patio was a grassy area twenty feet deep. A birch tree in the middle of the yard provided shade. Its branches and leaves, along with the seven-foot-tall wooden fence with slats a quarter of an inch apart, provided decent privacy.

She walked over to the fence on each side of her yard and peered through the slats to the neighbour. Neither was outside. She listened for any voices. But there were only birds chirping and the occasional delivery van rumbling down the street.

She returned to Cafrec, sitting on the grass instead of on her standard-issue lawn chair. It was white and hard—not at all like the green loungers of Ami's upgrading-hungry parents. Those chairs were so comfy you never wanted to get up.

"We're in the clear," she said. "You can have the chair. I'll sit on the grass."

"No thanks. Grass is more comfortable."

Breel chuckled—*He's probably right*—and sat in the chair and motioned for him to continue. He spent fifteen minutes venting about President Tatem. Breel moved closer so he could talk quieter but still had to keep motioning for him to lower his voice every few minutes.

When he finished, he leaned back, hands balancing himself. "Okay, sorry about that. Onto the discussion at hand. What do you think of all this?"

Breel crossed her legs. "It sounds like Centia was to lead us to Intercludae, figured she wouldn't be able to, and asked Mr. Tucap for help. Someone had already instructed him to teach us Lex Code, so he added the directions to Intercludae in the coding examples."

But as she said this, she frowned. How could a fictional place be real? And if it were real, why didn't Famut tell her? Knowing they were heading to Intercludae greatly increased her interest in doing this. But there was still a nagging doubt.

"That's a summary, not what you think," Cafrec said. "You don't seem convinced."

"Well," she said, "it's just... what if it's a trap? What if the government's telling anti-government citizens that Intercludae is real to see who journeys there? They could be waiting on the other side of the walls to arrest us for treason."

"That's a pretty elaborate scheme."

"Yeah, but... what if? I promised my parents I wouldn't draw anymore and that I'd keep myself safe. Following these instructions isn't keeping my promise, and I'll only do that if we know this is all Uncle Famut and Centia's doing."

"I'd say it could be the government except for the fact that Centia wanted to talk to us. Plus, Mr. Tucap said he knows Centia and went to school with Famut."

"What if he's lying? Uncle Famut never mentioned him."

Cafrec lay on the grass, fingers interlaced behind his head. He was far too comfortable given their situation. "Doesn't mean they don't know each other."

"Well, since Uncle Famut and Centia can't tell us anything, it comes down to whether we trust Mr. Tucap. You've known him longer than me."

"I never would've imagined him a defector. But I also didn't know there were others like Centia and Famut. You know what I mean?"

"Maybe?"

"I mean, why would I think he'd defect if I didn't realize it was a possibility? I naively thought Centia and Famut were unique. But maybe they weren't."

"What're you saying?"

Cafrec thought for a moment. A bird flew into Breel's yard, landing on the birch tree. "Mr. Tucap does his job well. That is, when you don't consider his people management skills."

Where was he going with this? Breel shifted in the chair, already sore. "So..."

"I think he's telling the truth. So many people I work with are so obviously pro-President Tatem. Sickeningly so, like your friend. They think he's the greatest thing ever. Mr. Tucap never did."

His voice was creeping louder again. Breel put a finger to her lips. "Shh," she said.

"Right..." Lowering his voice, he continued. "He never said anything against President Tatem or his government but wasn't an obvious Hargamite, either."

"He's just one of those people getting through his day to day."

"Exactly," Cafrec said. "Except, apparently, he was secretly going against the government, taking orders from other defectors..."

"And training us to do what we need to do. But for what?"

Cafrec shrugged. "It seems he wasn't told. I guess that keeps him safe. You can't tell the government what you don't know."

"You're saying we can trust him. This isn't a trap."

Cafrec sat up. "Yeah, I don't think it is."

"Okay. I trust your judgement. But I just don't understand what's supposed to happen. We leave Lexum via the pipe in the northeast wall, as it's closest to the house I grew up in. After walking north five miles, we enter building twenty-five. Then the entrance is a refrigerator. The directions to the pipe are the only part that makes sense."

He shrugged again. "I suppose it'll be clear when we're there."

"But what then? Assuming it's Intercludae, why hasn't the government found it? How'd it get there? Why're we directed to go there? What do we do when we arrive?"

Cafrec laughed. "You're one with the rhetorical questions today! I have no idea. We need to trust in Famut and Centia."

"I do. But what if we're caught? Like I said, I made a promise..."

Cafrec diverted his gaze to the grass.

"Yeah, dumb question," Breel said.

"No, I don't think it is. If we go, we must to be positive it's what we want. We need to accept the risk of capture, which means Mortae. Are we ready to risk our lives by leaving everything we've ever known to go to Intercludae? Even if it's not a trick, and Mr. Tucap is on our side, we can still be caught. Is it worth it?"

The thought of capture was terrifying. But Cafrec was right. They had to accept that risk. She had always trusted Famut, and thus, by extension, she now trusted Centia and Mr. Tucap. Famut wouldn't want her to go to Intercludae if there was a huge risk of capture. He'd have made the risk as small as possible.

Before she could respond, Cafrec said, "It's worth it for me. I've thought about all this a lot. When Centia told me we'd be officemates and gave me hints of what would happen, I made my peace with it then. I'm not that close to my family, anyway. I told you they're all

Hargamites. But I know that's a harder decision for you. You'd be leaving your family, risking your life, and breaking your promise. Are you okay with that? I know you said you want to see what Famut and Centia were up to. It seems to me that if they also involved Mr. Tucap, others are probably part of it, too. That means the stakes and risk have increased."

"Nothing's changed for me," she said. "We're still leaving Lexum, as we figured before. I couldn't stay knowing about Intercludae existing. I wonder how Mr. Tucap does it."

Cafrec shrugged. "Yeah, I'm not sure. I'm glad you're still on board, and hopefully, one day, your family will understand."

Breel's stomach clenched at the thought of leaving Lexum and the dangers it entailed. But she grinned, her hands tingling. She was going to fulfill her dream...

* * *

They talked until it was time for Cafrec to beat the curfew. He stood at her front door, hand on the handle but not opening it.

"You know," he said, "for years I wondered if this Breel existed and, if so, what she'd be like. If she'd be brave enough to follow Centia and Famut's plans. And you are. I'm glad I don't have to do it alone. Are you scared?"

Without a doubt. But stronger than fear was the excitement bubbling inside her. If all went well, she'd discover what had happened to Famut. Soon, she'd feel a pencil in her hand again and be able to relax in the only way she knew how. "Yeah. Are you?"

"Guys aren't supposed to admit that stuff, but yeah, a little. I mean, look at what they did to my cousin! Well..." He trailed off, eyes on Breel.

"Well?" Breel asked, heart thumping against her rib cage. Her foot stepped forward, as if stuck in a tractor beam. There was a mere two feet of space between them.

He smiled. "Goodnight, Breel."

A moment later, she closed the door behind him.

Her body heavy, she dragged her feet across the floor and slumped onto the couch.

Cafrec didn't like her—that was the only explanation. *If he liked me, he'd have kissed me.*

In a social circle so small, finding someone to marry and have children with before turning twenty-five seemed impossible.

Chapter Twenty-Four

Sleep was elusive. The discovery of Famut having dated Centia, Mr. Tucap being on their side, and the coded instructions, as well as the upcoming journey with Cafrec to Intercludae, were overwhelming. Not to mention the newness of being a Leader of Today and all that entailed.

Then there was Cafrec. Why had he paused at the door? Had he wanted to kiss her but decided not to at the last moment? More realistically, it proved he didn't like her in that way. Maybe he stared to convince himself she was real, that she really wanted to join him on this journey.

By the time Breel arrived at work, she'd fantasized about the moment of entering her office many times over. Cafrec leaping from his desk to greet her, eyes sparkling. Crossing the room to take her in his arms and kissing her until their mouths were sore.

Her nerves tingled as she opened the door. Cafrec, sitting at his desk, turned to face her. He smiled, and his eyes *were* sparkling, but he didn't leap to his feet. Breel hid her disappointment.

"Morning, Breel," Cafrec said after she closed their door. "How was your evening? Get up to anything fun or interesting?"

"Hung out with a coworker." She sat at her desk.

Cafrec leaned forward. "I hope they're fun to be around!"

"Oh, yes."

He grinned and turned back to his binder. Breel pulled hers from the shelf. She was now past the personalized examples. The content was dense, though no denser than programming textbooks. Come lunchtime, she knew many Lex Code functions.

They ate lunch during a seminar. Mr. Tucap presented again; however, unlike the prior week, his presentation was about an interesting use for code. She paid such close attention she had to remind herself to eat.

However, if possible, Mr. Tucap's presentation skills were worse than last week. He stopped to yawn, covering his mouth at least a dozen times. In the latter half, he leaned against the wall, his speech slowing. He appeared sick but, if so, the government had deemed him healthy enough to work.

Poor guy... He seemed less scary now that she knew he was on their side. How many of his actions were for the benefit of Intercludae? *Maybe his boring presentations are an act. Maybe he's super strict so no one suspects he's not a Hargamite.* It had to be a hard line to walk, but he did it exceedingly well. Never would Breel have suspected him.

Mr. Tucap changed to a slide describing how code could lock and unlock doors. Breel sat straighter.

"This code is a second layer of security above and beyond ID cards," he said. "Someone swipes their card, and the system prompts them to enter a code to gain access. The code can be anything, such as a password, another line of code, or a calculation result."

"That's amazing," said a man in the back.

Breel nodded and ate her sandwich.

"Now," Mr. Tucap said, "this knowledge is not to leave the room. It's experimental, and the government may or may not use it for certain Governmental Office areas."

While interesting, such security was surely overkill. Not only that, but Mr. Tucap's presentation made little sense unless they were to write the code. But since they were in the Department of Education, that seemed unlikely.

An hour before the end of the day, Breel and Cafrec met Mr. Tucap. Unlike their last meeting, he wasn't sweating profusely. However, his head was against the back of his chair. Bags were under his heavy-lidded eyes.

"I'm glad you listened to that seminar more than last week's," he said. Breel's heart skipped a beat. "I notice everything up there. The presentations are important to your task, so pay attention. Hand me your assignments. I'll come by your office when I'm done looking them over."

Once back in their office, Breel said, "I didn't think the presentations were important."

Cafrec looked up from his binder. "Maybe just this one. Perhaps that's how we get into it? Unlock the entrance by writing a program."

"Maybe."

But Breel wasn't convinced. After all, if others were in Intercludae, it was doubtful they'd all be programmers.

Mr. Tucap stopped by twenty minutes later, closing the door behind himself. He handed back their assignments and leaned against the wall beside Breel's desk, much like he had during the presentation. "Your work is good. Keep this pace up to get through the binder this week."

"Yes, sir," Breel said.

"What about our actual jobs?" Cafrec asked.

Mr. Tucap waved a hand, dismissing the question. "It's not your problem. Have a good evening."

He sauntered to the door and left without another word. *He's doing our work; that's why he's so tired!* Mr. Tucap was having to do his work during the day and theirs at night, somehow hacking the system to make it look like Breel and Cafrec had done it. For the first time, Breel felt bad for him.

* * *

Breel and Cafrec met a few times throughout the week, after the evening news, to discuss their plans, including what to bring. Cafrec had inherited two flashlights from Centia, which the government had given her and Famut for the times their work kept them later than the curfew. Breel and Cafrec agreed to use the lights. Given it was only a five mile walk from the pipe to Intercludae, they decided not to bring food and water. It was just as well, as it would've been difficult, if not impossible, to do so.

They discussed potential dangers, such as whether the carnivorous animals—lions, hyenas, and poisonous snakes—they learned about in class were real. There was no way of knowing without going beyond the walls of Lexum. Even worse, if the animals were real, arming themselves with weapons was impossible.

"That's what I fear the second most, after Mortae," Breel said. "Big, sharp teeth and... my flesh being..." She shuddered.

"I doubt they exist," Cafrec said.

Breel flushed. *He better not see me as some wimpy girl needing protection.* "Why's that?"

"It's a convenient lie for Tater to tell, right? Anyway, if it were true, why would Centia instruct us to walk through the desert? She knows we wouldn't have weapons."

Breel had to admit there was logic to that.

* * *

On Friday afternoon, they placed their Lex Code binders on Mr. Tucap's desk. They waited while he reviewed their work, leaning back in his chair, foot on the edge of his desk. His eyes were still heavy-lidded, but he had more energy than earlier in the week.

"Very good," he said, flipping to the second page. "Yep. Yep. Good, good. Good work."

It was validating that Breel wasn't failing as a Leader of Today. "Thank you, sir."

"Now..." He planted his foot on the floor, spring-boarding himself into an upright position. "You'll need to remember everything you've learned." He tapped the binder.

"Of course, sir," they said in unison.

"Everything. Including what I presented on Monday."

"Yes, sir."

The entrance to Intercludae is a program!

He glanced at his monitors. "You better get going so you don't miss the bus."

There were no last words of wisdom or instructions as Breel and Cafrec rose and walked to the door. Before Breel could open it, Mr. Tucap called them back.

"Yes, sir?" Cafrec asked.

A bead of sweat dripped down the side of Mr. Tucap's face. "Good luck."

And that was all.

Mr. Tucap had impressed upon them how important it was to leave at the end of the week, so they would go that evening. After tidying their office, somehow, they ended up reaching for the door handle at the same time. Their hands collided.

"Oh, sorry," they said in unison. They laughed.

Cafrec stepped closer. Breel's breathing quickened as his sparkling eyes bore into her. He smiled uncertainly and stepped closer yet again, only half a foot from her, as if in a trance.

Breel's heart sang. *He likes me! But... what do I do?* Before she could decide whether to step closer or wait for Cafrec to close the gap, voices came from the hall. Cafrec pulled away.

CHAPTER TWENTY-FOUR

"We need to go," he said.

Leaving was the last thing she wanted to do. But there'd be other opportunities. "Right," she said. "Go. Yes."

They went their separate ways with the plan of meeting at the pipe at nine—when it'd be sufficiently dark and before the curfew. They had considered Cafrec going to Breel's house and heading out together, but if the DOE came across them, it'd be hard to claim they were visiting their families, which was what they agreed to use as a cover.

After eating and watching the news, Breel lay in bed, lost in her thoughts. *Cafrec likes me.* It was impossible not to smile like an idiot as she replayed it over and over in her mind. She had more important things to think about, but putting Cafrec aside to instead ponder embarking on this journey was a struggle.

Oddly, this close to go-time, she wasn't nervous. After all, Famut had been involved, planning for years to get her there. It meant going was the right choice.

If everything Famut had told her was true—and why wouldn't it be—she'd be able to draw whenever and wherever she wanted. Intercludae meant freedom. It meant carving her own path in life. Thinking for herself. Learning whatever she wanted.

Her fingers tingled at the possibility of being an illustrator. She could even teach drawing. The possibilities were endless.

Chapter Twenty-Five

A couple of hours later, Breel's legs shook while walking down Crescent Road. If a patrolling DOE officer saw her, her only hope was that they believed her story about visiting her family.

Dusk had turned into night, the streetlights doing most of the illumination. They'd carefully planned their way using a map from a history textbook. Breel had memorized how many streets she needed to pass before turning onto a side street.

She made it to Forest Road—the closest street parallel to the north wall. One side had four-bedroom homes, the other a forest. At least, that was what everyone called the mahogany forest—as the steel wall on the other side was visible through the leaves, it wasn't much of a forest.

It took fifteen minutes to reach the intersection of Forest Road and Tatem Avenue. Cafrec would meet her beside the wall across from the intersection.

Delivery van engines roared in the distance, and leaves rustled in the wind. No other sounds. No one and no vehicles in sight. Confident she was alone, Breel slipped into the trees.

Walking was easy until the last forty feet, which had little light due to the overgrowth. She walked into branches, ignoring the cuts and scratches. But finally, there was the wall. Behind her, streetlights illuminated part of a shadowy house. Everything else was dark.

She stood against the cool wall and listened. For a few minutes, there was only the rustling of leaves. Then there was pattering feet. Her chest tightened. Someone was running in her direction!

"Breel," Cafrec said. His voice was soft.

She put a hand to her chest and exhaled. Her heart rate slowed. "I'm here."

A light from one of Cafrec's flashlights bounced around. Breel frowned—they'd agreed not to use the lights until they were outside of Lexum.

"Keep talking but quietly," he said. His words were staccato as he caught his breath.

"This way, I'm here. Over here."

Cafrec appeared a moment later, his breathing audible. The flashlights were off. "DOE officer," he said, panting. "We gotta find the pipe."

The DOE have the flashlight... Panic coursed through her. If the map was correct, the pipe was east of their position and not too far.

"We only have one chance at this," Cafrec said.

They ran along the wall. Moving softly proved impossible as they snapped twigs with every step. Each was like a bang in the night.

"We know you're out here!" the DOE officer said. His flashlight was closing in fast.

With a voice that deep, he must be huge. Breel shivered at the thought of him shooting his tranquilizer gun. Avoiding Mortae kept her going, despite the stinging in her chest.

She ran, hand along the wall, following Cafrec. After a minute, a *thunk* sounded, and she ran into him.

"Ouch!" he whispered. "I hit it."

The pipe jutted five feet from the wall. It was a metal culvert, three feet in diameter.

"You first," Cafrec said.

The flashlight was closer. No time to argue. Breel stepped inside, her feet clanging the pipe like a gigantic "WE'RE HERE" sign. Moisture seeped into her pants. An off-putting wet smell worsened the farther in she climbed. A soft clang told her Cafrec had followed.

The pipe slanted downward. It was littered with random collections of refuse. Most were damp and broke apart, but others were hard and furry. Breel shuddered to think what dead animals they were crawling through.

After twenty feet, they came to a bend. Breel slipped, landing on her stomach, the wind knocked out of her. She slid around the corner, picking up speed as several piles of wet who-knows-what hit her face. Her arms flung out to grab something—anything—for purchase. But the culvert had slick walls. Before she could regain control, it evened out. Speed slowing, she righted herself and continued on all fours.

Cafrec's breathing was audible and comforting. Knees and palms echoed despite attempts to stay quiet. Beyond the noises she and Cafrec made, the pipe was silent. The DOE officer hadn't followed.

Probably not allowed to. But could they follow if they ask for permission?

If so, and they caught up to Breel and Cafrec, game over. Mortae. There was nothing they could do to stop it. Breel's insides quivered. She pushed the thought from her mind. It was too late. No turning back now.

Thirty minutes later, light flickered ahead. Her breath caught in her throat, but she exhaled, calming herself. The flickers were too small for flashlight beams. They were fireflies living in the pipe. *They sure picked a strange home.*

Breel steeled herself and continued. The lights didn't move or change in size. However, they multiplied by the dozen. It was a strange, eerie sight.

Breel crawled along, drudging through another wet clump, when her hands touched nothing but air. Overbalanced, she tumbled out of the pipe, falling three feet before hitting the ground with a thud.

Good thing these leaves are here.

A small but steady line of water trickled from the pipe onto the concrete slab supporting it. Before Breel could call out to Cafrec, he landed on her.

"Sorry," he said.

But Breel ignored him and the pain in her leg as she stared at the sky.

The lights weren't flashlights or fireflies. They were stars. Hundreds—no, thousands—blanketed the sky. Some were big, others small, some bright, and others more twinkly than the rest. No one had ever told her of their beauty. And the moon—it was a ball of light which allowed them to see the little they could. How much the Leaders of Tomorrow missed because of the curfew!

"Wow," she said.

"Quite something, aren't they?" Cafrec said. "I sat on my porch gazing at the sky for hours the first cloudless night after I became a Leader of Today."

Cafrec handed Breel one of the flashlights. She turned it on and swept the beam around, muscles seizing as she imagined a wild animal baring its teeth, springing to attack. But no animals were in sight. Nor were there buildings, trees, or DOE officers. It was just them, the pipe, and a desert with the occasional bush and rock. Much of the tension in Breel's shoulders released.

"It's a wasteland," she said.

The walls of Lexum were half a mile away. Unbeknownst to its citizens, Lexum was on a steep hill. City lights illuminated some sections of the wall, but most were in shadow. The wall spanned in either direction straight to the horizon. Lexum was an island unto itself.

The desert was windier than the city. She pulled her hair back as it whipped into her face and turned to Cafrec, flashlight beam landing on him as he scanned the desert with his own light. She laughed. His clothes were brown, his pants and the bottom of his shirt wet. Leaves stuck to him. Scratches from the tree branches covered his face and arms.

Cafrec laughed at her, too. "You have something in your hair." He pulled out a twig and flicked it away. "Should we use the flashlights on our walk?"

It was a good question. On one hand, they needed to find building twenty-five, which could be anywhere. But DOE officers guarding the walls might see the light. Maybe they already had. As such, they agreed to only use the flashlights every ten minutes to keep on track. The moon and stars were bright enough to use rocks and bushes as guides for walking in a straight line.

With a bounce to her step, Breel, along with Cafrec, started the five-mile walk.

Chapter Twenty-Six

After an hour of walking through the desert, Breel and Cafrec had yet to come across the building. They shone the flashlights. No DOE officers followed. Ahead, there was nothing to see. They continued, trusting they hadn't missed it.

Breel picked up the pace, and Cafrec didn't complain. She burst for someone to explain Famut and his secrets. To explain why he pretended Intercludae was fictional and didn't tell her and Cafrec they were two cogs of a plan. She especially wanted to know about his supposed disappearance.

They were the only living beings in the desert—the silence was eerie. But that was a good thing. Even the smallest of animals would mean bigger carnivores couldn't be far off.

Breel shone her flashlight again. The beam landed on buildings, perhaps a thirty-minute walk away. "Cafrec, look!"

"I see them!"

They upped their pace again, a spring in their steps. Breel looked behind them—the lights of Lexum were smaller, though still visible. They dared a couple more uses of the flashlights.

Fifteen or twenty minutes later, they were close enough to notice holes in the exterior walls of many of the buildings. The wind had blown siding off others, revealing mahogany underneath. A small number were brick, but many were missing or smashed. Half of a metal roof hung off one building, teetering over the small space between it and the next. Most buildings were one-storey warehouses or factories with the entrances facing away from them. The sea of buildings stretched at least as far into the horizon as Lexum.

It wasn't much longer before they reached the buildings. They were careful to walk between those with intact roofs and nothing hanging off their sides. The clearance was thirty feet but tight because of blown shingles, parts of walls, and mounds of undeterminable metal and other factory supplies.

They found themselves on what looked to have been a two-lane dirt road. Over time, the desert sands and wind had swallowed it, making it nearly indistinguishable from the rest of the desert. A dented roof, settled into the ground, blocked their way to the other side. Across the road was another row of warehouses. Beyond were endless grids of the same.

It was unbelievable. No one had ever mentioned this place, but surely President Tatem knew it existed.

Breel's flashlight beam landed on a building with half a smokestack. The other half was on the ground in pieces. A second smokestack lay in ruins in front of the door.

Each gust of wind resulted in a cacophony of wood creaking, metal groaning, and objects rolling into each other. Breel breathed deeply to calm her nerves.

"Looks like a bunch of factories," Breel said. "But what is this place? Why was it abandoned?"

"I have no idea," Cafrec said. "Looks like factories and an entire town."

He pointed to where his flashlight shone across the road. They walked to it through a gap between buildings, wading through mounds of rotted, corrugated cardboard. Coming to another road, they stopped. Across the way were rowhouses which stretched far in the distance.

"House" was a generous term. Each was two storeys and eight feet wide. There was a five-foot-wide hole in the peaked roof of the house in front of them. The door hung on such an angle that the lower-right corner touched the ground. The window on the first floor was open to the elements. None of the windows had glass.

They returned to the first road, as per instructions. Illuminating the brick building in front of them, Breel's flashlight beam found the doorframe. No door. Blocking the entrance to the building was a pile of shingles. A metal plate hanging crooked above the frame said it was building 39.

It took twenty minutes to walk to building 25 due to the size of the factories and warehouses and needing to walk around—and sometimes over—the refuse. Building 25 was as large and nondescript as the rest. The front door hung off its hinges. Many bricks were missing or chipped.

They walked inside and entered a dark, cavernous room. Cement pillars, in various states of disintegration, held up the roof. Stacks of mouldy, ripped boxes were along one wall. Metal shelving units had tipped, knocking over boxes. Walking stirred up dust that stuck to their wet pants and shoes.

Some shelving units were standing. The nearest housed laptops stacked ten high and covered in inches of dust. The corner held a stack of various-sized square objects, nearly reaching the ceiling. One stuck out farther than the rest—a drawing of a house.

Breel gasped. "This is artwork!"

"What is this place?" Cafrec asked. It seemed he hadn't heard her.

Breel shrugged and gave the artwork her full attention. Her hands tingled with anticipation. It was impossible to go through a stack twice her height. She'd only ever drawn on a standard-sized sheet of paper. But here, many drawings were on large cavasses. Most of them were covered by other canvasses; however, birds, trees, and a head of hair peeked through. It was enthralling to see what could be possible at Intercludae.

"Breel, look at this."

Breel groaned but reminded herself she had to keep to the mission. She turned to Cafrec. He stood in front of a cardboard box with four-foot-high walls. In it were differently shaped brass and wooden objects. Some had strange brass buttons; others had strings. Cafrec picked up a wooden stringed object. One end had a long neck, and the other was fat and oval-like.

"It's light," he said. He pulled a string. When he released it, a deep twang reverberated throughout the warehouse. He pulled another string. This one was higher pitched.

"These are musical instruments," Breel said. "Like the ones playing music when President Tatem comes on the news. Oh!" She clapped her hands as it dawned on her. "This must be where they brought everything after President Tatem took over."

She'd never thought of it before, but everyone's possessions had to have gone somewhere. *That means President Tatem knows about this abandoned city.* She gasped.

"Cafrec," she said, suddenly realizing.

He was examining a ceiling-high and six-foot-long shelving unit filled with books. Some were on their sides, others standing up, all with the spine facing in. The pages had yellowed.

"Hmm?" Cafrec asked. His eyes were still on the books.

"This city has tiny houses and huge factories and warehouses. I think it's the suburb of Lexum where the lower class lived."

Cafrec tore away from the books. "Yeah, I think you're right. They did all the jobs the upper class didn't want to do, so all the factories were here. Then, after the civil war, it was abandoned." He turned back to the books. "I could look around all day..."

"Me too." Her thoughts drifted to the stack of art. But, pulling herself together, she said, "But we don't have all day."

Their mission had been waylaid long enough. Though hard to ignore everything, they searched for the refrigerator. It wasn't beside a shelving unit holding cardboard boxes or near a precarious stack of dining chairs. Nor was it among a heap of broken bookcases—all far taller than any in Lexum.

But five minutes later, there was a yellowed refrigerator standing against a wall, a pile of floor lamps beside it.

Breel opened the door. It looked nothing like the refrigerators in the food production videos. There were no shelves and not even a bottom. Someone had removed the bottom to reveal an oak trapdoor in the warehouse floor. In the centre was a small keypad and, above it, a brass handle.

"Wow! We found it!" Breel said.

"Go us!"

Cafrec hugged her. Breel was too stunned to hug back. Her heart thumped rapidly. Did Cafrec feel it against his chest?

Cafrec let go of her as if struck by lightning. "Sorry, um, automatic reaction, I guess."

"Meh." Breel waved a hand, trying to sound nonchalant.

Pushing on as if it never happened was the best course of action, so she leaned into the appliance to examine the keypad. It was a small version of the keyboards in Lexum. Above it was a metal strip with text burned into it: *Enter the name of the fantastical place.*

"You do the honours," Cafrec said.

Breel punched in *Intercludae*. At first, nothing. Her stomach flipped once. Twice. Then the familiar whirring of a lock disengaging.

"Incredible," she said as her stomach continued its gymnastics.

"It really is Intercludae!"

Soon, they'd learn what Famut and Centia had been up to, and she'd draw again!

"You ready?" she asked. Her grin probably matched his.

"All set."

She handed Cafrec her flashlight and pulled the handle. The door was at least twenty pounds, but it opened and easily rested against the back of the refrigerator. On it was another metal strip with text burned into it: *Close both doors.* Cafrec passed Breel her light and shone his into the hole. It was underwhelming: a ladder descending about thirty feet into darkness.

"You go ahead," he said. "I'll close the doors behind us."

"Down we go," she said.

Breel climbed inside.

Chapter Twenty-Seven

Cafrec closed the refrigerator door and then the trapdoor. The first eliminated the little light they had, and the second shut with a bang. When Cafrec shone his flashlight, Breel covered her eyes.

"Looks like we're in a sort of metal tube," he said.

Breel blinked to refocus her searing eyes. They were in another metal culvert. Every step echoed as they descended the ladder.

Her body jolted when her foot hit the ground. She alerted Cafrec the bottom was near and stepped back. There was but one direction to walk—down a tube, the sides of which only the tallest people could simultaneously touch. A metal sheet lay across the floor to even the walking surface. Someone had inset lights into the wall every ten feet. They were dim, but better than nothing. The end of the tube wasn't in sight.

Cafrec stepped beside her, and his fingers wrapped around hers. Her heart leaped and pounded as if she had just run straight to the tube from Lexum. *Cafrec's touching me on purpose this time! But for comfort or because he likes me?* She forced the thought from her mind and squeezed his hand back.

They walked in silence, only the faint hum of the lights interrupting the clanging of their footfalls, which echoed throughout the tunnel.

It took fifteen minutes to see the end. Some sort of metal sheet blocked their way. Breel shivered even though it was anything but chilly.

"Is it a dead end?" she asked.

It certainly looked like one. As they got closer, Cafrec's flashlight beam landed on opaque glass at eye level. It was a few inches high and spanned the width of the obstruction.

They stood in front of it. Nothing happened. Yet, this had to be the entrance to Intercludae. After all, it'd need to be difficult to enter. Without a handle, this was certainly difficult.

"Do we knock?" she asked.

"I guess so." He rapped on the door three times.

Nothing.

He raised his hand to knock again when a bored male voice said, "Your names?"

The voice didn't have the same commanding tone as a DOE officer. *This must be Intercludae!*

Cafrec gave their names. "Stand back," said the voice.

They did and covered their ears as a horrible metal scraping rang throughout the tunnel, reverberating off the walls. The barrier swung toward them, revealing white light from beyond it, and stopped a couple inches from the side of the tube.

A redheaded man stood in front of them. He looked to be a couple of years older than Breel and Cafrec. "You coming in?"

The moment they were inside, the door scraped closed.

"Welcome," the man said as machines whirred in the distance.

His clothing was unlike that of Lexum. He wore a short-sleeve shirt and multipocketed vest and pants the colour of the desert sand. No sweater. No collared shirt. Black boots instead of shoes. He maneuvered a tall, backless chair in front of the door and sat facing them. The glass in the door was transparent from this side, showing a clear view down the tunnel.

"It's an honour to meet you both," he said, shaking their hands.

"It is?" Breel asked.

"Oh yes. Very much so. Name's Praesio. I'm one of the guards here."

"And where is here?" Cafrec asked.

"Intercludae, of course."

Breel cheered and jumped into the air. Cafrec laughed as they hugged. "We made it," said Breel as they released each other.

Breel basked in the moment. All her life, Famut had been working to get her to Intercludae. Now, she was there. She'd escaped from the clutches of Lexum. All that was missing was Famut welcoming her and Cafrec to Intercludae.

I'm here, Uncle Famut. I'm finally here!

She'd arrived safely. The next step—besides drawing!—was to see about getting her family to come.

Praesio was laughing. "I was excited when I finally got here, too," he said.

"You came here?" asked Breel. "Like us?"

"Well, not exactly like you. But yeah, I did. Was a DOE officer. Didn't like the laws I had to enforce."

"So Intercludae is a community of ex-citizens of Lexum?" Cafrec asked.

"That's right. Would love to chat, but I need to return to my post. I'm not the one to tell you all this, anyway."

He swivelled around to look through the glass. A weapon leaned against the wall within arm's reach—a gun with a long barrel rather than one of the tranquilizer dart guns the DOE officers carried.

"Who's supposed to tell us?" Breel asked.

"Our leader." Praesio didn't turn from his post.

"You have a leader?" Cafrec asked.

"Of course. Head on in. They'll show you where to go."

They left Praesio. Ahead was a ten-foot wide, fifty-foot tunnel that led to a cavernous area with lots of equipment and people mulling around. Much of the equipment was weapons, particularly racks of guns, but also vests like Praesio wore and tools. The ceiling was low enough to make anyone claustrophobic. The air was musty and thick. To the left was a doorway. To the right was another ten-foot-wide walkway that appeared to lead to a room.

People leaned over stacks of papers on a table in the corner, each wearing the same uniform as Praesio. Another uniformed group at the far end were pointing long-barrelled guns into a crowd of DOE officers and citizens of Lexum in the Quaddro.

Breel gasped before realizing it couldn't possibly be the Quaddro. And it wasn't. A projector beamed the Quaddro images on a screen covering the entire far wall. The images moved, some DOE officers even shooting dart guns into the group of Intercludae residents.

"Brilliant, isn't it?" a man, perhaps in his mid-fifties, said as he approached them from the table. "It projects a replica of the Quaddro. The goal is to take out the DOE officers without harming other citizens of Lexum."

"You're preparing for war?" Cafrec asked.

"In a manner of speaking."

Breel's insides quivered. *But I don't want to kill anyone!* Before she could protest, he extended a hand.

"Manum Gaimster. Second-in-command here at Intercludae."

"Oh!" said Breel. "Are you related to a mathematics teacher?"

"Yes, my son. On our side, too."

Breel smiled. Her favourite teacher hated President Tatem, too! *I wonder how many others are like him and Mr. Tucap, still living in Lexum.*

"And you're Breel Sorep and Cafrec Masna," Manum said. He unsnapped one of his pockets and slipped something inside. Nothing on his uniform suggested his authority.

"How d'you know that?" Breel asked.

"That's a question best left for the boss. This way."

They followed him to the doorway. Everyone watched, even those shooting at the projected Quaddro. Most weren't much older than Breel and Cafrec.

The doorway opened into a hall branching in three directions. They walked down the middle one, passing by a drawing of a pine tree in front of the setting sun.

"Oh, wow!" Breel said. The detail was exquisite—the oranges and yellows of the sun, the needles on the tree, and the shadows on the branches and grass.

"Yes, you'll see a lot of that here," Manum said. "You'll have a chance to look later."

They entered the third room on the left. Beds lined the walls. Above each was a drawing—a wheat field lit by the sun, a loon swimming on a lake, and a rock formation were the ones closest to the door. It was all Breel could do to pay attention to Manum, instead of admiring the drawings.

"This is our medical," Manum said. "Take time to clean yourselves up. The adjoining room has showers and clothes for each of you. I'll be back in half an hour."

They entered the shower room, which had six stalls. Breel's stall had a table with clean clothes (black pants and a navy-blue shirt), a towel, hairbrush, soap, and shampoo. At the other end was a curtainless shower. The floor sloped to the drain in the middle.

The warm shower was refreshing. As she scrubbed every inch of her body, the water turned from brown to—finally—clear. The shampoo was a light pink and smelled like strawberry.

Twenty-five minutes later, she exited in clean clothes.

Cafrec was waiting. "You look great," he said, eyes lighting up. "So weird seeing you not wearing a uniform."

Breel's cheeks burned. "I know what you mean. You look great, too." And he did. He looked like an individual, not some robotic worker lost in a crowd.

Manum was standing near the door when they returned to the medical room. "Bet that feels better. This way to the boss."

They backtracked down the hall, and he knocked on the first door.

"Enter," said a male voice.

Manum led them inside. It was slightly bigger than a standard Lexum bedroom and as sparsely decorated. A collapsible table served as a desk on which sat an older desktop computer. A bookshelf held stacks of books and papers. Behind the desk was a window showing a sunset. A moment later, it changed to a thundercloud. The desk faced the fake window rather than the door. Someone with shoulder-length black hair sat at it. Between the desk and door was a set of four chairs facing one another, a table in between with food on it.

Manum left. Breel swallowed hard, her muscles twitching.

The person at the desk stood and faced them. Breel's jaw dropped, and she put a hand to her mouth.

He looked as she remembered, though his face was more weathered. "Uncle Famut... is it really you?"

No... it had to be a dream. Going to Intercludae was a dream, too. That was the only explanation for her uncle being in front of her. She pinched herself and winced. He was still there. She was still standing, not lying in bed.

Famut grinned. "You bet it is. Welcome to Intercludae, Ree."

He hugged her. It took a moment for Breel's body to cooperate, for her arms to wrap around him. It was that moment in which she knew it was real. He was alive. Famut wasn't dead. Hugging him—the only hugger of the family—felt so... familiar. Her body and soul had missed this. Suddenly, she was sobbing. Her arms tightened around him as she soaked his shoulder with her tears.

"We... we thought you were dead," she said, her words muffled.

"Yeah. I'm sorry about that. Long story."

She released him so she could look at him once more. He was in front of her. Alive. Actually alive. His eyes glistened with tears. His glasses frames were thin, black rectangles. They weren't quite as thick as her father's. Her body shook as she suppressed more cries. He smiled and took her hand.

"I've missed you too, Ree," he said. "So very much."

"I just... I can't believe..." She forced herself to take a breath. "I've imagined this moment for years, fantasizing that you weren't dead."

He looked away. "I'm so sorry my supposed disappearance, or rather assumed death, hurt you so much. I had no choice."

"Why?"

He sighed. "We have much to discuss. But first..." He turned to Cafrec and hugged him. "Good to see you, Cafrec. Sit down, you two."

Breel's body was numb as she sat across from him. Her mind spun. She had arrived in Intercludae and was with Famut again in the same day. All her dreams had come true in one fell swoop. All that was missing was her parents and Trafis being in Intercludae with them.

"I know you have questions," Famut said. "But first, how're you doing?"

"Fine, I think." She wiped away rogue tears.

"Good. And now you're a Leader of Today. Both of you at the Department of Education. I'm so proud of you." Now he was the one wiping his cheeks.

"How d'you know...?" she asked.

"In a moment. Trafis doing fine?"

"Yeah."

"Your mother?"

"She's fine."

"Good. She was always very kind to me."

There was an uncomfortable silence. Though Famut took interest in a fluff on his arm, Breel kept her gaze on him, not wanting to look at anything else. His eyes were farther apart than what she'd been drawing, and his pupils were larger than average. That was why she could never get the drawing right.

"And my father's fine, too," Breel said.

Famut didn't respond. Instead, he turned to Cafrec. "And, Cafrec, how're you?"

"I'm fine."

"I'm sorry about Centia," Famut said.

Breel cocked her head. *How'd he know?* Famut sighed, his smile gone. He had thin lips. Her mistake had been making them fuller, like her father's.

"Centia and I worked hard to lay out clues for you to solve together. She was supposed to accompany you."

His voice cracked as tears welled in his eyes. He stood, facing the window to observe the chirping birds in the trees on his fake window. When he spoke, his voice wavered. "She was the only woman I ever loved. I always thought I'd see her again. We were aware of the risks, more for her than me, but accepted them." He returned to his chair and, looking at Cafrec, said, "I suppose I was too optimistic about her survival."

"I'm sorry, Uncle Famut," Breel said.

"Me too," said Cafrec.

"How'd her Mortae go? My informant told me about it after it happened but didn't give details."

His informant... It must be Mr. Tucap! That's how he knows about Centia and where we work.

"What do you mean?" Breel asked.

"Did she try to escape?" Famut asked. "Did she scream?" His gaze fell to his lap, blinking away more tears.

"You would've been proud of her, Famut," Cafrec said. "She was silent and didn't try to fight. She held her head high. I've never seen a braver Mortae victim."

Famut managed a smile. "That's my girl. I'm sorry you had to witness that happen to your cousin."

Cafrec shrugged. "It wasn't your fault."

But Famut shook his head. Voice cracking, he said, "Yes, it is."

"Why?" Breel asked.

"We have a lot to discuss."

"We do," she agreed. "I mean, the government said you disappeared, so, like many others, we thought you were killed."

"I left to come here. That's what those disappearances are about—our side fleeing for Intercludae. Some succeed, some don't. Those who don't are usually killed by the DOE on the spot. Too high a risk for a public Mortae. I suspect Tater somehow encouraged the belief that all disappearances are deaths—anything for people to not realize that citizens are escaping." He motioned to the table between them. "Please eat while we talk."

Breel had focussed so much on Famut she forgot about the food. There were three glasses, a pitcher of water, three plates and cutlery, and a steaming bowl of noodles, tomato sauce, and vegetables. As Famut poured water for each of them, Breel's throat suddenly felt like sandpaper. She drained the glass he passed her within moments.

"I'll start from the beginning," Famut said, "and you'll understand. You ready?"

"Ready for what?" Cafrec asked.

"To know the truth."

Chapter Twenty-Eight

Famut repositioned himself, crossing his leg before starting. His fake window changed from a stream to a dense forest.

"As you know," he said, "as a doctor I hoped to work at the hospital treating patients. But one year my coursework shifted to a lot of biology and genetics courses. I contacted the government, thinking it was a mistake. There was no mistake. They said one day I'd learn why."

Breel rolled her eyes. *Typical Government of Lexum, explaining nothing.*

"It was clear a year after I became a Leader of Today when I was one of two doctors chosen to become geneticists. The other was Centia. They chose us to go that route because in school we had the highest biology and lab work marks. We weren't happy about it but obviously had no choice."

Unhappy was an understatement. Famut had told Breel how lucky he'd been with his Nito Test results, as he loved his job. But he'd then complain about lab work and missing patient care.

Behind Famut, the window turned to geese flying in formation. "While it wasn't what I dreamed of doing," he said, "I thought it was important work for citizens of Lexum to have children. After a few years, though, everything changed when Centia and I met with our Head, the Director of the Department of Health, and President Tatem himself."

Famut had never told Breel this. *Probably wasn't allowed to tell anyone.*

"Wow," she said. "What was that like?"

Famut grimaced. "He just has this... this aura. I really don't know how to describe him. He's just... horrible. I felt on edge the entire meeting. Tater told us about a new project. They had ambitions, and it was time to place Centia and me in the roles planned for us. It was a top-secret project called Project Consillo. We were to tell nobody, under not just the penalty of Mortae but the penalty of Mortae of our families."

Cafrec whistled. "Scary."

Breel nodded. She'd never heard of secrecy to that extent.

Famut paused for a drink of water. Faint yelling was audible from the other side of the door. Famut sat his glass down and waved a hand. "Don't worry, that's just training. You should eat, Ree."

"I don't think I can," she said.

"It's great," said Cafrec. His plate was half empty.

"Not yet," she said. Eating would be difficult when she couldn't take her eyes off her uncle.

Famut shrugged. "Suit yourself. As you know, the Nito Test determines one's future career. Project Consillo went a step further— guaranteeing children to be a genetic fit for a career. The Nito Test would continue as a formality only."

"What do you mean?" Breel asked.

"When Centia and I were Leaders of Tomorrow, the government started genetics research. All citizens were unknowingly part of the experiment, since the government collects a DNA sample at birth. Researchers examined which genes were responsible for certain traits and aptitudes. You remember me telling you about DNA and genes, right?"

They nodded. Famut had explained DNA as the instructions her body inherited from her parents and genes as sections of DNA with certain jobs—such as making her hair curly, her eyesight poor, or her intellect high.

Famut continued. "When looking at Mortae victims, the government discovered a gene they named Creativity. It was most common in Mortae victims who showed creativity and innovation. They also found other genes of interest, including the Rebellion and Self-Thinking genes.

"With this knowledge, they conducted a longitudinal study with Leaders of Tomorrow, starting at birth and ending at death. Were citizens with these genes more likely to receive warnings? Were they more likely to be Mortae victims? Results said yes. For example, the Rebellion gene showed a high correlation of .81 and Creativity a high correlation of .75 for being Mortae victims. As such, someone with the Rebellion or Creativity gene has a much higher chance of being killed by Mortae. The correlation is higher for people with both genes."

Famut sipped his water. Breel took the opportunity to do the same as Cafrec refilled his plate.

"How could they do that without telling people?" Breel asked. The thought churned her stomach.

"Oh, that's not all," said Famut. "They also researched Leaders of Today to examine certain Career Groups. Which aptitudes are most common for each Career Group? How does that align with the Nito Test? When there weren't enough new Leaders of Today to fill jobs, they'd assigned citizens to less-than-ideal Career Groups. This is partly why some citizens failed the Demna Exam."

Breel recalled Mr. Gaimster reassuring the class that they wouldn't fail the Demna. The government had blamed the curriculum and a less accurate Nito Test, but apparently that wasn't it at all.

Famut said, "They assigned Centia and me to play God. We were to turn off all undesired genes, such as Creativity, and turn on desirable genes, such as Loyalty and Obedience. They also provided us a list of ideal genes for each Career Group—such as the Logic gene or the Public

Speaking gene or the Multitasker gene. Some Career Groups required specific sets of genes. Others were more open, such as requiring two specific genes and at least two from a list of five.

"Centia and I analyzed every egg and sperm sample. Sometimes we didn't have to do anything. But other times, we needed to select genes. Perhaps there was an egg that'd make the perfect bus driver, but there was the Creativity gene and forecasts suggested in eighteen years, we'd need a new bus driver. We'd turn off the Creativity gene and use that egg. If we deemed no eggs or sperm 'good enough' for a certain Career Group, we looked at the list of projected required Career Groups to determine which eggs and sperm aligned best to manipulate as few genes as possible. When we found one, we'd turn certain genes on or off as needed."

This is ludicrous!

But Famut wouldn't lie to Breel, and of course, unlike her, he had trained in science, medicine, and genetics. He knew about these things. As ridiculous as it sounded, Project Consillo was exactly the type of thing Lexum would engage in. President Tatem would stop at nothing to demand obedience.

"Throughout all of this, Leaders of Tomorrow still wrote the Nito Test. Researchers examined whether the test results matched the chosen genetic characteristics for the possible Career Groups. If they didn't consistently match above a certain threshold, they conducted more research. The government is nearly at the point where the Career Group suggested by the Nito Test match what was planned for genetically.

"However, more than one gene expresses most of those characteristics, particularly for the undesired genes. For example, some creative citizens don't have the Creativity gene—they express another creativity gene. The government keeps finding more and more of these genes, making it near impossible to force obedience genetically."

It was a lot to digest. Famut had certainly talked about genes, but never about genetic manipulation. And then there was the Nito Test. Breel gripped the arms of her chair.

"But what's the point of our job, then?" Cafrec asked, taking the words from Breel. "Breel and I create the programs used to analyze the Nito Test!"

"Yes, to determine the best Career Group. Those results aren't just given to the Department of Occupation—they're also given to the Department of Health to determine the genetic match."

Cafrec frowned. "I don't like the sound of any of this." If he hadn't said it, Breel would have said the same.

"I'm sorry," Famut said.

"What about school marks?" Breel asked. "Do they help getting into more prestigious departments or is that also assigned at birth?"

Famut shrugged. "Maybe they do. However, this only matters if there are multiple departments requiring the same Career Group—and even then, sometimes there are exceptions. Centia and I didn't like any of this. We told Tater as much at the initial meeting, but he already threatened our lives and our family's lives. We had no choice but to fall in line. A few years went by. Centia and I were best friends and, despite never talking about it, knew the other didn't care for the government or the visits Tater made to our lab. First, he came monthly, then quarterly, then, thank goodness, semi-annually.

"One day we realized we couldn't carry on like we were. We wanted to escape and overthrow Tater to turn the government into an elected body. That's what we have in Intercludae, just like Lexum used to be. Every position of authority, even mine, requires nominations and elections and a majority vote."

"But how'd all these people leave?" Breel asked. Realizing she was still thirsty and remembering the water, she topped up her glass.

"I'm getting to that," he said, not unkindly. "Centia and I recruited people we observed during Mortae. We kept in the Silver section as much as possible. We were even in Platinum more than once. We wanted citizens in Silver or Platinum to ensure we recruited careful people. If the disgruntled kept away from Bronze, it was a good sign. We'd peg a citizen who seemed to be faking their enthusiasm and observe them over the next few Mortae. That was mostly Centia's job. Once she had chosen someone who seemed to share our views, I'd strike up a conversation, asking what they thought about the Vucapi and if they deserved punishment. If they pretended well, we wanted them for our cause.

"We'd gain each other's trust to the point we'd be comfortable talking about our views on Tater and the government. Once that happened, Centia and I explained our plan of creating a democratic society. One in which everyone has individual freedom and choice in their career as well as creative pursuits. Perhaps more importantly, though, a society that doesn't kill its citizens for infractions. So far, you've seen the entrance and part of the training area, but when you tour the rest of the compound, you'll see many of our residents have artistic talents. We have artists, like you, Ree, who decorate. A choir, acting guild, and band entertain us, often together, several times a week."

"How many live here?" Breel asked as Cafrec stuffed his face.

"Just shy of one hundred and fifty. Centia and I worked for years at finding citizens. We also began genetically selecting eggs and sperm for our purposes. We turned on the genes we wanted—but carefully, in such a way that the desired genes the government wanted were also on. For example, several Loyalty genes but also Creativity and other such genes. Specifically, we sought genes for independent thinking and courage. But we were sure to only do this for some eggs and sperm, those that needed the least amount of manipulation. Maybe that makes us monsters, too; however, we felt our actions justified because it aided in overthrowing Tater."

Breel's jaw dropped. "So... you did exactly what you didn't like President Tatem telling you to do."

Famut blanched. "No, not exactly."

"There's no difference!" Breel said. "You manipulated genes for your own purposes. How could you—*you* of all people—do something like that?"

His gaze faltered and dropped to his lap. "Ree, when you live in a society that 'embraces the collective' and considers free thinking a sin, you need to gain the upper hand somehow."

I can't believe this. This isn't the Uncle Famut I know. She drank her water to try to enhance her calm before saying something she'd regret.

"I agree with Breel," Cafrec said. "President Tatem saw a need for change when there was civil war. His solutions ended the war but only created other problems. Your 'solution' doesn't solve everything. It just makes things worse! Playing with people's genetics is..."

Glaring at her uncle, Breel finished Cafrec's sentence. "It's disgusting. You're right. You are monsters."

Looking at him, she didn't see her uncle. She saw someone as ruthless as President Tatem who gave no thought to others' rights.

Famut wiped his eyes. "I see. I'm not naïve enough to have assumed you'd be fine with what we did. However, I thought that you'd at least understand. Centia and I made changes—small, gradual changes— until we had an army of people on our side willing to do what it takes to overthrow Tater. We couldn't pass up the opportunity."

Breel crossed her arms. "I'm sure you had other options."

"I'm sure there are tons of options," he said. "However, this one made sense to Centia and me, given our job. I'm not saying we're proud of ourselves, because we're not. But we had to try. Will you please listen to everything? Maybe it'll at least soften your views."

Breel glanced at Cafrec, who shrugged. "I guess," Breel said.

CHAPTER TWENTY-EIGHT

I suppose I owe him that much.

Chapter Twenty-Nine

"Thank you. We recruited Intercludae residents from birth via their genetics. Not every child, mind you. If everyone was an independent thinker, audits of our work would spot that. But as much as possible, we selected these traits in children destined for certain careers we desired, such as DOE officers.

"But we didn't want to recruit Leaders of Tomorrow to our cause, so we waited until they turned seventeen when those with the most schooling become Leaders of Today. We even did this for those with less schooling, agreeing younger Leaders of Today are too young. One of our informants at the Department of Enforcement had access to who received warnings. If any of our hoped-for children did, we talked to them about it. I did that with each of you, as well."

Breel nodded. "Many times."

"I wanted to ensure their safety yet not snuff out the light of their individuality. Once they became a Leader of Today, we worked hard at getting them to Intercludae. Now, we couldn't tell every child what we told you. As such, from the beginning, Centia and I were cautious in the personalities we selected for. We already had informants within every department—some of them even talented enough to become Head of a Career Group. Getting our hoped-for future Intercludae residents to work under them was easier, though not easy, with having someone high in the Department of Occupation assigning new Leaders of Today to their departments.

"One day, Centia told me her aunt wanted a baby. We got hard at work. It was obvious the egg and sperm would result in an intelligent, logical person, which it did." He glanced at Cafrec. "Given other aptitudes, computer programmer was the obvious Career Group. We just did some slight tweaking, really nothing above and beyond what Tater ordered us to do, anyway. Based on Career Group need projections, the baby would likely end up in Department of Education or Department of Enforcement. Either would've worked, as we have an informant in the Computer Programming Career Group of each."

Breel glanced at Cafrec after Famut's admittance to having played with Cafrec's genes.

Cafrec placed his half-finished second plate of food on the table. "I just can't believe it. Any of this..." He stared at the ground, shaking his head.

"I understand," Famut said. "Would you like a break before I tell you more?"

"Keep going," Breel said.

"All right. Breel, the next year the same thing happened with your parents wanting a baby. There were definite creativity skills; however, given how your genes play out, it made the most sense to assign you as a computer programmer since you fulfilled all those criteria and then some. You only fulfilled a few of the illustrator criteria."

"Oh," Breel said, her heart falling.

"I'm sorry, Ree. I must admit I encouraged your drawing in part due to guilt. But if I assigned you illustrator, rather than computer programmer, it would've flagged as an irregularity."

It sounded like he was covering his own skin. *I guess I can forgive him for that. But manipulating my genes is unforgivable.* However, recalling her promise to listen, she let him continue.

He said, "I was unsurprised to see your aptitude for programming, given your father. When it was likely the Department of Education would be in need again, we knew it was fate. We told our informant at the Department of Occupation that it was important you two become coworkers under one of our people, preferably Samit."

"Samit?" Breel asked.

"My friend, your boss," he said pointedly.

"He makes us call him Mr. Tucap or sir," Cafrec said, rolling his eyes.

"Ah." Famut chuckled. "He needs to put on a tough act to protect himself."

Breel and Cafrec exchanged glances. Mr. Tucap was too good in his insistence for his staff to not call him by his first name for it to be an act.

"I can see you're not convinced. However, Samit is a great man and school friend of mine, though our classes differed early on. He was one of the first who joined us, and he's done essential work, hacking into systems to allow us entry from here." Famut motioned to his computer. "So, Breel, we assigned you to be a programmer. The years ticked by. We had certain people on our side, such as a DOE officer and a construction worker from the Department of Infrastructure, who searched for a home base. Long story short, they found this abandoned suburb. This underground area was already in existence. Both long forgotten."

"We think it's where the lower class used to live," said Breel. "Is that true?"

"Yes. As you know from history, the upper class kicked them out of Lexum, forcing them into this suburb where the smell of the factories couldn't penetrate the main city. All those items in the warehouse are what Tater confiscated when he took over."

"It was incredible!" Breel said, thinking of the drawings.

"That's for sure. Now, as you both grew up, I told you about Intercludae, which is what I called this place. It means obstruct—

to obstruct the government. To go against their love of utilitarianism. I tried to say enough to pique your interest while ensuring I didn't tell either of you enough information to find it alone in case your knowledge fell into the wrong hands. You were children, after all. I gave you enough for inspiration and to figure it out together."

"You certainly inspired me," Breel said. "I've dreamt of this place my whole life."

Famut smiled. "Much to your parents' dislike. Anyway, while we had people in Intercludae, Centia and I had yet to see it. The plan was to arrive shortly before preparing to overthrow Tater, but that was years away. One day after a Mortae, though, I was casing out someone for our cause. Your father heard, Breel. Or at least heard enough to tell me something I'll never forget. He said, 'I always knew you were up to something. You're not going to be able to see my children anymore.' Just the way he said it... it wasn't that he'd disallow me from seeing you and Trafis. He said I won't be *able* to see you. I knew he'd report me to the DOE.

"I hurried to Centia's house. We agreed I needed to leave for Intercludae and never return. She'd come later, at our predetermined date, with both of you. That was the hardest goodbye of my life." He paused, blinking away tears. "I took nothing with me. It was a while later that I learned your father was in Platinum for his call. Thankfully, they didn't suspect Centia, and I rested easy for that."

Breel gasped. "That's why he was in Platinum! But why? Why did he turn you in?"

"Because he was scared for your safety," Famut said. "He didn't trust me. I can't blame him."

Breel rolled her eyes. "But you're his brother!"

"Tater encourages it, you know that."

"I guess," she said. "It's still not right. Okay, we listened to you."

"Yes. Do you feel a bit better about what we did?"

"There's something I don't get," she said, ignoring the question. "You're saying that you manipulated genes for citizens to be more likely and willing to oppose President Tatem."

"Yes."

"Why do it at all? I'm sure plenty of people exist in each Career Group who have the same beliefs."

He nodded. "Of course. However, as I said, we strategically planned for our recruits to work under or with people already on our side. To make those connections, we needed more than luck. We needed what we had at our disposal—gene manipulation. I know it sounds awful, and it is, but believe me when I say we changed as little as possible. Most of the time it was encouraging skills and aptitudes by making sure certain genes were expressed."

What Famut had done certainly wasn't right. However, Breel could at the very least appreciate him and Centia trying to do what they *thought* was right. As far as she knew, no one else had attempted to overthrow President Tatem.

"Once I arrived in Intercludae," Famut said, "those already here elected me leader. We vote in new leadership every two years, so here I am again. We train and in time found more tunnels that reach Lexum—in some cases, people escape via these tunnels. We receive intelligence from our people, such as Samit, who can make our communications untraceable. One of our DOE informants headed the search for me and told the government I'd died in the desert to put an end to the search. As I knew they would, the government told no one that I died. Maybe that was just as well. I was relieved, but my heart ached for you two and Trafis. I felt horrible for Centia, who had to pretend she believed my disappearance meant I was dead. She wanted nothing more to do with her family, as they didn't care about her loss. She never belonged with them, anyway."

"Yeah," Cafrec said. "Neither of us do." His plate was forgotten on the table.

"Even after all our planning," Famut said, "sometimes things didn't go right. Despite our best efforts, sometimes children followed the crowd. Trafis is unfortunately in the latter group."

Breel nodded. "He always tells me I need to do what I'm told and despises when I hate on President Tatem."

"Unfortunately, he's far from the only one. As for you two, our plan was for Centia to approach you together, after Breel became a Leader of Today, to give directions to Intercludae. But I suspect that didn't happen."

"No, it didn't," she said.

Cafrec explained how after Famut left, Centia told him he'd have an officemate named Breel, and when the time was right, she'd tell them more.

Famut frowned. "Centia and I emailed each other several times per week. Why wouldn't she tell me that?"

"I dunno," said Cafrec. "I think she was afraid of capture, of Mortae. She said we'd have enough clues to put everything together. I didn't know what she was talking about but didn't ask. Years passed, I rarely saw her, and when Breel was the only new Leader of Today in the Department of Education, I told Centia. She wanted to talk with Breel and me. But then... then Mortae. Do you know what happened? I mean, why she was a Mortae victim?"

"Yes," Famut said. "Tater accused her of creating Leaders of Today who will break the laws of Lexum. As you know now, that's exactly what she did. We'd been manipulating eggs and sperm for several decades to achieve our goals—not so much to disobey, but to think for themselves. I suppose there were too many children with undesirable traits in one audit and it prompted scrutiny. I'm surprised she was killed publicly, given all she could've told Lexum."

"She was gagged," said Breel.

Famut's eyebrows rose. "I've never seen that. I suppose Tater wanted to make an example of activities done behind his back. So, Centia didn't help you get here. Who did? Samit?"

"Yeah," said Breel. "He gave us these programming examples with directions coded into them. He said Centia contacted him, desperate for him to do something, as she feared arrest."

Famut nodded, silent for a moment as he composed himself and dried his eyes. "Good for Centia, always thinking ahead."

He fell silent. Breel took a moment to eat some of the pasta. Muffled voices came from the hall and disappeared.

Breel interrupted the silence. "What exactly was your plan?"

"Overthrow President Tatem," Famut said.

"Yeah, but I mean... how?"

He sighed and leaned forward, arms resting on his legs as he stared at his feet.

"I'll save the story of how we'll accomplish that for tomorrow. I'd been expecting you within the next few days or weeks. But I expected her, too. It's been many years since we last saw each other, but we've kept in contact with email thanks to Samit's hacking." He blinked back tears.

He was dismissing them, wanting to be alone in his grief. It was just as well. Breel's brain was full of everything she'd learned. It was deeper than she'd ever imagined. Overthrowing President Tatem sounded impossible. But Famut was the smartest person she knew. If she couldn't trust him to have a well-thought-out plan, she couldn't trust anybody.

However, she oscillated between two thoughts: *Uncle Famut was only doing what he thinks is right; he only had the best intentions* and *Uncle Famut is a monster for manipulating genes.* In truth, she wanted to forgive him, but part of her found his actions inexcusable.

Chapter Thirty

After Famut dismissed them, Breel and Cafrec returned to the training area, where a group marched in formation. Manum, the second-in-command, sat alone at a table, reviewing a stack of papers. He beckoned them over with the same inviting smile as his son.

"Is there anything we should do?" Cafrec asked.

"Did Famut give you a task?" Manum said.

"No."

"Nothing, then. Would you like a tour?"

They said they would. Manum called over a girl not much older than them, pulling her out of the marching unit. He put an arm around her shoulders. "This is Ragula Culum. Ragula, do you mind giving them a tour? Breel and Cafrec, afterward you can relax for the remainder of today and tomorrow while you get to know Intercludae."

He returned to his papers. Ragula shook their hands. She was short, but the uniform revealed her muscle, which more than made up for her stature. "I arrived nearly a year ago," she said. "Worked as a DOE officer for nearly two years."

"How d'you get to be here?" Cafrec asked.

"Well, that's quite the story. I didn't want to be an officer. Weight training classes were brutal. They grade us on how much muscle we gain as a percentage of body weight. All the guys complain, saying it's easier for women since we weigh less, but it's easier for them to gain muscle so..." She shrugged. "They immerse you in water to calculate your percentage of body fat and assume cheating it if fluctuates within a certain amount."

How is this relevant? But Breel let her speak.

"I was one of three girls in my year destined to be an officer. Our teacher took to me, encouraging me. He gave tips on increasing my muscle mass, things he never even said in class. DOE officers take three weight training classes, and by the second, this teacher and I had meetings under the guise of me requesting extra help. One day I trusted him enough to say I didn't want to enforce rules I don't agree with. He was understanding, and we briefly imagined living outside of Lexum. He reminded me to be careful about what I said, and I assured him I would. Later, I realized he purposely steered conversation toward this topic."

They'd yet to leave the room. Ragula's colleagues were still marching, every footfall shaking the ground. Breel leaned in to hear Ragula better.

"Fast-forward to when I became a Leader of Today. My Head took a real shine to me. I thought she wanted to protect me from my male coworkers, as most of them look down on female officers. Because of my high Demna marks and work performance, she gave me variety in my assignments rather than the same one all the time. Though, honestly, most assignments are the same, boring things. Protecting the walls is one of the most prestigious because you're the first line of defence. Being a personal bodyguard of President Tatem is the most prestigious, of course. I did that, too, for a short time."

It was surprising to hear that. "You DOE officers rotate as his bodyguards?"

"No, it's a longstanding position. I think my Head pulled some strings, under the guise of telling President Tatem that I'm one of her best staff. Anyway, one day, about a year after I became a Leader of Today, I was heading home and came face-to-face with my Head. She said there's a place for citizens of Lexum like me, gave me directions to Intercludae, and explained its general premise.

"To this day, I don't know how she got me to believe her, but I did. When I arrived here, I learned her job had been to give me variety, so I'd develop as many skills as possible. My weight training teacher's job was to prime me for wanting to seek Intercludae. He arrived right after I finished my last weight training class. He's Manum, and he actually taught most of us ex-DOE."

"Oh?" Cafrec said. "Why isn't he an ex-DOE officer?"

"Sometimes they are. It doesn't really matter anyway. DOE officers don't receive practical combat training, so they're no further ahead than anyone else. After all, Lexum experiences only a handful of violent episodes per year, unlike during the civil war. That's what we're trying to train up for, but everyone's learning, even Manum. Anyway, that's my story. How about that tour?"

* * *

Intercludae was huge. Walls were cement painted institutional gray. The ceilings were mostly unfinished—a sea of crisscrossing wires and pipes. The floors were concrete with the occasional rug to ease the pain of standing on such a hard surface. Once past the entrance and training area, Intercludae didn't look too bad—thanks to the drawings. Some walls even had murals painted right on them. As with the initial drawings they'd seen, nature landscapes were the most common— especially sunsets.

Gotta make up for being underground somehow, I guess.

Most of Intercludae was communal space such as the training area, cafeteria, and surveillance rooms, so with one hundred and forty-six residents, it meant few had a private bedroom. Families lived in the largest rooms and others shared in groups of two to four. Each person had a bed and dresser. Carpenters made all the furniture.

"Famut told us you're an artist," Ragula said as they passed a drawing of a birch tree.

Breel nodded, unable to take her eyes off the drawing. The artist had somehow made the leaves appear 3D. Knowing she could draw and share her artwork without fear, without repercussions, was exhilarating. There was no need to hide her talent. Excitement coursed through her veins as she pictured everyone admiring her work. They'd comment on the realism of her portraits and ask how she got to be so skilled. Perhaps they'd ask for drawing lessons, and she'd be both an illustrator and drawing teacher.

"People do commissioned drawings," Ragula said. "Maybe you can, too."

Breel grinned. "That'd be a dream come true."

She wanted to start. It was tempting to ask Ragula where she'd get paper and pencils. However, Cafrec was looking around, interested in everything, and she wanted to finish the tour. The drawing would have to wait.

As they continued, they learned some children had been born in Intercludae. "Supplying our own food and water means no one adds hormones to food so we can have children naturally. The oldest is eleven, born a year after Intercludae was founded. The first child in forty-nine years who didn't take the Nito Exam and wasn't assigned a Career Group."

"Do they go to school?" Cafrec asked. "What do they learn?"

"All the children learn the basics like reading and writing and whatever else they want. Famut and Centia did a great job of ensuring we have a wide representation of Career Groups so there's someone capable of teaching most any topic. Those who used to be teachers assist."

Ragula showed them a classroom with ten desks and a chalkboard.

It was off the main hall, along with the medical room and Famut's and Manum's offices. Farther down was a meeting room, surveillance room, cafeteria, and kitchen. While similar, the kitchen was far smaller than those in food production videos, with only a few of each appliance instead of dozens.

"All the other rooms in this section are living quarters," Ragula said. "Breel, you're rooming with me."

"Okay, cool," Breel said.

I hope she's at least capable of silence now and then.

"Cafrec, I'll show you to your room. We're normally not up this late but needed to be ready for your arrival at any moment in case the DOE followed. Since that potential danger has passed, I imagine your roommates are getting ready for bed."

Ragula showed Breel to their room, down a hall parallel to the main one, and left to escort Cafrec to his.

Breel examined the room. It was no bigger than ten feet by ten feet, the walls bare. On one side was a bed with an oak dresser, the top adorned with a dozen palm-sized chunks of pine of various shapes. On the other side was a second dresser and a bed with a couple of towels and toiletries. Breel opened the top drawer, pleasantly surprised to find clothing.

She took some navy-blue pyjamas and got ready in the adjoining bathroom. Ragula was back when she emerged ready for bed.

Ragula motioned to the walls. "I haven't hung artwork because Famut said you draw and suggested you decorate the walls."

"I'd love to." She smiled, fingers itching to start.

"I've been decorating my dresser." She showed Breel a hunk of wood with a few spikes and rounded edges. "A carpenter is teaching some of us how to carve. It's supposed to be a flower."

Breel inspected it closer. Yes, the spikes and edges resembled petals, albeit oddly shaped ones. She'd never seen anything like it. "That's really neat."

"You'll love how we can learn whatever we want. Everyone's willing to teach everyone else. The only rule is if someone teaches you, you teach them something in return. Anyway, I bet you're tired and don't wanna listen to me anymore."

Oh good, she's self-aware.

Breel climbed into bed. The mattress was thinner than her bed in Lexum, but not too bad. Her thoughts drifted to Cafrec and what his roommates would be like. A few minutes alone with him to discuss what Famut said would've been nice, but that'd have to wait for the morning.

While considering the long day's events and the life she had left behind, Breel wondered about her family. The DOE wouldn't have told them she was gone yet. Her heart ached for them. Just like with Famut, the DOE would say she'd disappeared, and they'd assume she had been murdered.

They'd be angry, no doubt. After all, she broke her promise. But one day maybe she'd help them to Intercludae, and they'd understand why she did it.

Her stomach ached at the anguish they'd go through first. Her father may blame himself. If Famut was right, he'd tried to keep her and Trafis safe by turning in his brother. But then Breel disappeared, so the government would say. A wave of guilt spread through Breel as she thought about it. She didn't want her father to blame himself. It wasn't his fault. Her actions had been entirely her own doing.

Or, maybe, he'd blame Famut. After all, the government said he disappeared, just like they would with Breel. Her father would blame Famut for putting all those thoughts into Breel's head.

But mostly, her mind was on how Famut was alive, but her family didn't know. On his being so close to reuniting with Centia after five years, but it sadly not happening.

Before she could decide whether she should check on her uncle, her exhausted body fell asleep.

Chapter Thirty-One

The next morning, Breel entered the cafeteria with Ragula, who thankfully wasn't a morning person, so not up to talking. One wall had a hole with a counter overlooking the kitchen on which the cooks set food for everyone to serve themselves.

The cafeteria had four long tables and chairs, many already occupied. Even though it was only seven thirty, some were leaving, having finished their breakfast. Cafrec was sitting with a couple of men in their mid-twenties.

Breel and Ragula approached the counter. Breel's eyes widened at the trays of scrambled eggs, sausage, pancakes, and toast. "We can eat all of these?" she asked.

Ragula laughed. "Yeah. No more menu picking."

Breel took a bit of everything, curious how eggs and toast would taste with pancakes and sausage, then excused herself to say hello to Cafrec.

His face lit up when she sat across from him. "Hey! This is Breel. Breel, my roommates Medi and Cemus."

"Hello," said Medi and Cemus, sitting on either side of Cafrec.

They were identical twins, wearing thick glasses. The only discernable difference was the side on which they parted their thick brown hair.

"What's your Career Group?" Breel asked.

They laughed. "That's the first question everyone asks," Medi said.

Or was it Cemus?

"We were doctors," said the other. "Well, we should get going. Nice to meet you." They stood in unison, taking their empty plates and cups.

"So? How was your night?" Cafrec asked with his perpetual grin. His plate was already half empty.

"I slept as soon as my head hit the pillow. Ragula had to wake me this morning."

"Same."

Breel scooped some scrambled eggs with her fork and stabbed a piece of sausage. The pairing worked well, so it was too bad Lexum could only experience eggs and toast or pancakes and sausage. "How're Medi and Cemus?"

"They're nice. Haven't had much time to talk, but we'll get along. I can't tell them apart, though."

"Have you seen Uncle Famut?"

"No."

After swallowing another bite, Breel said, "I'm going to see him when I'm done eating."

"Good idea. I'll come with you. If that's okay, I mean."

She nodded, grateful. There was nothing to fear in Intercludae, but Cafrec was more familiar than this, despite his also being new in her life.

While eating, others introduced themselves—a stark difference from her welcome at the Governmental Offices.

"Wow, finally meeting Breel and Cafrec!" said a woman perhaps ten years older than Breel. "It's so nice to see you."

"I've been waiting for this moment for a very long time," said a man around their age. He shook Breel's hand, pumping it up and down several times. His handshake with Cafrec was two pumps.

A man closer to Famut's age said, "We've all heard so much about both of you."

One bit of egg later, a familiar voice said, "Welcome, both of you."

Mr. Progrio—her computer science teacher—was standing across from them. He beamed.

First time I've ever seen a smile cross his face.

It changed his demeanour. His eyes looked inviting rather than intimidating, his expression relaxed rather than intense, and he stood at a respectable distance rather than inches from her face.

"I assumed you were murdered in private," said Breel.

Mr. Progrio laughed. *I didn't know he was capable of laughter.*

"No, I came here," Mr. Progrio said. "I would've liked to have taught the last two days; however, Erup was my nephew. I couldn't bear to watch his Mortae."

"I'm sorry," Breel said. She grimaced as her thoughts flashed to the piercing scream of Erup's mother and his body falling onto the platform.

"I'd finished my job anyway," Mr. Progrio. "I taught you both programming and helped you get to the top of your classes. Thankfully, my task was easy, as you're both naturals. I'm happy you arrived here safely. Sorry to have given you such a hard time in programming class and cluttered your assignments and tests with examples of President Tatem's supposed greatness. Famut insists we act like that to avoid suspicion."

"It definitely worked," Cafrec said. "I had no idea."

"Me neither," said Breel.

I guess you can't jump to conclusions about people.

Mr. Progrio said goodbye and left to sit with an older man in the corner of the cafeteria. Other residents welcomed them. During the occasional moment in which Breel could eat between conversations, she discovered pancake paired with scrambled egg tasted quite good. Before finishing breakfast, though, a *ping* sounded. Manum was standing on a chair, clinking a glass with a fork. The conversation died down.

"Thank you, everyone," Manum said. "The first bit of news is that Breel Sorep and Cafrec Masna arrived yesterday."

Breel sank into her chair as everyone looked in their direction, clapping and cheering.

"Yes, we're always excited when people successfully arrive. The other day I announced Centia was last Saturday's Mortae victim. Please continue bringing me all requests and issues to allow Famut some time. That is all."

He hopped off the chair, and everyone returned to their conversations.

Someone from the next table turned to Breel and Cafrec. He was a few years older with a buzz cut. "Hey, I'm Manicus. Centia was your cousin, right?" he asked Cafrec.

"Yeah."

"Wow. I'm sorry, man. We have a wall showing Leaders of Today we've recruited and the Leaders of Tomorrow we plan to recruit. It's always sad when we move a picture to the Memorial Wall."

"How many pictures are there?" Breel asked.

"We've got over eight hundred and fifty undercover Leaders of Today."

Cafrec whistled. "Wow, that's more people than I thought."

"Yeah. But is it enough?" Manicus shrugged. "It's hoped some will stay in Lexum permanently, or until they're a suspect and need to leave, whereas others stay only until they complete their assignment. But like Centia, sometimes there's no time to leave. As well, we always have a couple dozen or so new Leaders of Today we're actively trying to bring here within the next few months. We have around eighty Leaders of Tomorrow we're working on or will work on. But statistically, less than half work out. Some are Mortae victims, or they don't want to rebel, or they didn't end up in the right Career Group or department or under the supervision of the Department Head we wanted."

"How many become Mortae victims?" asked Breel.

"A handful a year. Not too many, thankfully."

Famut said he and Centia had manipulated genes in those they hoped to lead to Intercludae. If Mortae victim numbers were low, it seemed they must have turned on some sort of carefulness gene.

"I should go," Manicus said. "I'm a mechanic, so let me know if you ever need something fixed. Sorry again about your cousin."

Most residents had filtered out of the cafeteria, so Breel and Cafrec were able to finish eating. They were knocking on Famut's office a few minutes later. When there wasn't an answer, Breel tried the doorknob. It turned, so she walked in.

The rainbow on the fake window brightened the dark room, illuminating Famut. He was slumped in the same chair as last night and leaning against the generous arm.

"Uncle Famut?" Breel asked.

His eyes flew open and squinted as the window changed to a sunny lakefront. He got up and turned off the window, leaving them in darkness but for the hall light.

"Do you need anything?" he asked.

"No. We came to check on you," Breel said.

He sighed and leaned forward, staring at the ground with his hands on his head. "Please close the door."

Cafrec did so as Breel turned on the light. They sat across from him.

"I'm really sorry," Breel said.

"Yeah…" he said to the floor. "Well, it's been years since I've seen her. I mean, we emailed daily. But it's been years."

"I'm sure that doesn't make it any easier."

"Especially since you thought you'd be seeing her any day now," Cafrec said.

"It's not. I'm over the initial shock, but you here together without her... The joy of seeing you yesterday got me through, but today has been hard."

He sat up, wiping his eyes. Breel jumped when he smacked the chair arm. "Centia feared not leaving sooner, but thought she had time. Stupid of us for waiting until you're a Leader of Today, Breel."

"Why's that so important?" Cafrec asked. "I know you said you wanted everyone to be at least seventeen, but she was *almost* seventeen."

"We agreed on the minimum age so everyone's old enough to make the decision to come for themselves."

"But why was it necessary for her to wait for Cafrec and me?" Breel asked.

"To assist you in coming here. But since she was able to get Samit to assist, I guess we could've used him all along."

"What'll happen now?" Breel asked.

Famut dried his eyes on his sleeve and sipped his water. "The same plan, but without Centia. Now that you're here, it's time to put that plan into action. You'll hear the details later, but we'll enter Lexum and apprehend Tater. If all goes well, there'll be no more need for geneticists."

Breel imagined President Tatem's security cornering them and firing their guns, mowing everyone down. "Uncle Famut, I can't do that."

Famut managed a smile. "You don't know that." He leaned forward, speaking softly. "Listen, I understand being scared. Trust me, I'm scared. Everyone is. But we've been planning and training for years. Of course, you haven't, but we'll protect you. It'll be okay, you'll see." He patted her hand and sat back in the chair. Apparently, she didn't look convinced, because he added, "Tell me you realized we'd be doing something like this."

"Well... maybe," Breel said. "I knew you had some plan. I didn't realize it was so drastic. I mean, what skills do I possess? I draw and program... but drawing is useless for invading Lexum, and Mr. Tucap is a far more experienced programmer. Do you really need Cafrec and me?"

Famut frowned. "Of course. We need both of you."

He was adamant. Perhaps it was worth listening to what he had to say. "Maybe if we heard more," she said. "How do we even enter Lexum?"

"We have a surprising number of people undercover, across all departments and most Career Groups. Some are high up and get us a lot of intel. Many are aware of others we haven't recruited but who are likely to join our cause when we make our move. The plan is to overthrow Tater and turn Lexum into a society with an elected government that allows adults to have children without government intervention, gives everyone choice over their career, and abolishes Mortae."

"But how'll we do that?" Breel asked. "Everyone believes societal benefit trumps individual benefit."

"Many believe individuality is important, and many more will agree our way is better than the tyranny of Tater."

How's that possible when Hargamites are the majority?

"How d'you know?" Cafrec asked.

"I've been around a lot longer than both of you," Famut said. "As Centia and I wrangled others for our cause, paying attention to subtle expressions and body movements, we noticed that many pretend to be into Mortae. But we, of course, had to be cautious with who we brought onboard. Our sources told us who's trustworthy and who we're better off not approaching.

"Being a geneticist meant I saw another side of people. After governmental approval, those wanting a child meet with a geneticist. I did this after they reassigned me from patient care but before starting

Project Consillo. Some braved making special requests, and most of them weren't requests made by couples believing societal benefit trumps individual benefit. They'd ask for their child to be tall or have a nice body or be smarter than them so they wouldn't experience the same bullying as their parents for not getting into a prestigious department.

"They knew we were capable of such illegal feats and braved asking us. Many of my colleagues reported these instances, but it was one person's word against the other. The government would believe the citizen with the cleanest record. They assumed the other citizen was lying and sentenced them to Mortae."

"But that doesn't answer how we'll get in," Breel said.

"We have help from the inside. That's what I'm trying to say. Many not yet on our side will be when they hear our goal. So don't think of it like we're a tiny group of insurgents. We're bigger than you think. I know it's scary, but it needs to happen so everyone can be free, not just those of us in Intercludae. Have I convinced you?"

"You clearly have it all planned out," Cafrec said.

"True," said Breel. "But you still haven't told us how we'll do it."

Famut checked his watch. "I have some work to do. There's a meeting in the cafeteria in two hours and during it you'll learn more. Please attend."

It wasn't clear why he hadn't just told them now, but at least the answer was coming.

Chapter Thirty-Two

After leaving Famut, Breel returned to her empty room to be alone while thinking through everything.

There was a notebook, package of pencils, eraser, and pencil sharpener on her bed with a note on top: *Something to get you started—Ragula.* Breel's fingers tingled as she ripped open the package of pencils, and she sat on her bed, back against the wall and feet dangling over the edge.

The feel of the pencil in her hand was magnificent. Freeing. She placed the spiral-bound notebook on her lap and turned to the first page. She drew a head, keeping her hands busy as she thought.

Apparently, taking part in overthrowing President Tatem was a condition of being in Intercludae. It was unclear whether it a condition for everyone, or just her and Cafrec, given their relationship to Famut and Centia.

If others had a choice, would they fight against Lexum? It couldn't possibly be the case; after all, most residents were young and recruited before learning about Intercludae. The odds of everyone being willing to infiltrate Lexum and overthrow President Tatem had to be low.

Breel added eyes to the head of her drawing.

But if others chose not to invade Lexum, there may not be enough people to succeed. Maybe they needed Cafrec and Breel because Famut was two people short.

And what then? If not enough people, chaos would ensue. Residents of Intercludae and citizens of Lexum would die. Maybe President Tatem would infiltrate Intercludae, arrest the remaining residents, and kill them at Mortae. Or perhaps do something worse... whatever that might be.

Glasses appeared on the head—Famut's glasses. Finally, after five years, she'd get his glasses and face right.

Then there were those in Lexum such as her parents and Trafis who hadn't chosen sides and were just trying to get through each day. Such events would affect them and everyone else. The DOE might kill them in the chaos. Failure to succeed would lead to President Tatem enacting new laws, affecting everyone even more.

She drew Famut's wavy hair as she reflected on Trafis. He wasn't happy with his Career Group. It was up to Famut, Breel, Cafrec and the others to storm Lexum so Trafis and others like him would get the chance to try something else, to find something that'd make them happy. She had to help Trafis and everyone else trapped in Lexum. For far too long, President Tatem had reigned, dictating every aspect of their lives. Everyone deserved the same opportunity to live the life they wanted.

Breel looked at her completed portrait of Famut—*finally*, it looked just like him—and her heart burst with happiness.

* * *

The cafeteria was full when Famut and Manum stood at the front to address the group. Many sat in groups. A couple dozen children—from ages three to twelve—sat at a table at the back, reading books or drawing.

Famut spoke with no preamble. "Our plan from the start was to infiltrate Lexum once Centia, her cousin Cafrec, and my niece Breel arrived, because they're the last keys to this plan."

Breel and Cafrec glanced at one another. "Keys to the plan? What's that mean?" Breel whispered to Cafrec.

He shrugged. "No idea."

Before Breel could consider what he meant, Famut continued. "We've planned for this for years. Our Department of Enforcement source tells us the next Mortae occurs at noon two days from now. You know the next steps. We contact our undercover sources. They get in position. We divide into five sections: East, West, North, South, and Tater Sections. The Tater Section gets Tater. Everyone arrives at the Quaddro as the citizens of Lexum do. The East, West, North, and South Sections station themselves in those directions around the Quaddro to surround it and prevent escape. The Tater Section will present a bound Tater to Lexum and take control of the microphone to state our case.

"Ideal scenario: we overthrow Tater, overtake any who oppose us, and create the beginnings of an elected government that allows individual freedoms and benefits."

Everyone cheered.

"And the worst case?" someone asked as the cheers died down.

"Mortae for all of us," said another.

"That won't happen," said Famut. "The many DOE officers on our side are prepared to follow through on their duties for our cause. We've prepared for this for years. We're ready."

"Famut," said a man with blond hair seated in front of Breel. "What percentage of Lexum is on our side?"

The woman beside him laughed. "Only a data geek would ask that."

Famut paused. "Admittedly, I don't know exact numbers. But we're nearly one hundred and fifty here, and if we count the Leaders of Today and potential Leaders of Tomorrow on the inside, we're nearly a thousand."

"That's only four percent," said the data geek.

"Yes. But those are only the ones we've actively recruited or are in the process of recruiting. Centia and I have always suspected at least twenty percent have our views."

"Twenty percent versus eighty percent?" asked the data geek. He frowned.

The room buzzed with whispers. Manum spoke above the noise. "We have the element of surprise. We've been through all this before."

"I know," said the data geek. "It just... it's suddenly real. That's all."

Manum stepped closer to the crowd. "I understand. But we've worked toward this for this for a long while and you're all trained in combat, as are many sources who trained in secret when possible. Not only are there more of us than DOE officers, but DOE officers receive next to no combat training. We'll easily overtake them."

"That's right," Famut said.

"We can do this," Manum added. Sincerity rang through his and Famut's tone. No one in the room could say they didn't believe in their cause.

"Infiltrate Lexum!" someone shouted. "Down with Tater!"

The room erupted into calls of "Down with Tater" as everyone leaped to their feet, arms in the air in an eerie similarity to Mortae. A shiver shot down Breel's spine.

It took a minute for the crowd to settle. Famut said, "You know your role. You know what's at stake. You know what we're up against. Now get to it."

The room cheered as everyone filed out. Famut motioned for Breel and Cafrec to stay. Once everyone left, Manum approached Breel and Cafrec.

"I promised you a day of rest," Manum said. "I'm a man of my word. After you speak with Famut, you may do what you will today."

Breel had intended to draw during her rest, but after talking to Famut, she wanted answers, specifically why she and Cafrec were "keys" to the plan.

Manum left and Famut sat across from them, straddling a chair with his legs and laying his arms on the back. "There's something else I need to tell you. You heard me say you're integral to the plan. You'll be part of the Tater Section."

Breel's heart dropped. It was the exact task she hadn't wanted. "You mean... kidnapping him?"

"Arresting him. If all goes well, he won't fight it."

Breel and Cafrec exchanged glances. It was tempting to back out, to say no way. Famut said they'd be protected, but how was that possible if they engaged in the most dangerous job of them all?

"We haven't been trained for combat," Breel said.

"Don't worry. Manum will head that section. He'll protect you."

"But why us?"

"We need you to enter Tater's house."

Breel frowned at his words. *He's making no sense.*

"How can we do that?" Cafrec asked.

"DOE officers guard his estate. Our sources at the Department of Logistics will schedule the appropriate people to guard his estate that morning."

It wasn't an answer.

"Ones on our side, you mean," Cafrec said. Famut nodded. "But wouldn't it be easier to capture him at Mortae?"

"That's what we thought, too. We tried twice and failed each time."

"I never knew that," Breel said.

Famut waved a hand. "Before your time."

"But you'd think someone would've said something about it over the years," said Cafrec.

"No," said Famut. "If citizens speak of an assassination attempt, the punishment is Mortae. Tater believes hearing about them makes citizens more prone to plan one."

CHAPTER THIRTY-TWO

"What happened?" asked Breel.

"In short, four Intercludae residents went from behind the Quaddro's platform, so they weren't noticed by anyone. But Tater's security faces outward during Mortae. When our people came around the side of the platform, his security was well-positioned to kill them all. In another attempt, we used twice as many people. Only two returned to Intercludae and only one of them lived.

"Since Mortae was impossible, we tried the Governmental Offices. Tater works on a floor requiring special access via an ID card. Several informants took turns determining the schedule of his secretary. Then, an Intercludae resident dressed in a uniform and borrowed an ID card from an informant. She joined Tater's secretary on the elevator. The plan was for her to shoot the secretary with a dart gun, use his ID card to gain access to Tater's floor, and apprehend Tater. But the plan failed. Later, Samit learned Tater's security stand in the hallway outside Tater's office door when he's in the room. They saw an unfamiliar person on the floor, saw the secretary's body, and shot her without pause.

"We concluded apprehending Tater at Mortae or his office were out. But an informant said Tater dismisses his security while at home, which means he's most vulnerable there. It's also the easiest way to capture him, as there will be fewer people around. By presenting an arrested President Tatem to Lexum, we'll show we needed no offensive to overthrow him. I'm sure not having a fight between us and his security and DOE officers will help our case."

No violence was appealing. Even better, having no DOE officers, including his security, improved their odds of survival.

But he's still not making sense... how are Cafrec and I keys to the plan?

"Why us?" Breel asked.

"They'll let us onto the grounds. We need you to open the door to his mansion. No one else can do it."

Cafrec said, "But we can't either. We don't have his ID, and I assume he has one."

"I'm not sure you want to know the answer. And I..." He hung his head, moving his arms to massage his knees. "I'm ashamed of it."

"Why?" Breel asked.

"First, you must understand," he said, avoiding their eyes, "Centia and I believed it was for the best. After our other failed attempts, we devised this new plan. We needed someone to do it and for them to have a backup."

"Backup?" they said in unison.

"Yes. You're each other's backup."

"Let me guess," Breel said. "You manipulated our genes, turning on or off certain ones so we'd have the abilities or characteristics that you need. You did the same genetic manipulation with both of us, so we'd have a backup in case one of us is killed?"

"In a manner of speaking, yes."

What does that mean? It was a lot to take in. She was even more uncertain about what to think regarding his actions.

"In a manner of speaking?" she repeated.

Famut exhaled. "I can understand if you hate us after this—Centia and me, I mean—but we agreed it was for the best. Like I said, our own DOE officers will be on duty around the perimeter of the estate when we arrive. Beyond the non-DOE Leaders of Today who come and go, we'll only have to worry about Tater and his wife. As I said, his personal security is dismissed when he's home."

Breel blinked. "He has a wife?" No one had ever mentioned President Tatem being married.

"I never knew that either," said Cafrec. "And you keep avoiding our question."

"Yes, I'm getting there. And yes, he has a wife. Xorem is housebound because of ill health. Sources suspect she's the reason Tater started the genetic projects.

"Many years ago, they were unsuccessful in having a child. They were the first couple to use the labs. In reality, Tater had no desire for children and ordered the doctors to lie and say Xorem's ill health prevented pregnancy. He demanded we keep their sex cells. We figured it was in case he changed his mind."

Breel groaned inwardly. *Here he goes ignoring our question yet again.*

"Can you just let us know what you did and why we're the key?" Breel said.

Famut nodded. "I'm almost there. Fast-forward to when we started planning for Intercludae and ultimately ending Tater's reign and genetic manipulations. Centia and I knew there was only one way into his house, and it'd take years to come to fruition. We did it once, and we did it a year later for a backup.

"We chose you two to unlock his house because we needed people who'd be close to us, who we'd have lots of contact with to influence. We needed to encourage your genetic traits that are necessary for our plan."

Breel asked, "What traits did you give us?"

"You, and a few others, needed very little genetic manipulation. Most DNA already had the genes of interest already turned on, or off."

He's making no sense. Breel told him so.

Famut gripped his legs tightly, fingers turning white. When he spoke, he stared at their feet. "Stay with me. ID cards don't work by scanning per se. The system matches the DNA of those in the household with the DNA of the cardholder. If the cardholder's DNA has at least a twenty-five percent match of anyone in the household, it allows access. It's done this way to account for relatives, including children accessing their parents' and grandparents' houses. Access to Tater's house operates the same way. We needed someone, and a backup, with enough of DNA of the Tatem household to get us inside."

Breel's stomach lurched. No. Famut couldn't possibly mean what he was implying. "What'd you do?" she asked.

"You're not actually saying..." said Cafrec. His voice shook.

Famut lowered his gaze. "Yes. Cafrec, you have your mother's and Tatem's DNA. Breel, you have your father's and Xorem's DNA."

Chapter Thirty-Three

Breel put a hand to her mouth, but it didn't stifle her outburst. "No... no... You can't be serious!"

Famut's expression was devoid of emotion. He didn't smile or say "gotcha!" Everything he said was true.

Breel could've dealt with manipulation of a creativity gene or a special skill. But not this. He gave her a different mother. And not just any woman—Tatem's wife. It was sick. It was downright wrong. And to think he and Centia did the same with Cafrec. *Poor Cafrec... he's President Tatem's biological son.* Bile rose in her throat.

"I'm so very sorry," Famut said, eyes downcast.

"I can't believe I'm related to him. To"—Cafrec swallowed hard—"to President Tatem."

"I'm sorry," Famut repeated. "If it's any consolation, we were careful about which genes we gave you."

Like that matters.

Looking at Famut's face made Breel want to punch him into next week. Gritting her teeth, she asked, "And Trafis?"

"He's not related to Tatem or Xorem."

Lucky him...

"How could you do this?" Cafrec asked.

"I'm very sorry."

"You used us!" Breel said. Her yell echoed throughout the empty cafeteria.

"We did. It's the only way to get into his house. I'm sorry."

"Stop saying that," Breel said. Her uncle's eyes were wet, but she didn't let that stop her. "Nothing gives you the right to screw with our DNA!"

"But that's the whole point," Famut said. "I don't agree with it, but we had to achieve our goal so that in the future no one's DNA is manipulated."

Cafrec stood. "Sounds to me like you allowed the benefit of society to trump the benefit of the individual." He managed to keep his voice steady. "In this case, the individuals were me and Breel."

Famut's jaw dropped, and he lowered his gaze.

"Hadn't thought of that, had you? Come on, Breel."

Breel left with him.

* * *

Breel's room was closest. Thankfully, Ragula was elsewhere. Breel slammed the door and sat on her bed, head in her hands.

"I can't believe it..." she said. "I feel so... violated. My DNA feels violated."

She wanted to gag. Her actual mother was Xorem—President Tatem's wife. Given who she married, it was doubtful she had good qualities.

She's attracted to power, obviously. That's why she married him. My biological mother's weak and stupid.

Cafrec sat, putting an arm around her shoulders and pulling her close. His hug didn't cause her anger to decrease in the slightest. "Don't you feel violated?" she asked.

"Yeah, sure. I guess."

"You didn't even sound angry back there!" she said, her voice getting pitchy. Her limbs shook. Ragula's carvings on the dresser caught her eye. It was tempting to chuck them across the room, but she couldn't do that to Ragula. She was innocent.

"Well, of course I am. I'm angry to find that out, to know I'm not who I always thought I was. But I'm so different from my family. It makes sense I'm related to someone else."

Breel crossed her arms. *Angry!?! He doesn't sound angry at all!*

"What bothers me most," he said, "is them doing to us exactly what they don't like the Government of Lexum doing. I understand why they thought it was for the best, but I'm sure there are other ways. They should've thought longer and harder about how to enter his house."

"I agree. I just don't understand how..." She paused; otherwise she would've tripped over her words. "How can being related to President Tatem not bother you?" Saying it aloud was like poison.

"Well, I'm nothing like Tater, so I'm less mad about that."

He glanced at her with his sparkling eyes. She gasped. They were President Tatem's eyes. And his hair... he had the same thick head of hair. Yes, he certainly was President Tatem's son. It was so obvious now. But the saving grace for Cafrec was not acting anything like him.

What does Xorem look like? If Cafrec looks like President Tatem, I must look like her! Everyone else in Breel's family had straight or slightly wavy hair—was Xorem's curly? Was Xorem taller like Breel, her father, and Trafis? She couldn't be short like Breel's—

Breel gasped as it hit her—she wasn't genetically related to her mother. Feeling faint, Breel leaned forward, putting her head down. *My mother... isn't my mother...*

"You okay?" Cafrec asked.

She shot him a dark look.

"Okay, okay, stupid question."

Her head feeling better, Breel sat back up. "I feel so dirty and tainted and..."

Cafrec pulled her close, his fingers digging into her arm but not enough to be painful. "I understand, Breel."

"Don't you feel all that? Doesn't your DNA feel violated?"

"I didn't know DNA could have feelings." He flashed her one of his characteristic grins.

His remark improved her mood a little. Even his smile was like President Tatem's, but where the latter was creepy and caused shivers to run down Breel's spine, Cafrec's was friendly and open.

If Cafrec can look so much like President Tatem yet act nothing like him, perhaps that means I look like Xorem but act nothing like her.

"What you're feeling makes perfect sense," he said. "I know you're close to your family."

Breel nodded. Her fingers curled around the edge of the mattress. *This couldn't be true, it couldn't.*

But it was. And as much as she didn't want to admit it, it made sense. Criba was short, with straight brown hair and perfect eyesight. Breel was tall with curly black hair and couldn't see a van parked in her driveway without her glasses. Criba was meek and quiet, whereas Breel was more outspoken like her father.

"I am close with my family," Breel agreed. "But now that I think of it... I know it's true, just like you do."

"Yeah," Cafrec said. "Like Famut said, I never belonged in my family. Though it's odd, Centia's from the Masna side of the family, and I was closer to her than anyone else, even my mother's side."

Breel's fingers loosened their grip on the mattress, her body less tense. She was still angry, but its intensity was waning.

It was only then that her brain realized Cafrec had an arm around her this entire time. The scent of his strawberry shampoo was strong.

At least Cafrec was with her. This wasn't something she wanted to navigate alone. Going through the knowledge that they were both the offspring of someone else made it more bearable. Together, they could handle it.

Something brushed her hand. She jumped—*spider!*—but it was only Cafrec interlacing his fingers with hers. Breel's heart skipped a beat. This time, they weren't in a pipe walking toward Intercludae and who-knows-what danger. No, they were sitting side by side on her bed. *Can he hear my pounding heart?*

"Breel, I said I've known about you for a while, and how excited I was to meet you?"

"Yeah." He was about to tell her how disappointed he was in the real her.

"Well, I really built you up in my mind. Stupid, I know, but I did."

"I'm sorry." The words tumbled out.

He frowned. "For what?"

"For being crappy in comparison."

For not living up to your dream girl, was what she really wanted to say.

He laughed. "Don't be ridiculous. Breel, I love you. I've loved you since the moment I saw you."

For a moment, all thoughts of being related to Xorem, and Cafrec to President Tatem, disappeared. It was like when drawing allowed a temporary escape from Lexum.

Cafrec looked at her expectantly. But fear gripped her like a vise. *What am I supposed to say? No one's ever told me they love me!*

"Oh, wow," she managed.

"Wow? The response every guy wants."

"Sorry."

Oh no... am I supposed to love him, too? Certainly, she had feelings for him and loved being around him. But was that the same as being in love with him?

"I shouldn't have said it," said Cafrec.

"That's okay. I... I just didn't expect it. And I... I wanted you to like me."

He flashed a smile. "Really?"

Breel nodded. A weight lifted when Cafrec leaned into her. Her heart fluttered. Even though she'd never been with a boy, she knew what was coming. She'd wanted it since the day she'd met Cafrec. His hand gripped her tighter as his lips touched her own.

For one magical moment, everything was okay.

* * *

A knock stopped their kissing.

"Probably Ragula," Breel said.

Cafrec removed his hands from Breel's hair, and she moved to sit beside him, a much more respectable position than straddling his legs with her own.

"Come in," Breel said.

Her muscles tensed when Famut walked in. Only hours before, she had been elated to see him. Now the sight of him made her want to scream.

"Can we talk?" he asked.

"No," said Breel. "I'm not ready to talk to you."

He held up a hand. "I understand why you're angry. But we don't have time for this. You have an important role, and we need to brief you on the mission."

She glared. "Maybe we don't want any part of that mission."

His face fell, shoulders slumped. Eyes tearing, he said, "Then Centia's death was for nothing. All of this will have been for nothing. You have every right to be angry. But this will help everyone. We'll be able to do what we want for a living. You can draw, Breel! Illustrate books or something. And when you marry, it's up to you how many children you have, and it's up to the roll of the genetic dice and the genetic dice alone what your children will be like."

"Not sure I want children who'll share twenty-five percent of Xorem's DNA."

Famut shut his eyes and bowed his head. "I'm sorry. To both of you."

"It isn't just us," Cafrec said. "What about our parents? They're the ones you deceived."

"You're right. I'll come clean once we've overtaken Tater. In the meantime, I know you're angry, but we need you. Please."

"I'll do it," said Cafrec. "But only because what you've done is the lesser of two evils."

Famut shifted his feet. "Sometimes to win, to do what's best for everyone in the long term, you need to do things that don't make you proud."

Tension released from Breel. Cafrec could do it without her. She wouldn't have to tag along. After all, she was just the backup.

Having Cafrec go without her was what she wanted to do. But, if she were honest with herself, she had to accompany Cafrec. They were a team, and she couldn't abandon him. Plus, she might as well put her genetic taint to good use, so at least it wasn't for nothing.

Famut stared at her, lips pursed and hands together as if in prayer.

"Fine, I'll do it too," she said.

Famut exhaled. His arms fell to his side. "Thank you."

"But, Uncle Famut, we're done. Through. Unless it's something about this mission, I don't want to talk to you ever again."

He removed his glasses to dry his eyes. Despite everything, a wave of guilt passed over Breel. But she steeled herself and said nothing.

"You have today to rest," he said. "In the morning, you'll meet with Manum after breakfast."

He left. When Cafrec's eyes met hers, for once they weren't sparkling. "Don't you think that was a little harsh?"

"After what he did to us? No."

Cafrec shook his head. "He just lost his girlfriend and now you, too?

The way he talked about you when I was growing up... he thinks highly of you."

"I used to say the same. But after we overthrow President Tatem, I'm done with Uncle Famut. Done."

Cafrec frowned. "You can't mean that."

"I do mean it. Stop scolding me, and don't you dare try to change my mind."

"I don't think I could no matter how hard I try."

Chapter Thirty-Four

Breel and Cafrec met many residents while exploring Intercludae. It was a good activity to keep their minds off what Famut and Centia had done.

True to her word, Breel didn't speak to Famut at lunch and supper. As it was, both times he left to eat elsewhere. Ragula said he'd started eating alone after Centia's death. It was just as well for Breel, who didn't have to actively ignore him.

After breakfast on Sunday, Manum escorted them to a near-empty room. It had a few tables and chairs and a row of floor-to-ceiling metal lockers. There was nothing on the walls. They sat at the table, across from Manum. It was like being in the room with an older Mr. Gaimster.

"Yesterday, Famut told me why you're needed for the mission," Manum said. "The only others who know are those who've had leadership roles." He glanced at them and then looked at the ground.

"You don't agree with him either," Breel said.

"No. But who am I to judge a man for his actions over eighteen years ago?" Breel frowned, and he added, "Of course, I'm not in your position. Your reaction is understandable. Nonetheless, we need you, so Famut and I are grateful you're on board.

"There are eight tunnels to Lexum that end at strategic places—two on each side of the Quaddro. Each exit is under the patio of someone's backyard. Our sources must remove the patio slab and open the door for us to exit. Our informants ensure our own people live in these eight houses. However, it's rather difficult, since we're talking a period of many years. Four tunnels are compromised. Of those, a newer house covers one after a fire destroyed the old, smaller house. Two are now the backyards of non-sources, as our people had to move to smaller houses. In one case, the source's spouse was a Mortae victim. In the other, a tragic accident killed their youngest two children, and their eldest child was a Mortae victim because of their innocent part in it. The last tunnel was compromised before a source moved into the house and the resident found and reported the door to the tunnel. The report made its way through the channels and some DOE officers searched for the supposed doorway. But they didn't receive the entire report because our people intercepted before it could be fully transmitted; as such, they didn't receive its correct location or details. Thankfully for us, though not for the reporting citizen, the reporter had a shady record as a Leader of Tomorrow, which suggested pathological lying. The government assumed they were lying to waste resources, and they were sentenced to Mortae. We felt awful and are glad that's the only such case. To be safe, though, we won't use that tunnel.

"Of the four remaining tunnels, one is on the west side, two on the north, and one on the south side of the Quaddro. For those of us going to Tater's house, we'll be taking the west tunnel. Once in Lexum, a delivery van will pick us up. The driver frequently delivers to his estate and can get us through its gates."

"Estate?" Cafrec asked. "Famut called it that, too."

"Yes. He lives in an expansive house on a large plot of land with gated access. Tragpraev Sunt arrived in Intercludae eight months ago after working as Tatem's dedicated housekeeper for many years. He's provided valuable intel regarding the layout and Tatem's schedule. Tragpraev will brief us on those details later."

Breel raised a hand. Manum smiled. "You're not in school anymore," he said.

"Right..." She lowered her hand. "You actually trust this Tragpraev after working so closely for President Tatem?"

Trusting him sounded too risky.

"Yes, we trust him," Manum said. "If all goes to plan, we'll approach a lone Tatem without detection. Our ex-DOE officers apprehend him, and Famut and I tell him our demands. We assume he won't step down willingly. In either case, we go to the Quaddro and address Lexum, an apprehended Tatem with us."

"And that's that?" Cafrec asked.

"In the ideal situation, yes. We assume enough citizens will be on our side who'll agree to a massive shift from his reign to our proposed changes."

Breel raised an eyebrow. Were Famut, Manum and the others being too positive about their chances? But Cafrec did say Centia was very organized. And they'd been planning this for years, putting people in strategic places for the final showdown.

I guess I just need to trust them.

* * *

Breel and Cafrec attended a Tater Section briefing. While waiting for Tragpraev and Famut, Manum introduced Breel and Cafrec to the three ex-DOE officers in their group. All wore the sand-coloured vest and pants.

"I handpicked these three for our mission," Manum said. He beamed at them, and they returned the smile.

Manum put his hands on the shoulders of a man perhaps ten years older than Breel. He was a head shorter than Manum. "This is Lexo. Often top of his class and has the fastest reflexes I've ever seen."

"Nice to meet you," Lexo said.

Manum patted Lexo's shoulder before moving to the next ex-DOE. She was around the same age as Lexo.

"This is Praxa," said Manum. "She scored in the top ten of everyone who's ever taken the moving target shooting portion of the Demna."

Praxa smiled but said nothing as Manum gave her shoulders a final pat. He moved to the final ex-DOE who wasn't much older than Breel. He had a head of unbrushed red hair.

"Oh, I know you!" Breel said.

It was Praesio—the resident who'd been guarding the door when they'd entered Intercludae.

"Yes," Manum said as he rested his hands on Praesio's shoulders. "Praesio's a very accurate shot. Part of the Demna Exam for DOE officers involves shooting dart guns at both stationary and moving targets to test accuracy and speed. He had the highest mark of any DOE officer in the last twenty years for the stationary target portion."

They were clearly skilled in their job. But it didn't ease Breel's anxieties about their mission. "Why just three of you?" she asked.

"Don't worry, we'll protect you," Praesio said, puffing out his chest.

Lexo smiled. "We need low numbers to avoid detection as much as possible."

Beside him, Praxa nodded.

"Exactly," Manum said. "Can't be traipsing through President Tatem's house with a crowd."

Famut arrived with another man at that moment, both right on time. *Probably wanted to avoid me for as long as he could. Good.*

Tragpraev Sunt was middle-aged—too old for Famut and Centia to have manipulated his genetics. He was at least six feet tall and perhaps twenty pounds overweight. He wore a midnight-blue sweater. His pecan-coloured hair was a couple of inches long with nary a strand out of place.

"It's important for our newest members to hear about your background, if you don't mind," Manum said to him.

Tragpraev nodded. He stood, hands clasped in front of him, as if there were a rod up his spine. Everyone else sat down. "I was President Tatem's housekeeper for ten years, a Hargamite through and through." His speaking style—slow, deliberate, and rather formal— was strikingly similar to President Tatem's. "I worked hard to be in a position in which I could be his housekeeper. Like all housekeepers, I started out working in citizens' homes. Reporting citizens often got me into Platinum. Before long, I was promoted to be the housekeeper of President Tatem's office. I even saw him occasionally. When his personal housekeeper died twenty years into my career, I was on the replacement shortlist. President Tatem himself interviewed me, which included a practical test, and gave me the job.

"I was joyous to be working directly for him, to be at his beck and call. It's what I wanted my whole life. I also saw firsthand how much he loves his wife, Xorem. She's sickly, and he always ensures she has what she needs. But I learned a lot about him as the years went by. He treats his personal gardener, cook, and everyone who lives and works in the household like scum. Including Xorem, despite his love for her."

He adjusted his stance, spreading his feet farther apart, hands at his sides. "He expects perfection from everyone. Bed made a specific way, not a speck of dust on anything, and shoes shiny enough to stare at his reflection. It was a dangerous job given that he sentenced seven of his personal staff to Mortae in my ten years there. After witnessing him doing that to his cook over burnt toast two mornings in a row, my love for him began to wane. Soon it was just a job."

Breel shook her head. *How could anyone ever want to work for President Tatem!*

Tragpraev continued. "One day at a Mortae, Centia approached me. She noticed I wasn't engaged. Over time, we developed a mutual trust, and she told me about Intercludae. We agreed my knowledge was unique and highly valuable. She encouraged me to stay on the inside and feed her information. But after a year, it became too dangerous. I arrived here eight months ago.

"I'm more familiar with President Tatem's house than even he is. We'll drive through the gates to the back entrance and enter via the back door. We'll be walking right into a staff-only hallway, so we should be able to get to him before he notices us. We'll take out any staff we come across."

Breel raised a hand but stopped herself. "As in… kill them?" she asked.

"No," Manum said. He stood beside Tragpraev. "We'll use the DOE tranquilizers. They'll be out for an hour."

The government claimed the DOE only used a few dozen darts per year. President Tatem would, of course, praise his own policies and ideals for this. But it was obvious that the fear of Mortae—the fate of all tranquilizer victims—kept most in line.

"Breel and Cafrec," said Manum, "your job is to get us into the house. Then you'll accompany us for the rest of the mission without further roles other than to witness history unfold."

He made it sound straightforward and easy. But things were rarely straightforward and easy.

Chapter Thirty-Five

Later that day, when Breel headed to her room to sleep, she found a wall of headshots. They were two sets of collages drawn by members of the creative arts group. One contained a drawing of each Intercludae resident and the other of each source in Lexum. Their drawings were incredible—like something from an ID card. Breel grinned as she thought about how soon she'd join that group and have others with whom to share her drawing hobby.

Some of the Lexum residents were familiar. A woman Breel had seen in the crowd at Mortae. Mr. Tucap. Another man identical to Mr. Tucap, albeit with dark, curly hair. Mr. Gaimster. Even the driver who delivered Breel to her house.

Breel wanted to keep looking at the collages, but Manum had instructed everyone to get a good night's sleep, so she continued down the hall.

Manum said they'd sound the wake-up alarm at seven, dress, eat during a briefing, and then divide into their teams and head for the tunnels. They had two hours to walk to Lexum, the Tater Section leaving first.

According to Tragpraev, President Tatem worked from his home office if Mortae occurred in the morning, so they didn't need to catch him before he left for the Governmental Offices. They'd be at his estate by ten, allowing two hours to get inside, locate and apprehend him, and arrive at the Quaddro for the Mortae.

"I'm jealous you'll see his mansion," Ragula said. She was in the North Section. "I never saw inside it when I was a bodyguard."

"Believe me, if you could take my place, I'd gladly give it to you."

"I can't believe your Head programmed your and Cafrec's IDs to do everything President Tatem's can do."

That was what Famut told everyone. For all intents and purposes, it was close to the truth. When using such terms, it didn't bother Breel. However, his messing with her genes and her parents' rights was never far from the top of her mind. When she explained to Ragula how angry she was at her uncle, Ragula didn't understand. So, she tempered her feelings with everyone except Cafrec and Manum. As much as she wanted to scream at Famut, at least he kept his actions a secret from most Intercludae residents.

Breel lay on her back, staring at the concrete ceiling, unable to sleep.

"Are you scared?" Ragula asked.

"A little." She'd had little time to think about it. After all, her world had been turned upside down within a week. She'd only been in Intercludae for forty-eight hours. Her brain had yet to process being a Leader of Today, let alone anything else.

"Same," Ragula said, "but yeah, only a little. Famut's been preparing for years; he knows what he's doing. And Manum's great—he'll protect everyone. I hope there's lots of time afterward for us to get to know each other."

Breel agreed and shut her eyes. But the more she tried to sleep, the more her head spun. Her parents, Trafis... they'd see her with the Intercludae residents, including Famut. They'd suspect she had been part of this for years. Duknum would take it as ammunition against his brother.

It was hard to know what her parents and Trafis would do at the Mortae. Breel worried most about her father. He'd certainly want to protect their way of life, and his brother's involvement could conflict him. And Trafis... a week ago he'd have considered her an outcast deserving Mortae. But after voicing his dissatisfaction with his Career Group, who knew? As for her mother, the indecision between following her daughter and the rules would tear her apart. It was impossible to know which she'd choose.

* * *

An incessant, piercing clang jolted Breel awake. Ragula had warned her the wake-up alarm was loud, but this was another level entirely. Breel covered her ears for a good fifteen seconds. Afterward, it echoed for at least twice that long.

They arrived at breakfast later than most. Unlike during other meals, the room was quiet, sizzling with anticipation and excitement. Everyone had waited for this moment far longer than Breel.

She slipped into the seat beside Cafrec and kissed him.

Ragula sat across from them. "Do you have anyone here?" Breel asked.

"Nah. I mean, some potentials, had a couple dates, but nothing yet."

Partway through breakfast, Manum stood on a chair, Famut on the ground beside him. Manum spoke briefly, rallying the group and reminding them of what they were to do.

Famut added, "No matter what happens, thank you all for everything you've done for our cause. Today is the culmination of our efforts, the efforts of those still in Lexum, and the efforts of those we've lost."

They had fifteen minutes to finish eating and get to their section's assigned area by eight. Only those with children were staying—they'd monitor the situation and contact inside sources when needed.

While Cafrec bade good luck to his roommates, Medi and Cemus, Breel entered Intercludae's training area with Ragula.

"Good luck," Ragula said.

"You, too. See you at Mortae."

They'd meet at the Quaddro, and Ragula would have a gun loaded with tranquilizer darts. It was hard picturing Ragula shooting anyone, even with a nonlethal weapon.

Breel crossed the room to meet the Tater Section. It was on the right side of the training area, near the entrance to Intercludae. There was a door off to the side, which Manum said they'd go through. No one else was there. Breel turned, frowning.

"You're in the right spot," Famut said, approaching. He stood away from Breel, eyes downcast. "Ree—"

"No."

He pursed his lips but was quiet. Breel looked away from him and was relieved to see Manum and Tragpraev walking over.

Manum held three dart guns with foot-long barrels and one of the longer-barrelled guns. He passed a dart gun to Breel. "I know you haven't trained on it, but just in case."

"Okay."

She took the weapon and nearly dropped it, not expecting it to weigh so much.

"Once Cafrec arrives," Manum said, "I'll give you two a crash course. I'll take a .45 calibre too, the same as Tatem's security, and the .22 calibre rifle." He motioned to the long-barrelled gun. When Cafrec arrived, Manum demonstrated with his dart gun. "Just open the chamber, load the darts, then point and pull the trigger. The chamber holds five darts, but I'm sure you won't have to use any."

Nonetheless, he handed them each a bag of darts and instructed them to tie it around their belt loops. Like the gun, the bag was heavier than expected.

"I know you're nervous," Manum said. "We all are. But I taught every ex-DOE officer we have in Intercludae. I handpicked Praesio,

Lexo, and Praxa and trust them with my life."

It was good to hear, but Breel's stomach still squirmed.

The three ex-DOE officers arrived, carrying the same weapons as Manum. Praesio and Lexo bade everyone good morning. Praxa smiled shyly as she nodded at Breel and Cafrec.

Does she ever speak?

The thirty-two members of the West Section stood a distance away and would later go through the same tunnel. In the meantime, they and the other sections had last-minute briefings and target practice.

"This is all of us," Famut said. "Let's go."

He and Manum led the way to the door. They walked into a room approximately the same size as Breel's bedroom, but it looked far smaller due to everything in it. Directly across from them was a hole in the wall, leading to the tunnel. On either side of the wall was a rack of weapons: dart guns, rifles, and .45 calibre pistols. Monitors—three rows of six—were on the other walls.

A man sat at a desk in the corner, viewing two more monitors on the desk. On the floor beside him, a young girl played with a doll. The man waved at them and returned to the monitors.

"Every tunnel begins in a similar surveillance room for monitoring," Manum said.

Breel looked closer at the screens. Several pointed to various places within Intercludae: the entrance, the training area, and the main hallway into the offices and bedrooms. But most showed video from Lexum including the Quaddro and the main entrance of the Governmental Offices.

"Your surveillance is impressive," said Breel.

"Samit was instrumental in getting us hacked into various Lexum feeds," Manum said. "Well, off we go. It should take us about an hour and forty-five minutes to get to the other end," Manum said before stepping through. "Questions?"

There were none. In case they came across opposition, he directed Lexo, Praxa, and Praesio to lead, followed by him, then Famut, Tragpraev, Breel, and Cafrec.

They stepped into the tunnel. Compared to the one Breel and Cafrec had gone through, this one was rougher, more oval, and about six and a half feet shorter in diameter. It was barely wide enough to walk side by side, and sometimes, due to the uneven tunnel width, it was impossible. Ceiling lights every few feet gave enough of a glow—albeit a dim one—to find their way.

Unlike the others, who walked two abreast, Famut walked in front of Tragpraev. Praesio and Manum were silent as they walked together, leading the group. Lexo and Praxa talked in hushed voices. Breel and Cafrec spoke to Tragpraev while they could, as Manum had warned there'd be no talking once they reached the city limits.

"What was it like working for President Tatem?" Breel asked.

"If you think about it, all citizens of Lexum work for him." Tragpraev was quick with his reply.

"I thought we work for the Government of Lexum," Breel said.

"Is there a difference? But to answer your question, I enjoyed it for a while. I loved seeing what no one else saw, to be envied by so many, to be trusted by our one and only President Tatem."

"But you said he was strict."

A light above Tragpraev illuminated him as he walked. As before, his posture was impeccable—even when walking, he kept his head up. "He was. But I did my job well, so I wasn't afraid. At least not until my feelings for him and my job changed. In the year I served as a spy, I was far more valuable to Intercludae than I ever could be to President Tatem."

It sounded like an impossible task. "That must've been hard to do," Breel said.

"Very. But one of our inside guys, Samit, is a computer genius. He hooked me up to part of the network only Intercludae can access, which allowed me to communicate with others for advice."

Someone else mentioning Mr. Tucap. Evidently, he was very important to the cause.

"He's, or he was, our boss," Breel said.

"Yes, Famut mentioned that. We couldn't have done half of what we've done, or know half of what we know, without him. He's the key to maintaining communication with our inside sources. Despite talking with others, though, I think I had a much harder job as a spy than most. After nearly a year, it became more difficult to hide my true feelings. I feared President Tatem suspected my loyalties, so I left. At least my knowledge is still useful to the cause. But it tore me apart to leave my wife and daughter."

Breel's jaw dropped. She'd assumed he was single. Her heart went out to his family. How awful for them. But then, she recalled her own family and how she'd made the same choice. In fact, most everyone in Intercludae had made that choice.

We've all hurt our families.

They would find out in a few short hours if it was worth it.

The tunnel narrowed, forcing them single-file. Tragpraev continued. "As with many others, the government told them I disappeared. It's hard for them, but in the end, it'll be for the best. I trusted Centia, and through emailing Famut before coming here, I learned to trust him, too."

"Are they Hargamites?" Cafrec asked.

Tragpraev laughed. "My wife and daughter? Oh, not at all. My wife called me a sycophant. I guess I was one. She didn't understand my obsession, especially since being his housekeeper meant working longer hours than most. She's not on our side per se, but no, not someone I'd call a Hargamite."

Tragpraev was silent, perhaps thinking about his family and what they were about to do. Breel's thoughts turned to how quickly her life had changed as her brain started the demanding task of consolidating everything. Just the other day she was sitting in the Lexum Exam Centre, writing the Demna Exam. Now she was a fugitive, had genetic links of which she'd been unaware, and was about to break into President Tatem's estate.

All this and I'm barely a Leader of Today.

But that put her in the majority. At least two-thirds of Intercludae had been Leaders of Today for no more than five years. Most of the older ones opted to remain in Lexum since they had more invaluable experience and knowledge. Plus, most of them had families they didn't want to leave or whose lives they didn't want to risk while journeying to Intercludae. Instead, they contributed by searching for and influencing others and assisting certain citizens to find Intercludae when their time came. They only fled to Intercludae once the government became suspicious—such as Famut and Tragpraev.

With half an hour left of their walk, Manum stopped and faced the group. "We're about to head under Lexum." He smacked the side, dirt crumbling. There was a light screwed into the wall, rather than the ceiling, as a marker. "No more talking. Once we get to the end, we wait for our contact. He'll get us out, and we'll board the delivery van to head for Tatem's estate."

They continued. After curving toward the west, the tunnel straightened and began a slight incline.

Breel walked unconsciously closer to Cafrec. This was really happening. In a short while, they'd be pulling up to the estate and using their DNA to enter President Tatem's house. She swallowed bile. Knowing the intrusion of her DNA helped others didn't improve her opinion of what Famut had done. But she didn't want to arrive angry. An angry mind wasn't a rational mind. The time to consider Famut's actions was later. She took Cafrec's hand and breathed deeply in an attempt to calm herself.

Twenty minutes later, the tunnel ended unspectacularly with a metal ladder. Manum walked to the front and climbed it, a short twenty feet up. He knocked on the door.

Metal scraped. Breel shielded her eyes as light poured in. Manum exited the tunnel, and everyone else followed suit.

Chapter Thirty-Six

Breel blinked as she stepped out of the tunnel. Dots of light impeded her vision as her eyes adjusted to the sunlight. Someone took her arm. Moments later, a door opened, and she was escorted into a house.

It took a moment for Breel's eyes to adjust. They were standing in a dining room where Famut was embracing Mr. Tucap. Breel did a double-take. No one had told her Mr. Tucap was the citizen who lived here.

"So good to see you again, my friend," Mr. Tucap said to Famut.

He faced everyone, his smile reaching his eyes. "Cafrec, Breel, everyone, hello. Glad you're all safe."

Maybe Uncle Famut's right and Mr. Tucap's toughness really is an act, just like Mr. Progrio.

A loud knock on the front door made Breel jump.

"No time to waste," Mr. Tucap said. "That's your driver."

They followed him down the hall. His house was the same size as Breel's, so he was single and childless. Mr. Tucap peered out the door.

"The driver parked as close as possible," he said. "I'll go outside and signal when the coast is clear. Leave two at a time. I've hacked the surveillance to run a fake video feed for another fifteen minutes. Good luck. I'll see you at the Quaddro."

Manum paired everyone with an ex-DOE officer. First to go was Famut and Lexo, then Cafrec and Praesio, Tragpraev and Praxa, and

Breel with Manum.

Mr. Tucap and looked down the street in both directions. He waved them forward. One by one, each twosome disappeared into the van until everyone was inside without incident.

Unlike the van that had driven Breel to her new home, this one only had a driver and passenger seat, so everyone sat on the floor in the back. While the windowless back meant no one could see them, they were blind to the road ahead. The first stop sent everyone flying.

"Sorry," the driver said as everyone climbed out of each other's laps. "Red light."

"How long's the drive?" Breel asked.

"Not long."

She sat beside Cafrec, wedged into the back-left corner for some stability. Manum and his group checked their weapons. Praxa opened her bag of darts, ensuring each faced the same direction.

"We're driving up his laneway," the driver said a few minutes later. "Don't make any noise." The van slowed, brakes squeaking. Breel's stomach flipped. She froze to the spot, not daring to move even a finger. The driver lowered his window.

"State your business," said a bored female voice.

"I've got a delivery for President Tatem."

"Order number?"

"38923."

"Scan your ID." Seconds later, a *beep* sounded. "You're permitted entrance."

The driver closed his window and drove forward, slower than before. They wound their way through the estate, first to the left, then the right. A couple minutes later, the van stopped.

"We're here," the driver said. He remained in his seat, facing forward. "We're parallel to the house; the van's side door is beside the back. As I told you, Famut, I'm not sure how you'll get inside, as I only deliver here. I'm not permitted entry, so have no way in. Tragpraev wouldn't either since his name's tarnished."

"No need to worry," Famut said. "Thank you for the lift."

Famut exited and opened the side door. They were a foot away from a nondescript entrance in the side of a brick building. Beside it was an ID scanner and a small computer screen. Famut motioned to Breel and Cafrec. "Try it," he said.

Cafrec nodded for Breel to go ahead. She stood, hunched due to the low ceiling. Before hopping out, she took the opportunity to view the estate.

The driver had parked on an asphalt surface that could've fit a dozen more vans. Beyond it was a lawn at least the size of Lexum Secondary School with countless rows of trees and flowerbeds, a path meandering between them. In the centre was a fountain, water gushing out of a jet. Around the perimeter of the estate was a manicured hedge in front of a reddish-brown twenty-foot brick wall. The house itself was wide, two stories tall, and made of the same brick.

"Come on," Famut said.

Breel turned back to the task at hand. She jumped to the ground, wedged between the house and van with only two feet of clearance. She raised her ID to the scanner, holding her breath. *Beep.* Her body relaxed. It worked. But that only proved everything Famut said was true. She really was Xorem's offspring.

Cafrec stepped beside her as words appeared on a computer screen. "It looks like code," he said.

Indeed—it was a jumble of *if* statements. "I don't get it," said Breel.

Famut spoke. "Tragpraev said Tater added this for extra security. It's why Samit had you learn—"

"It's Lex Code," Breel said.

Famut nodded. "Yes. The old coding language."

Now Mr. Tucap's insistence for their learning the language, and his random presentation on security, was clear. Breel and Cafrec reviewed the screen:

```
CreateLocal (
    Door = Door Number
    CreateLocal id = Scanner Readout;
    CreateLocal entry = 0;
)
If ( door = 1 and id = 1 ) or if ( door = 2 and id = 1 ) or
if ( door = 3 and id = 1 )
    Set entry = 1
Else if ( door = 1 and id = 0 ) or if ( door = 2 and id = 0
)
    Set entry = 0
Else if ( door = 3 and id = 0 )
    Set entry = 2
End if

If ( entry = 1 )
    Run "Open sesame"
Else if ( entry = 0 )
    Run "Intruder"
Else if ( entry = 2 )
    Run "Delivery"
End if

/* Enter what the incorrect line should read to complete
the unlocking program, then hit Enter on the keyboard. */
```

It was a simple program to determine what should happen upon an ID being scanned. The variable "Scanner Readout" appeared to refer to whether the scanner should accept the scanned ID card. Depending upon which door was used and whose ID card was scanned, it'd either run one of three programs to either: open the door, do something if there's an intruder, or do something for deliveries.

While reviewing the code, a blank line appeared at the end with a blinking cursor, and then a keyboard emerged from the wall just below the screen with an electronic whirr.

Breel read the code again. This time, she examined the subtleties—those little coding annoyances such as punctuation and spelling. Then it hit her. "Here." She pointed to the second line.

"Oh, good eye. It's missing the semicolon to terminate the line."

Breel looked again—Cafrec was right. "Oh, yeah! What I noticed was the 'door' variable being saved with an uppercase *d* but being used as lowercase."

"I guess it's both," Cafrec said.

"Glad we have you two along," said Manum, patting their shoulders.

"You do the honours," Breel told Cafrec.

She punched in *door = Door Number*; into the keyboard, Cafrec confirmed it was correct, and she hit enter. With another whirr, the lock disengaged.

"Well done," Famut said.

Cafrec grinned at Breel. "We make quite the team."

There was no time to celebrate. Manum opened the door and stepped inside, checking both directions before beckoning in the others. Tragpraev went next, followed by Lexo. Praesio and Praxa motioned for Famut, Breel, and Cafrec to precede them.

They walked into a hallway that extended the width of the house. Numerous rooms, all doors closed, led off it. Carved mahogany surrounded all doorframes and the ceiling's edge. Framed pictures littered the walls. Each was of President Tatem in various poses: speaking at Mortae, sitting at his desk, addressing the citizens of Lexum on television, standing in front of a fireplace. The floor was mahogany—which occasionally creaked—with a red carpet down the middle.

They walked half the length of the hall before Tragpraev opened a door leading to a staircase. It was narrow—enough to turn anyone claustrophobic—so they climbed single-file. The floor here creaked with every step. It was a wonder the entire house didn't investigate.

Breel had never been inside a two-storey house, so she marvelled at how they had to climb four flights of stairs before reaching a landing. It led to a hall identical to the previous, except with a different collection of President Tatem portraits.

Near the end, Tragpraev pointed to a door. Praxa opened it while Manum and Praesio entered the room, guns raised.

Breel's heart raced, but for nothing—the room was empty. Her jaw dropped as they entered—it was at least the size of her house. One section of the room was a sitting area with overstuffed chairs facing a fireplace and bookshelves along the walls. The books were leather-bound, all the same dimensions. The room was bright thanks to a skylight and floor-to-ceiling window.

Directly across from the fireplace, interrupting the ubiquitous bookshelves, was a life-size portrait of President Tatem. In front of it was the oak desk where he gave his daily address. It was U-shaped, each section at least six feet long and half that wide. Two computer screens sat on one side and a stack of papers on the other.

The room overlooked the estate entrance. The brick wall extended here too, interrupted by a single gate with three-foot spikes at the top and two cameras pointed at it. A winding road through Swietenia mahagoni trees and up a hill led to the house. At the top, in the middle of a circular drive, was a fountain identical to the one in the garden.

On Manum's orders, Praxa closed the door. She, Lexo, and Praesio stood near to guard it.

Famut, his nostrils flared, rounded on Tragpraev. "I thought you said he'd be in his home office."

Tragpraev stepped closer to the desk, brow furrowed. "He normally is... I guess he changed his schedule."

Famut swore under his breath. "Now what?"

Tragpraev bit his lip, though his stance and demeanour suggested his normal air of confidence. "Give me a moment..."

Things are already going wrong... Breel glared at Tragpraev, whom everyone said was trustworthy, as he stood puzzled in the middle of the room. Famut and Manum stood by the desk, shaking their heads. The ex-DOE officers were near the door, guarding the room. Breel and Cafrec stood by the window.

There was a crack. The door swung opened, and an arm emerged. *BANG!!*

Chapter Thirty-Seven

Breel jumped, heart leaping to her throat, and covered her ears. *What was that?*

Her ears reverberated. Breel winced.

The door was off its hinges. Praesio, Lexo, and Praxa scrambled to their feet.

A strange sulfury stench filled the air as President Tatem himself walked into the room, flanked by four of his personal security. Their guns pointed at Manum and the ex-DOE officers. President Tatem aimed his own gun at Famut.

"How lovely of you to visit me," President Tatem said. His voice was faint, as if he stood at the other end of the house.

A vice seized Breel's heart. "No, don't!" Her voice sounded far away due to the endless ringing in her ears.

President Tatem chuckled. "Oh, but I did." He motioned to Famut, who had a hand on his stomach and a growing red stain on his shirt.

That was the bang—President Tatem had shot Famut with a pistol.

"No, no, no, no, no," Breel said, a hand to her mouth. She wanted to go to Famut, but her legs wouldn't move.

"I suggest you drop your weapons if you do not want my guards to riddle you with bullets," President Tatem said.

Manum did so, and Praesio, Lexo, and Praxa followed. Manum sidled up next to Famut.

"All of you!" President Tatem said.

Breel watched it happen in a haze. Famut fell, caught by Manum, who eased him to the ground. Remembering she, too, had a gun, Breel dropped it and ran to her uncle.

"No, no... Uncle Famut." She knelt beside him and held his hand, not caring that it was stained red.

His glassy eyes took a moment to find her. "Ree. Cafrec. I... I'm so sorry."

No... Breel's throat constricted. After all these years, she was reunited with Famut. He couldn't... he just couldn't... "Please don't, Uncle Famut. It'll be fine. You'll be fine."

"Sorry, every... one."

His hand slackened in hers. Breel cried out and bawled into his chest.

"Yes, yes, what a lovely family reunion for you," President Tatem said. "Get up. Get her up."

Cafrec pulled her away. His own crying was audible as he led her to the others sitting against the wall. President Tatem's security stood with guns trained on them. Breel slid down the wall, unable to take her eyes off Famut. He lay there still, unmoving. Dead.

"How'd this happen?" Manum asked, head in his hands. "This can't be real. It can't be real..."

President Tatem laughed. "But it is real. You really think you could outsmart me? That your little group could overtake my government? You are delusional, but he was most of all." He waved his gun at Famut.

"He's not delusional!" Breel screamed.

Another laugh. President Tatem's lips upturned into a twisted smile. "He *was not* delusional, dear. Your uncle is dead now. Are you unable to comprehend that, or do you have a short-term memory problem?"

"You're an animal," Cafrec said.

President Tatem rubbed his hands together, grinning. "I am not used to such sass. This is quite enjoyable."

"How d'you know?" Cafrec asked.

"I have my spies, as do you."

A chill went down Breel's spine. Famut and Centia's grand plan never had a chance, and now her uncle was gone. As for everyone else, what were the odds of their survival?

"Who's the spy?" Cafrec asked.

President Tatem stroked his chin. "One of my spies happens to be in this very room. Who do you think? Could it be previous Department of Enforcement officers? My ex-housekeeper? My spawn? My wife's spawn?"

Breel gasped. *He knows about Cafrec and me!* Thankfully, either the others missed it or knew enough not to ask.

"It's gotta be them," said Praesio, pointing at Breel and Cafrec. "They just arrived at Intercludae!"

President Tatem rolled his eyes. "Wrong. Shoot him for his idiocy."

"No!" Manum said.

Too late. Another deafening bang, another sulfuric smell, and a second corpse.

Manum cried out and returned to holding his head in his hands.

It was a moment before President Tatem spoke. "Think, people! Obviously not Breel—Famut is her uncle. And obviously not Cafrec, as he thought Centia was his cousin. Although would that not be poetic? Double-crossing their relative, supposed relative in Cafrec's case, to join me, another relative or relative in-law? But no. Clearly, Breel and Cafrec are not spies."

"It's Tragpraev," Manum said. His voice was monotone. He didn't look up from his hands.

What a risky thing to say!

President Tatem clapped, slow and drawn out. "Well done."

Breel gasped. But Tragpraev had seemed so genuine! *Before the war, he could've been an actor.*

Manum looked up, his jaw set, fists clenched. Praxa had one hand on his shoulder. "Don't," she said. Her voice was shrill. "Mr. Gaimster, don't."

"Yes, listen to your underling," said President Tatem. "Attacking me is ill-advised. What tipped you off?"

Manum looked up to glare at him. "I handpicked the ex-DOE officers for this mission. I taught them and know them well."

His voice caught as he spoke. He put a hand to his mouth, unable to peel his eyes away from Praesio.

"You know two of them well," President Tatem said. "The other you *knew* well since he is dead." President Tatem extended an arm. "Tragpraev, no need to sit with the riffraff." Tragpraev rose, and President Tatem hugged him as if he were a long-lost son.

"I'd never turn my back on you, President Tatem," said Tragpraev.

The hug ended, and Tragpraev gazed at President Tatem. There was no doubt he'd been a spy all along. He was still a sycophant. Every word from his mouth had been a lie.

"I can't believe this," Manum said. "Tragpraev... you're killing innocent people."

Tragpraev shrugged.

"Silence," said President Tatem. "This is my game now. Your game ended years ago, unbeknownst to any of you."

"Even if we die, there are plenty of others," Manum said.

President Tatem's smile sent more shivers down Breel's spine. He rubbed his hands together, eyes lighting up. "That is where you are wrong. Tragpraev is not my only eyes and ears. With their intel, do you honestly think I would allow the others to get this far?"

Chapter Thirty-Eight

President Tatem grinned as he surveyed everyone. "You did not think I know about the tunnels? Of course I do. Goodbye insurgents who entered via the south tunnel."

Nausea hit Breel. Beside her, Manum stared at his lap, body quivering as he sobbed. It was no secret that this adventure would be dangerous. She'd certainly been scared, but Famut and the others had been so certain of success. The horrors witnessed over the last few minutes zapped her sense of adventure. It was as if her heart gained fifty pounds. Even though she sat doing nothing, she breathed as if running a race. Her tongue was like sandpaper, making swallowing difficult.

President Tatem said, "Shall we proceed? Officers!" Eight DOE officers entered the room, joining his security. "Take them away."

A muscular woman with short, spiky hair cuffed Breel and escorted her to the hall. A woman in a thin nightgown blocked the doorway. She was Breel's height with shoulder-length hair. It was white and unkempt but strikingly curly.

Breel gasped. There was no question as to the identity of this woman. Xorem was an older, frail version of herself. She clutched the doorframe, her face gaunt.

"Hargam, what's going on? What happened to the door?" Breel had to strain to hear her quavering voice.

"Xorem." President Tatem rushed over, placing an arm around her.

"Xorem, I told you to stay in the bedroom."

"Yes, but—" She surveyed the room. Her eyes lingered on Breel longer than the others but gave no sign of recognition. She put a hand to her mouth when she saw the bodies of Famut and Praesio. "You killed two men?"

"No, no, not me," said President Tatem.

Someone who didn't know the truth would swear he was being honest.

"Yes, you did!" Breel said. "Xorem, don't believe him. He's evil! I saw him kill my uncle and Praesio with my own eyes."

"Do not believe a word she says, Xorem," said President Tatem. Xorem swayed, and he tightened his grip around her. "Sit, my dear."

He assisted her to the ground and sat beside her as she rested her head against his chest. After a moment, he looked up at the DOE officers. "Get moving!"

"Yes, sir," said an officer.

He led the group into the hall and down a staircase with Cafrec near the front and Breel in the back. They entered a sublevel—a maze of gray hallways dotted with doors, each with several locks. A DOE officer stood at the intersection of each hall, only they didn't dress in the usual black and yellow DOE officer uniform. Their clothing was the same gray as the walls. Like President Tatem's security, each had a .45 calibre pistol.

After a couple of intersections and turns, DOE officers forced the hostages into the locked rooms. Cafrec was the first to go, Breel shouting after him.

"Silence," said the woman holding her. Her fingers dug into Breel's arm.

A minute later, it was Breel's turn. The DOE officer pushed her into a room beside Manum with the butt of her gun. The door clanged, and three locks engaged. A single lightbulb cast a dim yellow glow into the windowless room. She sat on the cot, springs creaking, which barely fit beside the toilet.

As she gripped the edge of the bed, her tears splashed onto the concrete floor. She threw her flat pillow against the wall and collapsed onto the bed.

"I'm sorry, Uncle Famut! I'm sorry!" She pounded the mattress with her fists.

Famut had manipulated her genetics with the best of intentions. But instead of trying to understand his perspective, she had given him a hard time. It was too late to take back what she'd said, too late to make things right between them. Her only hope was that in his last moments, he knew she still loved and cared about him.

Somehow, despite her swirling mind, she was asleep within minutes.

Chapter Thirty-Nine

The whirring of disengaging locks woke Breel. She winced, her back, hip, and shoulders screaming from the pokey, unsupportive mattress. Standing in the doorway was a man wearing a gray uniform.

"You have a visitor," he said.

Breel blinked, unsure if she'd heard him correctly in her half-asleep state. "I... I do?"

"Yes. Get up."

Breel didn't move. A visitor couldn't possibly be a good thing. "I don't want a visitor."

"You don't get an option. Up or I get you up."

She rose, wincing, and flexed her muscles to loosen them, but the guard hurried her out the door. They walked through three consecutive, identical hallways before walking into a small room. An officer standing inside closed the door behind her. Across from them was a metal table and two chairs—her father in one of them.

Breel's stomach dropped. Duknum crossed his arms, frowning over the rim of his glasses. Explaining her actions was impossible. Determined not to say the first word, she stared back, not breaking eye contact. But that wasn't enough for him to speak. He only shook his head.

"You only have five minutes," the officer said. "I suggest you get to it."

Breel sat across from Duknum. He pushed his glasses up the bridge of his nose. "Why'd you do this to us? When the DOE told us you went missing, your mother and I nearly died of grief! Your mother's spent the last few days crying in my arms. Thank goodness our Heads are understanding."

Breel stomach dropped. *My poor mother… what have I done…?* She blinked away the tears that threatened to surface.

"All they said is you disappeared, so naturally we thought you were dead. Imagine our surprise when I got a call from President Tatem's secretary saying they found you, and one relative could see you. I knew things were serious."

"And you came instead of mother, so I wouldn't taint her."

He slammed his hand on the table. "No! They said only I could visit you."

Breel frowned. "What sense does that make?"

"I don't ask their reasons, Breel. I follow directions."

Breel resisted the urge to roll her eyes. Then it dawned on her. *He turned Uncle Famut in five years ago… They chose him because I'm less likely to influence him!*

Duknum continued. "I get here, and President Tatem himself told me of your betrayal of Lexum, of its government and citizens. Of your conniving with this Cavic person."

"Cafrec."

His icy stare hardened. "Like it matters. Do you know what happens to citizens like you, Breel?"

"I never expected to be caught."

"We're lucky President Tatem isn't sentencing the entire family to Mortae!" His words echoed in the sterile room.

"That's why you turned Uncle Famut in, right?"

"In part. It was for the safety of you and Trafis. I didn't like what he was telling you—it was dangerous. I warned him more than once, and he didn't heed my warnings. You weren't safe around him, and it terrified your mother. We told you what she went through with her sister. How could you do this to her? When your mother found out what you did..."

He choked on his words. Her father had never shown so much emotion. It made her own hard to keep in check.

Breel shifted, avoiding his gaze. "I'm sorry, I really am. I... I had to. I thought—"

But he slammed the table again, not wanting to hear her hopes for getting them to Intercludae. "No! You didn't have to. You promised to keep yourself safe! Why couldn't you be content with Lexum? You became a Leader of Today! You had a great Career Group in the most prestigious department!" His voice cracked. He sniffed and looked at the floor. "You had what so many others only dream of, me included!"

It wasn't surprising to hear it—Criba had told her as much.

"Instead," he said, "you let Famut's crazy beliefs cloud your judgment."

"They're not crazy. Society should benefit from its people, but people should do things to benefit themselves, too."

"Breel—"

She plowed through. "Do you know why the government doesn't allow citizens to become pregnant naturally?"

"Of course. So only approved citizens can have children."

"That's not all! It's so only certain eggs and sperm produce children—those with certain traits like obedience and loyalty."

He glared at her. "Lies. You sound just like him."

"No, it's the truth! They also mess with our genes to make us fit for a certain Career Group. They're close to not needing the Nito Exam. Instead, our genes will determine our Career Group."

He stood so quickly his chair fell over. "Stop this! President Tatem was right to not have your mother or Trafis come to hear this. I certainly wouldn't want to subject them to seeing you in this place."

"Your five minutes are up."

Breel ignored the officer. "Father, did President Tatem tell you what happened to Uncle Famut?"

Duknum—ever the rule-follower—headed to the door. "Yes. He lived in some underground place for years and led an army of insurgents, you included, back to Lexum."

"Sounds like President Tatem missed the part where he shot Uncle Famut with a gun from ten feet away."

His stride faltered. "He what?"

"He's dead. I saw it myself." Tears welled in her eyes.

Duknum had already recovered, face stony as ever as the guard opened the door. "All lies. You may be my daughter, but right is right. What you're doing is wrong, and as much as you mother begs me, I can't help you. I must protect the rest of our family. President Tatem will punish you how he sees fit. I won't stop him. Your mother and I never expected this from our daughter. This is going to destroy her more than it already has."

Breel caught herself before saying in haste that she wasn't her mother's daughter. She had already told him enough. He didn't need more information against Famut.

The moment he left, she sank to the ground and cried.

* * *

No sound penetrated Breel's cell. Without a window and no one talking to her except the brief visit from her father, it was impossible to determine the time of day. She could only estimate it based on when she received food. If she was correct in figuring they fed her twice daily, four days had passed.

Each meal—and that was a generous term—was always similar: a glass of water; chicken or pork; a bun, mashed potatoes, or rice; and vegetables. The meat was grisly and dry, the bun hard, the mashed potatoes lumpy, the rice sticky and dry, and the vegetables limp and white.

The job must go to the cook with lowest marks.

Famut's last moments—President Tatem shooting him, Manum catching him and easing him to the ground, and the precious little time Breel had with him, her hand stained with his blood—were seared in her mind. Try as she might, like the news, it played on a loop. Multiple times a night, she'd wake in a cold sweat, screaming as she apologized to Famut and begged him not to die.

Breel thought about Cafrec and the others in their own cells, sitting on the uncomfortable mattress. Everyone's spirits shattered after everything they'd been through. She thought of Cafrec the most and often wondered if he thought about her, too.

Occasionally, her mind drifted to those who took the tunnels after them. President Tatem said they killed those in the south tunnel and implied he'd killed the others, too. She imagined the DOE coming early to kill the homeowners, lying in wait for the knock on the door underneath the patio slabs. The DOE may have entered the tunnel when the door opened and fired. Or perhaps DOE officers entered the house after the homeowner greeted the Intercludae residents. Once everyone was inside, bullets rained down upon them. Either way, there would've been little time to react. But perhaps that was best, as it meant their deaths were painless and without knowledge of the betrayal. However it happened, Breel's heart ached for them.

That said, it was possible President Tatem was lying and Ragula and everyone else was alive. After all, Famut and the others planned this for years. They wouldn't instigate the plan without the utmost confidence in its success. Maybe the DOE officers infiltrated one or more tunnels, but the Intercludae residents resisted. Ragula had even said DOE officers had little combat training. Those at Intercludae were far more prepared for such a situation. There were likely to be casualties, but it couldn't have been many given their preparations. They would've fought through the DOE officers and stationed themselves around the Quaddro.

However, Breel and the others had failed to bring President Tatem to the Mortae. If the others made it to the Mortae, what happened to them? The North Section may have stormed the stage while another section rained darts upon the DOE officers. It would've been chaotic, but it was possible they still could've captured President Tatem.

Only... Breel's stomach flipped. Neither her father nor the DOE officers acted as if that were the outcome. Her father had spoken to President Tatem—he wasn't a captive.

It was impossible to know what had happened to the other hostages. Having nothing to do meant thinking about it endlessly. When her mind tired of it, she replayed her life over and over: conversations with Famut, arguments with Trafis and her father over Famut's influence and beliefs, Famut's disappearance and her father's indifference to it.

But she spent most of her time replaying events from the last couple of weeks. Talking with Cafrec at the departmental event. Discovering he was Centia's cousin (or thought he was). Learning his views on President Tatem. Mr. Tucap feeding them clues to Intercludae and following the directions. Kissing Cafrec. Was there anything she did wrong? Was there something she could've done to change the course of events?

The obvious answer was that she could've refused to accompany Cafrec to Intercludae. But she didn't.

Throughout her childhood, Famut had touted the benefits and lifestyle of Intercludae. There, she could draw as much as she wanted and work toward her dreams. Don't want to be a computer programmer? Work toward another Career Group. Want to switch Career

Groups after you've started working? Learn the skills and knowledge needed for something new. Just those ideas alone had been fantastical and alluring. Famut influenced her enough for her to hold the same convictions and beliefs, which of course spurred her into wanting to go to Intercludae to be an illustrator.

Neither Famut nor Centia had predicted things would go this badly. Had they simply been naïve? After all, the sensible thing to do was account and plan for possible capture. But Famut had always assumed the best, so he likely didn't have the foresight to make a contingency plan. After all, it'd been Centia, not Famut, who had contacted Mr. Tucap to tell Breel and Cafrec how to find Intercludae if she didn't survive. By the same token, it was likely Centia's idea to give Cafrec a genetic backup.

Because of their and her own actions, she was in jail. Her father certainly believed she'd be sentenced to Mortae, and of course, that was the most logical conclusion. It was doubtful President Tatem cared about having his and Xorem's "spawn" murdered.

Her mind had drifted back to Cafrec when the locks on her cell disengaged. A gray-uniformed officer with a crew cut stood in the doorway.

"Stand up," he said. "Face the wall."

Breel obeyed, relieved to be exiting her cell and have her Mortae before going stir crazy. He cuffed her arms in front of her, placed a cloth bag over her head, and escorted her out of the cell.

Chapter Forty

It was a lengthy walk through the hallways and up a staircase. Due to the blindfold and the officers hurrying them along without so much as a railing to hold onto, she tripped at the third step. The officer hauled her to her feet and forced her to walk faster. She tripped a few steps later, crying out as her shin smashed against the step. The officer grabbed her arms and got her to her feet yet again.

She managed to reach the top without falling a third time. Her shin was tender—it would undoubtedly be a colourful bruise soon. More walking and then, despite the bag over her head, the world was lighter. A breeze blew. Birds sang.

Officers forced her into a vehicle. They secured her cuffs to something, metal clanging, and removed the bag from her head. Breel squinted, expecting a bright light, but the vehicle was as dim as the cell. She was in another windowless van, this one with a bench along either side. Chains shackled her cuffs to the bench. A wall separated her from the driver.

It was a mobile cell but far better than the one she'd come from as Cafrec, Manum, Lexo, and Praxa were there, too. Some had ripped clothing, and Lexo had dried blood on his shirt. Given the state of everyone's greasy hair—not to mention the smell—it looked like they'd been in jail for four or five days.

Everyone exchanged wordless glances. Manum was the first to break eye contact and stare at the ground.

Lexo broke the silence. "Did anyone else get a visit from a family member?"

Everyone nodded.

Glad it wasn't just me.

"My mother," Manum said.

"My father," Breel said.

"My father, too," Praxa said.

"My ex-girlfriend," said Lexo.

Cafrec said it'd been his mother. "I'm officially kicked out of the family."

"I'm sorry," said Breel.

"Doesn't matter now, anyway."

The ride was smoother than the last, perhaps because they were sitting on benches or because the shackles prevented too much jostling. It wasn't long before the van stopped and the back door opened, sunlight blazing in. The shackles weren't long enough for them to shield their eyes, so everyone squinted. DOE officers unshackled them from the van before shackling them together via a long metal chain looping through their cuffs.

They walked onto the driveway of a house as nondescript as all the others. Breel frowned. *Where's the Quaddro?* Two DOE officers led the group to the front door. Breel was first in the line, followed by Cafrec, Lexo, Praxa, and Manum.

A DOE officer said, "You were my favourite teacher. I thought you were a smart, good guy."

Manum made no reply, and the other DOE officer scolded his partner for talking to the prisoners.

They walked into the living room, where President Tatem himself was sitting. Breel's breath caught in her throat. He was the last person she'd have expected. She felt a chill go through her.

President Tatem instructed them to stand along the window. A DOE officer stood in front of each of them, pointing a .45 calibre handgun. The guns didn't bother Breel. President Tatem wasn't about to miss the opportunity to publicly murder five people.

President Tatem stood and examined them one at a time. He reached Breel last. She was determined to not break eye contact and stared right back into his soulless eyes. When President Tatem finished the staring contest—neither of them having blinked—he backed up a few steps to view all the prisoners.

"There is something you must see," he said. "One punishment for your escapades. May it serve as a reminder of the consequences of betraying the government and your fellow citizens."

A DOE officer unshackled Manum at the far end of the line and escorted him out the back door. President Tatem followed. Breel and the others remained, the four other DOE officers' weapons trained on them. It was at least five minutes before the DOE officer and President Tatem returned—less Manum. Breel's stomach tightened.

Oh, no... what'd they do to him?

There was no explanation. Instead, the same DOE officer unshackled Lexo and disappeared with him out the back door.

And on it went, with each leaving and not returning. Breel's legs shook. Standing was difficult. The minutes ticked by until only she and Cafrec remained. Her breathing was audible, chest heaving with each inhale and exhale. She put an arm around Cafrec, and he followed suit. His heart pounded against her chest.

All too soon, the DOE officer returned, trailed by President Tatem.

"No!" Breel said as he unshackled Cafrec.

"Silence," said President Tatem.

Breel bit her tongue and turned to Cafrec as the DOE officer led him away. Cafrec turned his head to kiss her, but their lips only brushed. As he disappeared around the corner, Breel collapsed to the ground, soaking the carpet with her tears.

When they returned to retrieve her, her legs shook so much two DOE officers assisted her outside. President Tatem stopped at the patio and eyed her, upper lip curling into a smile, as she passed him.

At the far end of the backyard was a cold, stainless-steel shed—a smaller version of the ones they had visited on a class trip to the fields of the Department of Food.

"Enter the shed," said a DOE officer.

In Breel's confusion over this command, some of her unsteadiness dissipated. However, panic gripped her. What was in the shed? There'd been no gunfire, so the DOE hadn't shot the others. But there were other ways to murder someone. They could've injected them here, instead of at Mortae, and tossed their corpses in the shed. Opening the door was the last thing she wanted to do. Just thinking about seeing their corpses splayed across the floor, their faces frozen in fear, made her jelly legs return.

Please, no. Not more corpses. Especially not Cafrec!

"Walk." The DOE officers raised their guns. Breel approached the shed at a slow, shaky pace. She reached the door and raised her hand. Gulping air, she tried to breathe deeply to regulate her racing heart. Even though she didn't touch the shed, a whirring sounded. A seal broke. The door slowly opened. It was so thick it took a moment for there to be enough clearance to walk inside.

She didn't want to enter but the guns trained on her gave her no choice. She'd only walked a step toward the pitch-black interior before the most putrid smell to ever waft into her olfactory receptors did just that. Her hand immediately went to her nose. But plugging it wasn't enough.

"Get inside! Get inside or we'll shoot!"

She didn't want to walk into that shed. A gunshot pierced her ears. Breel jumped, waiting for the blood, for the pain. It didn't come.

"That was a warning shot. In the shed!"

Survival instincts kicking into gear, she darted inside. As soon as she cleared the door, the whirring sounded again, and it closed—locking her inside. Lights extinguished the darkness, slowly, bathing the shed in an eerie yellow. No corpses splayed across the floor. But each wall had floor-to-ceiling shelves—filled with dozens of corpses all in the early stages of decomposition.

Chapter Forty-One

Breel shut her eyes, bile in her throat, for fear of recognizing a corpse. But the vision had already burned into her memory. She collapsed to the floor, landing in a sea of vomit, spewing out her guts.

After exhuming her stomach contents, she yanked on the door handle. Nothing. She slid down the wall and sat, landing in the vomit. Breel had no capacity to care. She pulled her knees up to her chin and held her nose as tears streamed down her cheeks.

A horrible sinking thought came to Breel: *Where are the others?*

She didn't want to look, but she had to check. Summoning her strength, she opened her eyes and scanned the corpses. They were all on their backs. Shelf after shelf, she recognized no one—until she got to the second wall. There was Medi—or Cemus—with eyes staring blankly at the ceiling. The other twin was on the next wall. Cafrec, Manum, Lexo, and Praxa weren't there. Neither was Ragula.

"This is what happens when you disrupt the fine inner workings of Lexum." Her blood chilled at the sound of President Tatem's voice. It was mechanical, a recording coming from within the shed. "This is your punishment for betraying me, betraying my government, and betraying the citizens of Lexum. Did you not realize we would catch the insurgents in the tunnels? Did you not think it would lead to their deaths? Think again.

"It is not my wish for citizens to die. With death, we lose citizens with skills that benefit everyone. But these people are no longer citizens. You are not a citizen of Lexum if you betray Lexum by putting your individual needs above society's needs to form a separate community and attempt an uprising. These insurgents deserved to be slaughtered for their crimes. And so, they were."

There was another whirring. Breel wasted no time in running outside and across the grass. But she didn't make it far due to the tears blurring her vision, the cuffs limiting her movement, and her shaking legs. She tumbled to the ground.

"Get up. Get up or we'll shoot."

The temptation to stay on the ground, the soft grass, to be killed here instead of in front of her parents, Trafis, and all citizens in Mortae was strong. But if Cafrec were alive, he had to be worried about her, like she was about him.

Cafrec, think of Cafrec. She got to her legs, picturing him with his smile and flopping hair in an attempt to evict the images of the corpses of Medi and Cemus.

The DOE officers led her back to the van. Seeing the others already there, some of the tension in her body dissipated. She kept her eyes on Cafrec as they shackled her to the van. He stared into the abyss. Lexo leaned over, still retching. Praxa was crying, though not as hard as Manum, whose sobs shook the bench.

Clearly, they'd been to the same shed, as they hadn't escaped the sea of vomit, either. Rather, it was clear that, like her, they'd contributed to it.

It was impossible not to relive the scene in the shed. The corpses, the unimaginable smell of putrefaction, the horror of seeing the paralyzed faces as she checked for Cafrec and the others. Thinking of pleasant childhood conversations with Famut instead wasn't any better—they only ripped her heart in two and churned her stomach.

* * *

They arrived at another house, which had another shed. Again, the DOE brought them into the house, then to the shed one by one before returning them to the van. Breel didn't open her eyes this time. Nor the third or fourth times. While in each shed, she held her nose and leaned against the wall as she tried not to expel bile.

The van door opened shortly after leaving the fourth house.

Oh no.... what now? There were no more tunnels, so conceivably no more sheds. Still shackled together with **Breel** at the front, the DOE escorted them toward a plain white building. She'd only gone a few steps before there was a pull on her cuffs. Manum, at the end of the line, wasn't moving.

"Walk!" shouted a DOE officer.

When Manum didn't move, the DOE officer went to grab him. Manum acted fast. One moment he was standing beside the DOE officer. The next, the DOE officer was on his knees, the chain around his neck. Manum pulled on it, veins popping in his muscular arms.

The remaining DOE officer already had his weapon aimed at Manum when someone yelled, "No! Do not shoot!" It was President Tatem running from a car that had tailed the van, the remaining three DOE officers with him. He grabbed the gun from the man. "He is the one most known by the citizens. We cannot kill him like this."

"But he's killing Gulari!" the gunless DOE officer said, his voice panicky and high-pitched.

"Let him," said President Tatem. "Or try to rescue this Gulari and risk being killed yourself."

The DOE officer looked to Gulari and Manum and back to President Tatem. Then, with a sigh, he stepped back.

All the while, Manum pulled on the chain wrapped around Gulari's neck.

"Mr. Gaimster," said Praxa, shackled beside him, "don't do this. You're not a killer. You don't want to do this."

But Manum was doing it and had, in fact, already killed Gulari. He loosened the red-stained chain, and the man fell to the ground. Breel stared at his partly severed neck in horror.

Manum... no... Praxa was right—this wasn't like Manum. The events of the past few days had sent him over the edge—an edge from which he'd now be lucky to return.

Manum turned to President Tatem, chain still in his hands. "You're lucky you're over there," he said.

"Not luck," said President Tatem. He pointed to his head. "Brains. Congratulations on killing a citizen of Lexum."

"Congratulations to you, too," Manum said. Voice cracking, he said, "Why'd you kill them, make us see the aftermath? These were people I knew! People I taught, lived with, and cared about for years! People I..." He choked on his words and let out a cry.

President Tatem grinned. "Yes. That is why I did it. Officers, carry on."

The DOE officers instructed them to continue walking, but Manum didn't move.

"Walk," said one of the DOE officers, pointing his handgun at Manum's head.

"Tater said to not kill me."

"That's President Tatem to you, to all of us," said the DOE officer. He punched Manum.

Manum screamed, cuffed hands going to his face but not able to reach as blood spurted, splattering Praxa.

"Obey or we kill this one," President Tatem said.

He pointed to Breel, and the DOE officer pointed his gun from Manum to her. Her heart stopped. Cafrec put an arm around her, which was a good thing, as her leg muscles were hardly working.

"How touching," President Tatem said, sneering.

"I'll walk," Manum said.

The DOE officer lowered his weapon. Breel inhaled and then exhaled immediately, her lungs desperate for air.

They walked into the building, through a long, sterile white hallway, and down several sets of stairs into a small room. It was empty save for chains hanging from metal loops along the wall. The DOE unshackled them from each other and put a ring of keys on the wall. They spaced the group out around the perimeter of the room and then shackled them to the chains along the wall so their arms were over their heads.

Two DOE officers had a weapon trained on each of them. President Tatem wasn't in the room, but he had to be nearby.

Beside Breel, five feet down the wall, Cafrec's eyes no longer sparkled; his expression held no emotion. Praxa finished rubbing her face into her arms to remove Manum's blood and stared at the wall. Lexo glared at one of the DOE officers pointing a gun at him. Manum looked ready to collapse and probably would have if not for the chains holding him up. Tears and blood streamed down his face. His cries echoed in the small room.

Breel's arms ached until she realized her legs weren't doing their part in holding her up. Putting more weight on her feet was an effort, as her body had little strength left. Her heart tried to escape its rib cage. Breaths came in quick gasps, as if she'd just come up for air after a long swim.

A commotion sounded from above. Since the DOE had murdered the other Intercludae residents, likewise unable to fulfill their task, it was obvious the noise wasn't anyone coming to their rescue. Even their Lexum spies wouldn't be that bold.

"You hear that?" she asked.

Cafrec nodded. "I'm sorry, Breel."

She frowned. "For what?"

CHAPTER FORTY-ONE

"Dragging you into this."

"You didn't drag me."

"Silence," said a DOE officer.

Why does he think he dragged me into this? After all, they told each other everything they knew about Famut and Centia. It just so happened he was the one who knew enough to bring up leaving Lexum. That must've been the cause of his guilt. If only she could talk to him, to assuage him of it.

The commotion got louder. There was no mistaking it. There was cheering and thumping from above. The Quaddro. They were below the Quaddro.

They were Vucapi.

This was their Mortae.

This is the end...

Somehow, she always knew her life would end with Mortae. Growing up, she'd sometimes wonder what would be on her mind in this moment. She tried to think happy memories.

Playing games with Uncle Famut and Trafis.

Beating Ami in a math test.

Drawing before my first warning.

Supper conversations with my family.

Tears rolled down her cheeks, first one and then a deluge. She moved her head to wipe them with her arm.

No, no tears. Be brave like Centia.

She blinked them away and worked on slowing her breathing, though it proved impossible with her racing heart.

For better or worse, they were only with their thoughts for five minutes. The DOE shackled their legs and unchained them from the wall. They adjusted the cuffs to be behind their backs. An officer collected all the keys, put them on a ring, then on the wall. Two officers sandwiched each prisoner as they escorted them out, starting with

Breel. They climbed a staircase, the crowd's roar louder with each step.

This is it... don't be scared. It'll be over soon.

The door at the top opened. There, smiling as if greeting a special guest, was President Tatem and his personal security. Beyond him, separated by the glass barrier, were the citizens of Lexum—a boisterous, ready-for-action crowd that both cheered ("Mortae! Mortae!") and booed the insurgents.

Breel stepped onto the platform, and her eyes scanned the crowd even though it was the last thing she wanted to do. There, in the front row of the Platinum section, only twenty feet away, were her parents and Trafis.

Chapter Forty-Two

Breel should've expected to see her family in Platinum, since that was where the Vucapi's immediate family always watched, but it was nonetheless shocking. A DOE officer flanked each of Breel's family members as well as those of the other Vucapi.

The two DOE officers forced Breel onto the bench she'd seen time and time again. There was a second one to make room for all five of them. *Breathe, breathe. Be brave like Centia.*

Without the glass barrier between the Vucapi and crowd, there was a clear view of her family—and the families of the others. Duknum crossed his arms, glaring. But through the glare was a flicker of something else—fear. Criba was hugging him while she periodically glanced at Breel between moments of burying her face into his shoulder as tears streamed down her cheeks. Trafis stared in disbelief, mouth open.

"Breel!" said Criba.

She stepped forward but stopped when her assigned DOE officer put a hand on her arm.

"Our first insurgent—Breel Sorep!" President Tatem's voice boomed into the microphone.

The crowd booed. As it died down, Criba's cries were audible.

"As a Leader of Tomorrow," President Tatem said, drowning out Criba, "she had the highest grades in her Career Group. Breel just became a Leader of Today, working as a computer programmer at the Department of Education. She had a couple of warnings, but nothing suggesting insurgency. This goes to show that even the most unassuming citizens of Lexum may spend years plotting against our way of life."

The crowd booed. Something sailed through the air, smashing onto the ground between Breel and her parents.

"I can explain," Breel said. "I wasn't plotting for years."

President Tatem ignored her. In fact, he likely didn't even hear her over the noise of the crowd.

President Tatem said, "She is related to the leader of the insurgents—Famut Sorep. Famut was killed in the ensuing battle when they broke into my house and attempted to murder me."

The crowd gasped as one. Breel eyed her father, whose expression hardened. More citizens booed and threw objects, none hitting their mark. The crowd moved closer to the platform, though still confined to their sections.

"That's a lie!" Breel yelled. "We didn't attack you! You killed him for nothing!"

But no one heard.

"Next is Cafrec Masna."

Two officers led him to the bench. Cafrec sat, looking at the ground and ignoring his family.

"I don't blame you," Breel said.

"You should."

Breel stole a glance at President Tatem. He had eyes only for the cheering crowd, soaking up their adoration.

"I don't," she said. "For years I wondered what had happened to Uncle Famut. If I didn't want to risk this, I wouldn't have come. This isn't your fault."

Cafrec was silent. Or perhaps his response was too quiet to hear.

President Tatem said, "Cafrec has a similar history to Breel with high achievement in school. Not only was he another computer programmer for the Department of Education, but he was also officemates with Breel. His cousin is Centia Masna, the geneticist recently sentenced to Mortae who had worked with and dated Famut Sorep. See the entwining of all this, citizens? Famut and Centia recruited their younger relatives to be part of their failed attempt to overtake Lexum."

He had said Cafrec was cousins with Centia—which President Tatem knew wasn't true. *Probably doesn't want everyone knowing about Project Consillo.*

Lexo and Praxa were next. According to President Tatem, Famut had recruited them both. They had clean records with top scores in everything they did. Then came Manum. His face was no longer bleeding; however, it was purple, and his nose was misshapen. There was a collective gasp.

"I see you recognize him," President Tatem said.

"He was my teacher."

"Mine too."

"I thought he was a true citizen of Lexum."

President Tatem continued when the crowd settled. "Yes, Manum Gaimster. An impeccably clean record. Model citizen and highly regarded by all. However, early on as a Leader of Tomorrow, he had many classes with Famut Sorep and evidently kept up their friendship. As Manum was a weight training teacher, there is no telling how many he brainwashed with his flawed ideals."

More booing. More citizens throwing objects, one hitting Manum in the chest. Whatever it was, either it didn't hurt, or he didn't care enough to react.

"What does all this show?" President Tatem asked. "It shows how only a few bad people can taint otherwise good citizens who 'embrace the collective.' Therefore, we all must be extremely vigilant. See any suspicious behaviour? It does not matter if it is your sibling, parent, child, friend, or a stranger. Everyone must report all and any suspicious behaviour whether it is witnessed or simply suspected. Citizens, what is the punishment for such behaviour?"

The crowd stirred once more with shouts of "Mortae! Mortae!"

If it weren't for the shackles, Breel's legs would've run halfway across Lexum before her brain could catch up. But she couldn't show cowardice in front of Lexum. No, Lexum would remember her as someone who died with her head held high—just like Centia. She focussed on a point just above the crowd, looking at the first building on the other side of the Quaddro.

"Mortae is a cornerstone of our society," President Tatem said.

Breel's heart raced, her breathing quickening. This was it. He'd espouse Mortae, and the Deliverer would kill them.

"It is the pinnacle of punishment for those who place individual benefit above societal benefit," said President Tatem. "Many of you know at least one of today's Vucapi. They plotted against the government, against the citizens of Lexum. They formed a secret society. But it is not just them. Officers have killed others like them, for there were too many for a single Mortae. These five broke into my estate and attempted to murder me. They deserve our cornerstone punishment."

"How dare they!" said some in the crowd.

"Mortae! Mortae!" said others.

President Tatem used the intermission to run his hand over his hair. "Others like them are still among us. Citizens have served as double agents, pretending to believe in the rights of society. However, what they really believe is that individual rights trumps society rights. Is that any way for citizens of Lexum to behave?"

"No!" said the crowd.

Breel kept looking at the building far beyond the citizens of Lexum;

however, the crowd was so vast their pulsating arms were in her peripheral vision. *They're excited... excited for me and the others to die. How did Uncle Famut ever believe he could change such ideals?*

"We know there are more citizens of Lexum part of their scheme," said President Tatem. "If you are one of them, make no mistake, we know who you are. We will arrest and kill you."

The wall—the wall at Intercludae with pictures of their inside sources. She gasped. The DOE had gone to Intercludae and found that wall. That was how he knew there were others and who they were. When the DOE stormed Intercludae, the parents and children left behind had undoubtedly been murdered. Her stomach churned at the thought of the DOE gunning them down.

"But I say this," President Tatem continued, "come forward of your own volition, and your punishment will not be Mortae. Do not come forward, and Mortae is your fate just like these five. I ask you: does plotting against the government benefit society?"

"No!" said the crowd.

"Does plotting against the citizens of Lexum benefit society?"

"No!" The crowd was getting louder.

"Should we condone this behaviour?"

"No!"

Breel winced. If her hands could reach her head, she would've covered her ears.

"What should we do with these five?"

"Mortae!"

"Say it again!"

"MORTAE!"

"And a third time!"

"MORTAE!"

Breel's ears rang. Even the call for Centia's Mortae hadn't reached this level. The crowd chanted it over and over, their energy building like a wave. Breel's breathing increased, and her body shook.

It was a good minute before President Tatem said, "The Deliverer!"

Breel was determined not to watch. She focussed on her point, urging herself to be like Centia. No crying. No pleading. No fighting against the DOE officers.

The crowd continued its "Mortae! Mortae!" chant.

As the Deliverer walked behind her, Breel's breathing became erratic, to the point of hyperventilation.

Calm down, calm down.

She laughed at the ridiculousness of telling herself to calm down, and, remembering her family was watching, regretted it. She looked to Cafrec, who stared back. His lips moved, but the roar of the crowd drowned his words.

The Deliverer was behind her, his lab coat grazing her back as he retrieved the needle from his pocket.

During every other Mortae, the crowd quieted in this moment. But not today. It only became more demanding and louder as everyone screamed, "Mortae! Mortae!"

"Silence, silence," President Tatem said, his voice a whisper amongst the crowd.

They didn't listen. He tried again, louder this time, but the crowd was beyond hearing. President Tatem, his hands in fists, looked at the Deliverer and raised a finger, telling him to pause. President Tatem faced the crowd again and screamed "Silence!" into the microphone.

But the crowd ignored him. The chant continued, arms punching the air with each word.

President Tatem motioned for the Deliverer to come forward and pointed to the microphone.

The wait was torture. *Just do it! Please, just get it over with and stab me.*

The Deliverer stepped forward, hand behind his back with the needle.

It was uncapped, his finger on the plunger, as if an arm were right there awaiting death. The change in routine must've caused him to not think about recapping it.

It happened fast. One moment, President Tatem and the Deliverer were standing side by side at the microphone. Then the Deliverer moved to stab President Tatem's back with the needle. But his security was quicker. One pushed President Tatem out of the way and the other pushed the Deliverer.

The crowd was finally silenced.

President Tatem stumbled from the push, but one of his security guards caught him.

The Deliverer got to his feet, holding the needle high and aiming it at President Tatem. His hood had fallen—it was Tragpraev.

BANG!

A recognizable sulfur stench filled the air. Smoke curled from the gun of one of President Tatem's security.

Tragpraev grabbed the microphone. As blood seeped through his shirt, he said, "I, Tragpraev Sunt, Tater's ex-personal housekeeper, killed the Deliverer." His knees buckled, and he fell.

President Tatem's security surrounded him and led him through the door behind the platform.

After President Tatem left, not a single soul in Lexum said a word. No one moved, not even the DOE officers in the crowd.

It lasted half a second.

Then everything happened at once.

Darts flew into the crowd and onto the platform. Most of those headed for the platform hit the glass. Citizens screamed. Many, including DOE officers, surged toward the platform, Bronze, Silver, and Platinum Sections forgotten. They came like a wave. But thousands of citizens—many with Leaders of Tomorrow—went against the wave to leave the Quaddro. It was a losing stance. The crowd trampled one man as if he wasn't even there.

"Move, Breel," Cafrec said. He and the others were already on their feet. Lexo bent down and placed a hand on Tragpraev's neck. He shook his head and followed the others, alongside Breel and Cafrec. The group ran as fast as possible with shackled legs to the edge of the platform before the hoard of Lexum could arrive.

Breel didn't see her family, but there was no time to think about where they were. They had but moments before the crowd stormed the platform.

They jumped the three feet to the ground. But before they could run behind the platform, a blonde head stood in their way. Breel's breath caught in her throat. Ami.

Breel froze. *What's Ami doing here? How'd she get from Bronze so quickly?*

Ami's jaw had dropped, tears flowing down her cheeks. "How could you?" she said. Her nostrils flared.

"Ami—"

"Shut up, Breel!" Ami said, face turning crimson. "I had a feeling about you! When I heard about your disappearance, I knew it as far too coincidental after your uncle's. I told the DOE everything I know about you."

Breel gasped. *Ami was awarded Platinum... That's how she got here so fast.*

"I should've figured about you years ago," Ami said. "Getting into the department I wanted wasn't enough, was it? You almost murdered President Tatem!" More tears streamed down her cheeks. "I hate you!"

Typical Ami, making things personal. Feeling the need to explain herself, Breel said, "Ami, I didn't—"

Cafrec pushed her forward. "Forget her, Breel!"

He was right. There was no time. Besides, Ami wouldn't understand.

Breel and Cafrec followed the others. Ami let them past undeterred. Steps later, a deafening crash stopped them midstride, followed by the endless sound of tinkling.

The glass in front of the platform had smashed. Breel resisted the urge to turn and look at pieces raining down upon hundreds of people. At least it'd slow some of them.

Ami wasn't the only one waiting for Breel. There, mere feet from Ami, was her family. Tears stained Criba's cheeks. Duknum stared, face red and fists clenched. Trafis's eyes were wide with fear.

"Come with us," Breel shouted as Cafrec urged her along. The others were already twenty feet ahead of them and turning around the side of the platform.

"Breel, come on!"

"It's my family!" she said. He stopped.

Trafis stepped toward Breel, but Duknum grabbed his wrist. A dart flew past, missing her father's face by inches.

"No, Trafis," Duknum said. "You won't be part of a rebellion who attempted to murder President Tatem! I failed at keeping one child safe, but I'm damn well keeping you safe."

For the first time in his life, Trafis decided for himself. He wrenched out of Duknum's grip and ran to Breel.

"No!" Duknum said, his voice high. It wasn't a shout of anger but of fear as his children disobeyed the laws of Lexum.

"We've gotta go!" Cafrec said.

The crowd had made it to the platform. The surge of citizens was massive enough to hide what those on the platform were doing, which was just as well—Breel didn't want to imagine what would become of Tragpraev's body. But many headed for Breel and the others, bloodlust in their eyes. Yet, there were others holding them off—secret rebels who'd been living in Lexum. There were enough of them to contain the flood, though it got harder by the second.

Breel looked at her parents. Her mother stepped closer, but Duknum grabbed her, too. "Criba, no!"

"Let go of me!" Criba said.

It was the first time Breel had ever heard her mother raise her voice or defend herself. She launched toward her children, ripping out of her husband's grasp.

Duknum's jaw dropped. Tears welled in his eyes. "Criba, don't you love me?"

"I do!" she said, crying with him. "But I need to be with my children. Come with us, Duknum!" Her lip trembled as she held out a hand to him.

As Breel turned to her father, a lump formed in her throat. Tears rolled down his cheeks, his shoulders drooped. *Father, please come. Please come.*

His jaw set. "No. I cannot break the law. I will not."

After seeing his reaction to his wife making her choice, it wasn't what Breel expected.

The entire exchange had lasted no more than fifteen seconds.

Chapter Forty-Three

Breel, Cafrec, her mother, and Trafis ran behind the platform. At any moment the crowd would overtake them, or a well-aimed or errant bullet would hit them.

Manum, Lexo, and Praxa were nowhere in sight, despite having come this way. They couldn't possibly have left the Quaddro already, not with their legs hampered by the chain and hands cuffed behind them. Criba helped Breel along, holding her up when she nearly fell. Trafis did the same for Cafrec. Occasionally a dart whizzed past, but none hit their mark.

They made it past the platform when someone called, "Cafrec! Breel!" A man wearing the Department of Education uniform stood in front of an open door behind the platform. Mr. Tucap. He waved them over, gun in hand. "Hurry!"

They ran to him, and, once inside, Mr. Tucap shut the door. They were in the same sterile white hallway that took them to the platform. Manum, Praxa, and Lexo were there, massaging their wrists—free from cuffs. Mr. Tucap had a ring of keys in hand and was already uncuffing and unchaining Breel and Cafrec.

"Follow me," he said the moment they were free.

No time for questions. He led them downstairs, checking the corners, gun straight ahead, before running into the next hallway. Before long, they arrived at the door they'd entered after Manum killed Gulari.

Mr. Tucap cracked the door open, gun cocked, and peeked out before opening it fully.

"Not much farther," he said.

They followed him outside and across the street. He turned onto the driveway of the second house on the road.

The door opened when they were steps from it. Everyone filed inside without a word.

A man stood in the entryway. Except for his Department of Health uniform, he was identical to Mr. Tucap—even his Career Group stripings. His picture had been on the wall in Intercludae.

"Sanctus, we're safe?" Mr. Tucap asked. "You hacked the surveillance feeds?"

"Of course," said his brother.

They embraced.

"This is Sanctus, my twin brother, and his wife, Vida," Mr. Tucap said.

He motioned to the living room. Vida—heavily pregnant—was a nurse from the Department of Health. Her hand rested on her rapidly moving chest.

Mr. Tucap turned back to his brother. "Thank you."

"Of course. We only just got here." He paused for breath between words. Sanctus sat beside Vida and put an arm around her.

"We won't stay long," Mr. Tucap said. "I don't want to put you in more danger."

Sanctus waved a hand. "Do what you need to do, Samit."

Mr. Tucap looked at everyone, observing Criba and Trafis longer than the others, as if noticing them for the first time.

"My mother and brother," Breel said.

No, not my mother... not really.

He nodded. "Of course."

"What happened?" Cafrec asked. "Everything went wrong!"

Manum sat on the ground between the entrance and living room, head in his hands. He seemed not to notice anyone else.

"As soon as I got you out of the tunnel, I fled here," said Mr. Tucap. "This is the house of Vida's aunt and uncle. It's been a planned safehouse for years. We're close enough to escape the Quaddro, and Vida's biologically related enough for her ID card to permit her entrance but not so related that the DOE will immediately consider searching here. It was always doubtful we'd get President Tatem to the Quaddro. After all, he has spies too."

"And Tragpraev was on our side?" Breel asked.

"Yes. After much discussion, we figured that was the only way. We needed someone close to President Tatem. Someone he'd trust. It was some other spy who told President Tatem about the plan, but when that happened, we agreed it made sense for Tragpraev to speak about it with President Tatem. Only Famut and I knew this. We agreed not to tell Manum or anyone else in the group going to President Tatem's house, as we needed pure reactions."

The reactions were pure, all right.

"Tragpraev suggested to us that he hide under the platform as backup in case something happened. While there, he killed the Deliverer. Tragpraev wasn't naïve—he knew his death was pretty much assured."

"So, you're saying Tragpraev pretended to be on President Tatem's side? That you planned all of this?" Cafrec asked.

"To a point. Yes, Tragpraev was a double agent. But we failed. Tragpraev was to kill President Tatem. But Tatem had clearly told his security to be even more watchful, and they stopped Tragpraev before he could stab Tatem with the needle. But even if our initial plan worked and we successfully got President Tatem to the Quaddro, the odds were against most of our people making it. Fleeing the scene was pretty much a given. The DOE officers on our side could only do so much to protect us in the Quaddro, especially since we didn't want to use lethal weapons."

Breel clenched her jaw. "They lied to us! Uncle Famut and Manum lied to us!"

She looked at Manum with disgust. But her heart went out to him as she watched him rock back and forth, crying. Lexo and Praxa sat on either side of him, the latter rubbing Manum's back.

Mr. Tucap said, "Famut and Centia believed it was necessary. We must make sacrifices. You're too young and new to appreciate that. Believe me, you aren't the only ones who knew but part of the truth."

"Still doesn't make it right!" she said.

"What's done is done, unfortunately."

"What happens now?" It came from Trafis, in a quavering voice.

He and Criba stood a distance from the others, huddled together.

"We wait," Mr. Tucap said. "We need to remain hidden while things calm down. Especially you who came from Intercludae—your faces will be all over the news. I'm sure mine will be too, since I fled immediately after you left my house. Without a doubt they investigated me, saw I'm your Head, and connected the dots. And Sanctus is likely a suspect as well."

"His picture was on a wall in Intercludae, along with others on the inside," Breel said.

Mr. Tucap's eyes widened. "Are you serious? There are pictures of everyone inside Intercludae? Whose dumb idea was that...?"

"No, they'll be gone," Lexo said. "I heard someone say that the pictures were to be burned before heading to Lexum just in case something happened."

Relief crossed Mr. Tucap's face. "Good."

It was tempting to challenge Lexo and remind him that President Tatem said he knew the identity of the Intercludae residents and their sources. But it wouldn't be the first Mortae in which President Tatem lied. *Saying he knows who people are, striking fear into them, is exactly what he'd do.*

Vida tended to Manum's face—the bruises were getting colourful—as Sanctus and Mr. Tucap brought chairs into the living room. Manum, Praxa, and Lexo sat near the entryway and Breel, Criba, and Trafis in the living room beside the television. Mr. Tucap, Sanctus, and Vida stayed on the couch.

Hiding was awful, though updating Criba and Trafis provided Breel some distraction. She skipped over jail and the sheds.

"What happened to all of you?" Trafis asked, pointing to her clothes.

Images of corpses flashed in Breel's mind, but she pushed them away. "You don't wanna know."

"I can imagine."

Breel glanced down at her filthy clothing, covered in dry vomit, which she'd worn for at least five days. No wonder Trafis and Criba were sitting a couple feet away. Breel shut her eyes as she wished away the memory of the lifeless bodies of Medi and Cemus.

"No, you can't imagine," Breel said.

As Breel spoke to Trafis and Criba, her mother said very little. She mostly stared at the ground, often with her head in her hands.

"I'm sorry for worrying you," Breel told her.

Criba met her eye for the first time since entering the safehouse. "Breel, we assumed the DOE killed you. Then we were forced to watch what was to be your execution."

Breel looked away. "I'm sorry. I thought it'd work out. I thought you'd understand once everything worked out."

"Well, it didn't. And your father..." She let out a cry and put a hand to her mouth.

She's mad at me. I guess I deserve that.

"I thought he would've come, the way he spoke to you," said Breel.

"I figured he wouldn't," she said. "Too much history with Famut." She turned, her back almost entirely to Breel.

Breel shook her head. There was the safety thing, sure. But Famut never treated her father poorly. *How much history could there possibly be?* But she didn't push her mother.

With every outside noise—which was near-constant for hours—a hush came over the room. No one dared move as shots were fired, people screamed, and voices called. As evening approached, the commotions lessened.

"How long do you think we'll stay here?" Breel asked.

"I don't know," Mr. Tucap said. "We also need to decide whether we attempt to kill President Tatem again or leave Lexum to regroup."

Manum's head shot up and—for the first time in hours—he looked at someone—Mr. Tucap—with bloodshot eyes. "No!" He smacked his hand against the wall. "We don't leave. We try again. My students weren't killed for us to just give up!"

"I agree," Mr. Tucap said. "We'll lay low for a while and then contact as many of our people as possible."

Placated, Manum returned to burying his face in his hands. Breel looked away, as watching Manum made her want to break down and cry, too.

Famut was gone, her father hadn't joined them, and President Tatem was still alive. Though she hadn't forgotten what Famut and Centia had done, the last thing she wanted was for their work and all the lives lost to have been in vain. She'd do all she could to overthrow President Tatem. She was a wanted ex-citizen of Lexum with nothing to lose.

Who had but one benefit.

She could draw.

Receive a Free Short Story!

Receive the exclusive and free short story *Warning* by subscribing to my newsletter at https://feliciaketcheson.com/nlsketching/.You'll also receive news about upcoming releases and exclusive content, and your email will never be shared. If you only want to read the story, simply unsubscribe after downloading your copy.

> *Can sixteen-year-old Cafrec avoid the consequences of disrespecting the president of his oppressed society?*

> *In a society where obedience is expected and defiance is punished, Cafrec is a dissatisfied teenager searching for a way out. When he takes a small, impulsive action in class, he quickly learns that even the slightest deviation from the norm can have consequences.*

Takes place two years before *Sketching Rebellion*.

Please Share Your Thoughts

Thank you so much for reading my book. I'd love to hear your thoughts about it. Please consider leaving an honest review to share your feedback. Short or long, all reviews are appreciated.

Author's Note

Genetic engineering is part of the *Sketching Rebellion Trilogy.* In Lexum, certain genes determine certain personality traits (such as whether one is creative or rebellious). But this isn't a scientifically accurate portrayal of genetics.

In reality, while we do inherit *some* of our personality through our genes, there are no personality traits determined only by genes. Instead, our personalities depend on many factors—including nature (i.e. our genes) and nurture (i.e. our environment).

I made genetics in Lexum less scientifically accurate to write the book in the way I wanted the story to unfold.

Thank you for understanding and for reading.

Felicia

Acknowledgments

Thank you to my family and friends who read an earlier draft of this book: my mom, Colleen Ketcheson, and brother, Edward Ketcheson; friend, writer and colleague Lisa King; and fellow Toastmasters Tim Condon, Sue Storie, and Gennie Walton.

To Edward: Growing up together seems just like yesterday. I admit, sometimes I miss the days of acting out elaborate, whacky storylines with our recurring cast of characters. The time I pretended to be a zombie all morning until I drank the cure (orange juice, for some reason) sticks in my mind. Always enjoyable were the many swordfights using plastic swords or cardboard wrapping paper tubes. But my favourite was tying skipping ropes onto the basement's support poles so our toys would avoid the dangers of the jungle on the forest floor. I'm sure our industriousness from these escapades and creating related trading cards, board games, and more amused Mom and Dad. As my first two series of books were based on our two worlds of pretend, who knows if I would've started writing without you! Thank you for not only making my childhood a blast but for giving me something to write about.

To Mom: Until 2020, you were the only person I was brave enough to allow to read my books. Over the years, you endured questions ("who's your favourite character?"), requests for assistance ("how should I tie up so-and-so's character arc?"), and random ramblings ("I finally decided how to end my book!"). Thank you for indulging me and being my first reader.

To Grandpa: I wouldn't have published this book without you. Throughout twenty-one years of writing letters to each other, you encouraged me to be a dreamer and goal setter, to publish my books, and most of all to not be afraid of rejection. But despite your words of wisdom, I never had the courage to try. I wish it didn't take rereading all your letters after your death for me to finally take your advice. The stuffed Snoopy with the book backpack you gave me—"if Snoopy can publish a book, you can, too"—sits on my desk so I can see him whenever I write. Thank you for your wisdom and faith in me—I finally listened.

To Lisa: You provided me with the tools, encouragement, and knowhow to get published. I'll never forget the day I told you about a book idea from when I was sixteen that I had yet to write. I took you up on the challenge to write the first draft within a few months and three years later, I have published it as *Sketching Rebellion*. Thank you for helping me get to this point—I couldn't have done it without you.

About the Author

Felicia Ketcheson is the author of *Sketching Rebellion*, which was a 2022 Killer Nashville Claymore Award finalist (Best Juvenile/YA category), and *Drawing Freedom*. When she was seven, she wrote her first book about a dog, cat, and bee. Four years later, she randomly started writing a short novel, catapulting her into the world of series writing. When she's not devising ways to destroy the lives of her fictional characters, she works as a systems analyst. Database developing is a passion she simultaneously loves and hates. She lives in St. Catharines, Ontario, Canada.

Photo credit: Lorne Devarajan

You can connect with me on:

🌐 https://feliciaketcheson.com

f https://www.facebook.com/feliciaketchesonauthor

🔗 https://www.goodreads.com/feliciaketcheson

Also by Felicia Ketcheson

Sketching Rebellion Trilogy
  Sketching Rebellion
  Drawing Freedom

Adult sci-fi technothrillers written under pen name Remi Cape
  Unshackled Intelligence. Unshackle yourself from the chains of mortality. https://feliciaketcheson.com/unshackled-intelligence/

Teen & adult memoir
  Life of a Salesman by R. Alex Jackson. Read about the secrets of a man who lived life on his own terms in this captivating memoir. A collection of stories written by Felicia's grandpa about his fascinating childhood and young adulthood. Compiled posthumously by Felicia and her mom. https://feliciaketcheson.com/life-of-a-salesman/